# Yours

BEAUTIFUL SINNER SERIES

## ELENA M. REYES

# SUMMARY

*I'm a man with an immoral compass. A convicted killer in one country and the right-hand to the devil in another.*

Javier Lucas offers death without mercy—something my enemies don't live long enough to tell, but the carnage left behind paints a brutal story. I have no soul. No regrets. This is who I am, and I embrace the darkness that flows through my veins while blood stains my skin.

And I've never wanted more until...

Our eyes met and my world took a pause. One flirty exchange and I vowed to tame her wildness.

*Fate is a word I now believed in.*

Because it led me to her. To my beautiful little criminal.

# ACKNOWLEDGMENTS

Before we get into YOURS and its yumminess; I need to thank a few people that I adore:

***K.I. Lynn, C.M. Steele, and Mary B. Moore:*** My girls. My chicas. My Boo's. You are a huge part of my life/success and I'm beyond blessed to have you as my peeps. Thank you from the bottom of my heart for being in my corner, for pushing me when I get stubborn, and for never letting me settle. You are such a huge part of my life and I'm thankful to have you in my corner. I love you.

***Marti Lynch:*** I can never say THANK YOU enough! Seriously, you have the patience of a saint with me and always come through. You are the best editor and friend an author could ask for.

***T.E. Black Designs***: BEST. COVER. EVER. Seriously, I can't stop staring at my pretty. Thank you!

***Michelle Myers:*** Babe, I legit can't thank you enough for the amount of work you did with me on this. You rode with me to the end, the long days, and made by baby so much better. Thank you for loving these characters and helping me become a better author. Love you!

***Ana Rita Clement***: Thank you so much for your insight and enthusiasm. I appreciate you so much, and I'm blessed to have you on my team. From the bottom of my heart, thank you!

***Elena's Marked Girls:*** You guys keep me going and always give me a reason to smile. Thank you for everything. For your unconditional support and encouragement. Please know that I love you—that you mean everything to me.

*Tiffany Hernandez:* Girl, you're the best PA ever! Thank you so much for all the hard work, for keeping me on track, and taking care of whatever I throw your way last minute because I've become the unorganized queen. It's because of you that I'm able to focus all my energy on writing and getting things done. You ROCK my world!

*Hubs and Kiddo:* You are my heart. My entire world. Everything I do, I do it for you.

# GLOSSARY OF SPANISH/COLOMBIAN SLANG:

Muñeca = Doll

Linda = Beautiful or Pretty

Hijueputa = Son of a bitch

Parce = Friend

Güevon = Lazy person

Brujeria = Voodoo/Witchcraft

Mamita = Term of endearment for a mother or used as a cat-call for hot girl. The same word could be used either way and has different meanings depending on how it's used.

Listo = Done

# QUOTE

*We're a brutal explosion of lust and hunger,*
*this raw uncontrollable yearning that I call home.*

~Javier Lucas

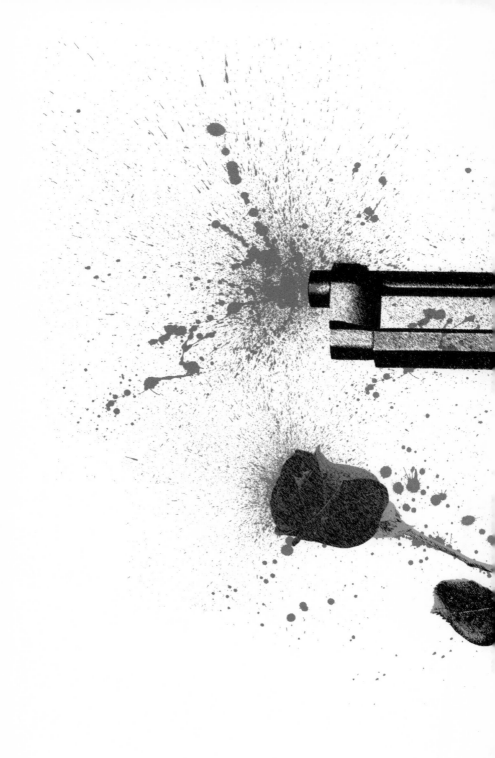

# 1

# Javier

*Colombia three years ago...*

THE STALE STENCH of old wounds greets my senses the moment I step inside the semi-darkened room. It's overpowering and undeniably human. That beginning stage of decomposition where lesions fail to heal and infection sets in, rotting a person from the inside out.

It's a scent I know. One I understand.

Because for every action, there is an often more damning consequence that even the most corrupt fear. All men have a weakness. One soft spot which renders them useless, and no one is immune to the karma of divine justice.

I'm here today as an example of that.

You pay in life for your wrongdoings.

My eyes sweep the room, and I nod at the man responsible for my role in today's proceedings. Alejandro, my cousin, sits just a few feet from the center in an opulent golden chair that doesn't fit within these walls while villagers gather around. Men and women line the back wall of an old abandoned building on the outskirts of Bogota while waiting on justice to be served.

Two men are on trial for their misdeeds and are tied together by greed. Stupidity.

For stealing from those who trusted—put faith in the empty words of a low-life opportunist.

Because you don't bite the hand that feeds. You don't take away the only source of sustenance these families have by emptying the poppy fields while using their labor under false direction—telling them it was a direct order—and attempting to sell the flowers to a European company whose loyalty lies with our family.

A novice mistake, and they'll pay with their lives for two reasons. One, for being scum. And the other, for trying to go behind his boss's back and making that idiotic purchase.

Everyone's watching the two men bound and gagged—bruised and bloodied—with horror-stricken expressions on their faces as the men take me in. The assholes wait, they beg with their eyes for a mercy they'll never receive.

Instead, the closer I get, the more they tremble. The smile on my face eviscerates whatever shred of hope they held on to.

I don't feel bad for them. Not at all.

I wouldn't be here if they were honorable men.

Hushed whispers meet my ears then, the murmurs of witnesses filling the space as I stop beside a small rolling cart. There's a tray atop it with two bullets, a .45 caliber Glock, and a machete.

It's all I'll need.

*"That family is nothing but an infestation of roaches in need of extermination."*

I catch that, and my attention snaps in the direction of the idiot who spoke. It's not hard to pick him out amongst the group. Not when the two women beside him take steps to the side with wide eyes. They're watching him, and then flick their eyes to me and then back again. Back and forth three times, and then they all but run toward the opposite side when I move in his direction.

There's a gulp, and two palms go up in supplication.

"Say it again, Güevon," I hiss out, my hand wrapped around his neck before his next inhale. My fingers tighten and his breathing becomes choppy, chest rising and falling fast—fighting to regain the missing oxygen he needs to live. There's a choking sound that slips from his parted lips while his body fights to break my hold, and still, I won't budge. I don't lose my stance even when his legs go weak. If anything, I take joy in the feel of his life slipping away beneath my fingertips.

I revel in the moment rationality sets in, and how easy it is to lose one's mortality becomes a haunting truth; he has no choice but to confront.

"Por favor, I didn't—" His fingernails try to break the skin at my wrist but fail. No strength whatsoever.

"I won't ask you again." Bringing my face closer to his, I arch a brow. "Repeat."

"Can't breathe," he chokes out, voice low while the color of his face reminds me of a fallen tomato out on the fields: dirty and ripped open under a heavy boot. It's a pathetic response that further fuels my dislike of him. Of his type.

A man without a backbone. Without conviction.

The kind that runs at the first sight of a fight but will feed the fire until someone snaps.

"If you can talk, you can breathe." Multiple guns click and many avert their eyes as I tilt my head to the side, catching sight of Alejandro walking over from the corner of my eye. "What did you say?"

"Q'hubo, Andresito?" My cousin stops beside us and I look over, catching the smirk on his face. He's calm and collected, methodically dissecting the idiot in my hold. "You have something to say?"

"No."

"Louder." Alejandro nods and I release the man, letting him fall to his knees. At once, his hand comes up and he rubs his neck, glaring at us from his position. "Didn't your father ever teach you manners? How to respect those above you?"

"You'll never be him." The hand on the ground bracing his weight tightens into a fist, his teeth grinding as he spits out words through them. He's amusing to watch, at least.

"An abusive adulterer? Is that who I should admire?"

"Fuck you," Andresito hisses out a second before the bottom of my foot meets his face. A swift kick and he's thrown back, landing on his back with an arm at an awkward angle. "Hijueputa!"

"Watch. Your. Mouth." My fingers twitch, and I hold myself back from putting a bullet between his eyes. We're not innocent—there's enough blood on my family's hands to cover a stadium, but his crimes are worse. Behind the disguise of a poppy farmer, Don Andres also dabbled in human trafficking and kept a horde of prostitutes at his disposal by forced addiction. Andresito knows this. His wife knew this. "I won't repeat myself."

"He ruined us!" The kid tries to wipe his face, but only succeeds in spreading the blood flowing from his nose across his lips and cheek. "My family is—"

"You're a bunch of sick fucks."

At my words, his eyes narrow and he tries to stand. "Maybe I'll return the favor?" He's unsteadied, almost drunk-like, and can barely manage to kneel with his face screwed up in anger. "He killed mine and I'll kill—"

"You." I finish for him, pulling my Ruger from the holster around my chest. His father died at Alejandro's hands, and he'll meet his end at mine as a second later I pull the trigger, killing the sole male heir to Don Andres's small estate. A few garbled breaths, and those scared eyes are on mine as his body stills and his life's essence seeps from the wounds. One to his neck and the other his chest; two bullets exit his body and ricochet off the concrete ground, his blood marking those closest to his corpse. "Anyone else have something to say?"

Not a word. Not so much as a sound.

"We apologize for this small inconvenience." Alejandro's voice reverberates throughout the space as he clasps my shoulder, giving it a small squeeze before releasing. His men lower their drawn weapons, and mine returns to its place. "Let's proceed."

"Agreed." Nothing else is said while he retakes his seat, and my attention turns to the men on the floor, a puddle of urine now surrounding their scared forms. That, and the rivulets of blood winding down to the divot at the center that leads to drainage in the cement floor. "How are you two holding up? Need anything?" Their response is a muffled sound and I look over at the man closest to their forms. "Remove the gag."

"Of course, sir." Alejandro's guard tears the covering, then moves back into formation, gun in hand and finger on the trigger.

"Gracias." He nods, and I tilt my head in Francis's direction. "I'm not going to repeat myself."

"I can explain, Javier. Just hear me out."

My eyes narrow and I pick up the machete, admiring the smooth wooden handle and slick blade. Not too heavy. Unbreakable if used with force. "That's not what I asked, Francis."

"Please."

"How have you been?"

"C-could be better."

"And whose fault is that?" Placing the machete back upon the tray, I prepare my single-use gun by loading the two bullets and cocking it with the barrel pointing at Francis.

I've known him for years.

I've welcomed him to share a meal or two with my family.

I offered him a job when his father fell ill, and later when he passed, my family took care of the bill. *Ungrateful son of a bitch.*

"I'm sorry." It's a whisper; two pathetic words that earn him a bullet to his right shoulder. His cry of pain reverberates throughout every inch of this room as his life's essence begins to flow.

At first, the .45 bullet's entry and exit create a small splash, but soon it begins to flow downward, staining his exposed skin.

He's a human map of bruises and cuts, of swollen flesh and pain. From where I stand, it's easy to make out the broken ribs and the fragment poking through the skin.

My cousin doesn't take kindly to thieves.

And while it's his product the men stole, these two are mine. I'm not the head of this operation, never want to be, but I do command respect.

Taking lives is my profession. My passion as a private Sicario.

But more than that, I am a Lucas first, and it was my mother they ran over with a pickup while rushing out of the field.

They left her for dead.

They left a woman whose life revolved around taking care of loved ones broken and now bound to a wheelchair.

"Fuck your apology." *One bullet down.* "Now, let's play a round of truth or death."

"We can find a solution, Javier. She didn't die—"

"You'd already be dead otherwise." The man beside him weeps, and I look over. "Something you want to say, Mr. Gil?" His head shakes back and forth fast, a bit of bloody spittle flying out with the frantic move. "Then be a good boy until I address you. Understood?"

"Yes." Low and meek.

"Speak up. You still have your tongue."

"Yes, sir."

At my nod, he lowers his head and sits stone still. "Tell me, Francis. Tell me why you did it?"

"He offered me money and a lot of American pussy."

"The world is full of opportunities, culicagado. Some good. Some bad." I take the remaining steps between us and poke the still-hot barrel of the Glock into his wound. He squirms, trying to move away while I dig deeper, forcing the tip inside the hole by force. Tears run down his grimy face, his nose running as the skin stretches and eventually gives way. One hard push, and the muscles there buckle. The barrel is deep enough to stay upright without my hand and I let go, crouching down to his level. Eye to eye. "The outcomes vary by scenarios. Investing in real estate is profitable, but stealing from those you owe your life to becomes a death sentence."

"Please don't kill me. I-I'll work off the debt."

"Open that mouth again out of turn, Gil, and I'll slit your throat," I say without looking over, and when he doesn't utter another sound, I smile at Francis and tap the handle. "Get up."

"I'm bound, Javi—" He doesn't finish as the back of my hand connects with his face, forcing his head to the side.

"There's enough slack for you to stand." Gil looks up at me and begins to rise before Francis, but I shake my head. One kneels while the other struggles to find footing, taking longer than my patience has time for, and I pull the gun out and hold it to his temple as positive reinforcement.

Once again, his scream rends the air and his body recoils, but Francis is smart enough to rise to his feet. "That's better."

"What can I do to make this right?" His low words meet my ears and I smile, rubbing the stained red barrel down his cheek and then tapping the skin there. "I don't want to die, Javier. Please."

"So, you want to make a deal? Is that right?" At my words, he nods. "Okay."

"Okay?" There's a hint of relief mixed with trepidation in his tone, and there should be. Nothing is ever as simple. Not in our life. "I'll do whatever it is you ask."

"You sure about that?"

"Yes." No hesitation, and I catch the nervous flinch from Gil. The way he folds into himself.

That man isn't a complete idiot; he just made the mistake that so many do. Greed isn't an awful trait; the problem lies in taking from the wrong hands because those at the top have been where you are.

The most notorious criminals start somewhere. An attack on our business isn't a foreign occurrence—it's something our family has prepared for—but not choosing their victim wisely will be a costly error.

"There's a bullet in the magazine, Francis. Just one." He nods and I hand the Glock over, taking a step back. "Kill him."

There's an important choice to be made here:

Be brave or fight.

Shoot him or me.

Not that he would ever set a single foot outside this warehouse, but when the will to survive is strong, you'll try anything. A few beats of silence follow, the sole cause of noise coming from the man still kneeling on the cold and dirty floor.

Gil begins to recite words that are familiar to me. A prayer from the Catholic church while Francis raises a shaking hand. There's a line on forgiveness for one's sins—on repenting for harmful thoughts —and throughout both, the man remains breathing.

Sweat beads on both sets of brows, and those in the room to witness don't dare speak.

"Shoot him."

"Javier, I'm—"

"Unable to follow simple instructions?" Because playing the role of a monster and being one are two vastly different things. "Is that what you're telling me?"

"I can do it." His shaking limbs say otherwise. His expression is one of utter fear.

"Then get closer and use both hands to steady the shot." Not that his injured shoulder helps, but it amuses me to see him grit his teeth while doing as I say. "You have five seconds to shoot."

Francis closes his eyes, and I move closer. He exhales roughly, and I smirk. "That's five." Before he can react, I have the Glock back in my hand and Gil lies dead with a bullet hole to the side of the head. Fragments scatter with the force of the blast. A lifeless body. Cold, vacant eyes.

I drop the gun between his bare feet and wait.

No reaction. Not so much as a twitch of a muscle.

My eyes flick to Alejandro, and he presses a button on his phone. At once, the buzz of speakers fills the space and Francis's voice filters through the room.

*"I told you this would be easy, parce. These people are mindless slaves. If the Lucas family says jump, they fall into line and ask how high."* The sound of an engine turning can be heard, and then the seat belt alarm follows shortly after. His companion doesn't give more than a grunt in answer, giving Francis the opening to run his mouth. I've listened to this recording. *"Cocky assholes sit comfortably atop while we do all the work."*

*"But isn't your dream to be them?"* Gil asks. A lighter sparks and you can hear his deep inhale from a cigarette. *"That's why you're doing this, no? The money, power, and easy pussy attached."*

*"Always for a willing whore!"* Both men laugh, but then Francis sobers. *"But apart from that, I said yes because both Alejandro and Javier denied me the money I needed. They cost me my wife, and I'm returning the favor by taking a client and making them lose a lot more than the fifty thousand dollars I asked for."*

*"They couldn't spare fifty?"* Gil's tone is incredulous with a hint of amusement. *"That's nothing to them. Not even a blip on their accounts."*

*"It isn't."*

*"Then why say no?"*

*"Javier—"*

"Turn it off." Alejandro does and then tosses the device to land beside the gun. Francis looks down at both, face pallid. "Say it again."

"Say what?" He doesn't look up at me.

"Finish what you said on the recording."

"You know?"

"We do." Every single member of my family does.

"How?" Now his eyes meet mine, and in them I find defeat. "I didn't talk around—"

"The pickup Gil offered was one of ours, you dumb motherfucker. It was a loaner he got from Emiliano a day before under the guise of being here on vacation. An idiot move, for a man who didn't hide his tracks well."

"Why?"

"We let you empty the fields. We let you make the transaction with him."

"I'm sorry."

"You will be." I take the few steps toward the tray with the machete and pick it up, slapping the metal against my palm before turning back to him. He's a mess: bloody and weak. "But this was the risk you were willing to take when you decided to rise against us, and all because we wouldn't give you the money needed to silence your mistress."

"It wasn't supposed to end like this." Francis hangs his head, shoulders slumped. "In and out is what he promised me and with the move, Ana would forgive me. She'd come back."

"Why put yourself in this position?" I ask, but the answer is of no true importance.

"Because I'm an idiot."

"Very true."

Francis takes in a deep breath and lets it out slowly. "For what it's worth, Javier, I'm so sorry about what happened to your Mrs. Ida...how we left her there. I regret that more than you'll ever know."

"And I'll see you in hell one day, parce." With that, I swing the machete clear across his chest, tearing open his flesh from shoulder to rib. Blood spills and his scream of pain overtakes every inch of the room while those inside begin a slow clap. One by one, the witnesses make their approval heard as the noise level drowns out Francis's pain. "Mercy or pain?"

"Pain."

"Pain."

"Pain."

It's a chant that grows louder, the small windows rattling, and I nod, lifting the machete high again. The next strike is down his injured shoulder, embedding deep before I leave a matching slice across the opposite arm.

The puddle beneath him grows. The strength in his body is depleted and he slumps forward on all fours. "Please end me, Javier."

"It'll come sooner than you think." One by one, I leave cuts across his body from the neck down. His face is left alone and only so his family can bury him without further trauma.

"Thank you." Those are his final words as the last blow is delivered to the back of his neck. My blade stays lodged as he falls, the final breath escaping while his mouth is now stained by the blood trickling from the corner.

"Let this be a lesson to those who ever try to rise against the Lucas family. Next time, I won't be as forgiving." Faces nod and people turn toward the door as the seconds begin to pass. They go back home to their families while Alejandro's men begin to remove the bodies, and it's when Gil is placed inside a bag and wheeled out that my cousin approaches once more, a damp towel in his hand. "Thanks, primo."

"Our get-togethers have always been entertaining."

"Would you have it any other way?"

"No." Alejandro claps me on the shoulder then, a laugh booming out of him. "You remember our last trip to Mexico?"

"How can I forget." There's a smirk across my face as I remember what led to the showdown with a local cartel boss. "Who knew turning down a gold-digger would cause such a mess. I lost my favorite gun in that exchange."

"There's a replica in the car for you."

"It's the least you can do." We both let out a chuckle, making our way outside and toward my SUV where I pause to admire the gaudily wrapped box atop the hood. "The paper is hideous."

"Shut it and smile."

"I'm going to miss you, asshole."

"And it won't be the same without you here." He turns and leans against the front grill. "Are you sure about Chicago?"

"I'm a wanted man."

"Aren't we all in this family?"

"True." I mimic his stance, and we both watch the sun begin to set across the skyline. "But something is pulling me in that direction, and I'm following my instincts. Besides, I've been made a very lucrative offer."

"How good?"

"Enough to keep me occupied for a year."

"And you trust this person?"

"He comes highly recommended." It's the best I can give him, and he nods. In this business, no one has morals and everyone has ulterior motives—myself included.

"Just remember that this will always be home, Javier."

"And blood is always thicker than water."

# 2

# Javier

*Two months later…*

THE ASHER BUILDING is synonymous with wealth and opulence, and yet, I know the truth behind these walls. Things hidden in plain sight that those walking past would never imagine the man behind a CEO's desk is capable of.

But then again, I'm not most people, and word travels fast within certain circles.

All it takes is the right connection—the right person pulling the strings—and doors open with endless possibilities for the right price. A price Mr. Asher is all too willing to pay for a man with my particular set of skills.

A young woman sitting at the receptionist's desk looks my way as I walk through the main entrance and head straight for the elevator. She's smart enough to not draw attention my way just as the guards ignore my existence. Instead, she quickly looks away and helps an elderly woman asking to speak with the investment specialist inside the branch.

No one speaks to me, and I don't wait long as the door opens a few seconds after I press the button, letting me inside a wide and empty car. The walls are glass and as I ascend, I take notice of multiple cameras on each floor and the heavy security watching all who enter.

To someone who doesn't know any better, it's a simple system—common—while I know the quality of the equipment will rival that of the White House. The sensors are there to read more than activity. More than account for who comes and goes.

At this point, someone inside the security room knows the size of my cock and to what side it hangs.

There is no privacy within these walls, and I respect that. Respect the man who's taken his family's bank and turned it into a profitable money laundering empire for corrupt and unapologetic businessmen around the world. Men like my cousins who could profit from the services offered.

He's dangerous, but I have no soul. He's wealthy, and I have no fear.

I pass floor after floor until reaching the last, and the door opens. Two letters stand out across from me; a large golden M and A that lead to a small hallway where a desk awaits. There's no one sitting there—no one to let their boss know I'm here, and just when I take a step past the table, my world stops.

Literally. Unequivocally.

"Take another step and I'll shoot you." There's a hint of amusement in her tone, and the decadent sound sends a rush of excitement down my spine. Every nerve ending vibrates as her scent, a sweet and floral tone, infiltrates my senses. The owner of the voice is close, invading my personal space, and my nostrils flare—my cock giving a harsh jerk behind the confines of my zipper. *What the fuck?* "Now, the question here is…are you feeling frisky?"

"Those are dangerous words for a…" I begin but trail off when she steps into my line of sight, hand on her hip and eyes, challenging. *Fuck.* This woman is beautiful: a tiny doll with a hint of wickedness behind those seafoam eyes and a taste of depravity in every sinful curve.

Because I take her in.

All of her.

From her dark auburn hair to the dangerous heels on her tiny feet; this woman is perfection. At no more than five feet and three inches, she draws something from deep within that makes me throb where I stand, but it's the cockiness—that tiny curl of her upper lip that brings forth the asshole in me.

I take a step forward, loving the way her chest expands.

I lick my bottom lip, savoring the way she follows the movement with unveiled interest.

*Who is she?*

"Who are you?" she asks without pause. No shame in the way she watches me.

"I'll tell you after I meet with your boss, Muñeca." There's a slight narrowing of her eyes and purse to her top lip at my words, and they make me want to bite her. To keep pushing her buttons to see if she snaps—if she scratches. "So be a good girl for me and let him know Javier Lucas is here."

"What did you just say? What did you call me?" My eyes skim down her front and pause on a small name tag attached to her white silk top. "I think I heard wrong."

"Mariah," I croon low, savoring her name on my tongue and the small hitch in her breath. There's a slight tremble that she quickly hides behind a rigid back when I close the space between us. "Muñeca…my little doll, I asked that you do your job and announce me. I promise to reward you after."

"Step back," she hisses through gritted teeth, her expression angry, but I catch the straining of two little nipples against her top. The goose bumps on her arms. "I'll give you to the count of—"

"Mariah, let me know when Mr. Lucas arrives," a male voice says from the doorway at the far back of the room. It startles her, and she jumps back as if burned while I hold my ground, never taking my eyes off of her. Never addressing the man I came here to see.

"He's here, Malcolm." I don't like the way she says his name. The familiarity and ease when she should address him as her superior and nothing else.

"You mean Mr. Asher?" The bite in my tone isn't missed by either, and I feel the man's eyes on me. Sense when he comes closer, and if I were a lesser man, I'd cower back.

But I'm not. Never will be.

"Is there a problem here between you and my cousin, Mr. Lucas?"

*Cousin? She's his cousin?* I'm better than to miss an important fact like this.

For the first time in my life, I'm speechless—a bit embarrassed—and all I can manage is a shake of my head, and yet, pulling my attention away from her is impossible. The jealousy that burns through me like molten acid unnerves me, but at the same time, excites me. It's shaken me, and by the coquettish look in those beautiful orbs, Mariah knows this.

Finds my reaction amusing. *Motherfucking dangerous.*

"Mr. Lucas seems to take his formalities extremely serious, Malcolm. Cut him some slack. It might be a cultural thing." My eyes narrow at her words, but her cousin merely chuckles to my right where he seems to be taking in my fumble.

"Is that so, Javier?"

"Not at all." I flick my attention in his direction for ten seconds —moments where I take in the familial resemblance and smirk— before meeting Mariah's challenge head-on. "I've just been caught off guard by your cousin's beauty. That's all."

"I am spectacular, *cousin*," she says, and then fucks me in a way that tests my control. I'm left hanging by a very thin thread and every muscle in my body tenses, coils when her delicate fingers land on my chest while closing the distance between us. There's playfulness in her words while her body language teases. "Can't fault the man for having impeccable taste."

"You are trouble."

"And I think you like challenges." With that she walks past me, leaving me in the open room with the man I came to work for and a hard cock.

"*Christ.*"

"Is not affiliated with my family." Malcolm gives my shoulder a quick squeeze before turning toward his office, and I follow, walking through and taking a seat on the other side of his desk. And while I try to gather my thoughts and explain my behavior, Asher walks over to a small bar on the back wall and pours a few fingers' worth of clear liquid into two glasses.

He hands one to me and I immediately bring it to my lips, taking in the floral with a hint of citrus notes in the gin. "Thank you."

"You're welcome." His first sip is slow, and I expect the narrowing of his eyes when he swallows. Once, twice…on the third, Malcolm tosses back the spirit and walks around to his chair, taking a seat with the Chicago skyline as his backdrop. "Now, tell me why I shouldn't shoot you."

"That's the second time within thirty minutes someone in your family has threatened to do so."

"And we won't hesitate, either."

"Neither will I."

Malcolm doesn't react as one would expect with my threat. No. Not at all.

Instead, his smile widens and his narrowed eyes crinkle at the corner from amusement. "You've got balls, Javier. More than you should for a man outside of his country."

"What's that supposed to mean? Outside of my country?"

"Simply put?"

"Speak your mind, but I will do the same."

He's smirking, not a single thread of fear. "This isn't territory the

Lucas family controls, nor is this a diplomacy. I hired you because I know you're the best and will be an asset to me."

"An asset?" Because my understanding is that I'd be in charge of his security for the next twelve months with a payout well over three million American dollars. I'm here to shape his guards and implement what I've done back home. "Explain yourself, Asher."

"I've done my homework."

"That makes two of us."

"Then you know I put out the call after the job you did for a client. News travels fast, and I'm not an easy man to impress." Placing the glass down, he rubs his chin. Dissecting me. Waiting for me to ask a question that will never leave my lips. I'm not a man who worries about the whys or maybes. Instead, I match his composure and wait.

And wait.

His patience matches mine and, in this game, neither is willing to bend. I know why he wanted me and why the call came, but the change in negotiation came much sooner than I expected.

"Ask me."

"How long?" There's no need for me to elaborate and he sits forward, opening the drawer to his right and pulling out two items: a file and a knife. Both are pushed my way and I open the folder, reading the contents inside. He's been busy. Most of the offenses here are well accounted for and I've never denied or hidden them, but it's the last page that makes me pause. "Who gave this to you?"

There's no mistaking the venom in my tone nor the tensing of my muscles for what it is…

A threat. A warning.

"I paid that contract out, Javier. No harm will come to them."

"Who did this, Malcolm?" I grit out through clenched teeth, crushing the paper in my hand. "Who the fuck was stupid enough to put a hit on the women in my family?"

"It's taken care of—"

"No. It isn't." With that, I stand, roughly pushing the chair back, and turn to leave, but before I reach the door, the knife once atop his desk embeds itself in the wall closest to me. My reaction is just as volatile, full of ire, and I grip the handle in my hand and pull it out. It's a beautiful piece, and by the weight, I can attest that it's solid gold. The blade is sleek, sharp, and I return the favor with a quick flick of the wrist.

"You haven't been dismissed, Javier. Sit down."

"Next time, I won't miss."

"Then you aren't interested in taking a walk with me and meeting the name on the sheet you've crumbled in your rage?" That stops me in my tracks. No rebuttal. Not a single word as I retake my seat, eyes on him with a neutral expression.

Malcolm Asher played his cards well, and I'm not stubborn enough to walk out with the silent offers he's made.

"I'm listening."

"Look at the last line and read it aloud."

"Castro Acevedo."

"Do you know him?" A nod is my response, seething at the nerve of this son of a bitch. Castro Acevedo works with the presidential family in Colombia, an enemy to mine. They all are. "This came as a direct order the moment you left the country. They want you to come back."

"I know they do."

"So much so, that they sent Acevedo here."

"Here?"

"Here."

"Where is he?"

"I'll give him to you on two conditions." And there it is. His upper hand. Malcolm stands then and takes his jacket off, placing it carefully over his chair. Then the cufflinks come off and the sleeves are rolled up. He doesn't answer me while he does this but does push across another piece of paper.

A smaller one with a single line written in neat penmanship.

*Three years and ten bodies. Do you accept?*

"I CAN, but I have a stipulation of my own." Grabbing a pen from beside his stapler, I scribble my condition and slide it across.

*I'll concede to an open contract with no end date under my discretion after the three you request, but in return, you don't interfere.*

"YOU'RE WALKING A VERY thin line, Lucas. My cousin isn't—"

"I want the chance to get to know her, Malcolm," I interject before he says something that will destroy any agreement we could arrive at. The click of his gun is quickly followed by mine as two hands raise, and we hold our ground. "I'd never disrespect her like that."

"Give me one good reason why I should allow this?"

Because while I don't believe in love at first sight, I won't deny she's caught my attention. That her sass has lit something within, and I want to see how dangerous her touch will be to:

My body. My mind.

I want her to burn me alive.

Keeping those thoughts to myself, I hold his stare. He might be the boss in Chicago, dominate the global market of finances, but I'm not some peon or low-level thug who came begging for a job off the streets. I'll give respect but demand it just the same.

It's the only way this agreement will work. I'd hate to hurt him or anyone in Mariah's family.

"First, she's a grown woman and makes up her own mind. Head

of your family or not, I won't allow you to take choices away from her."

"And second?" There's less hostility in his tone, and my stance relaxes a bit.

"She undid me." I'm not going to beat around the bush or deny it. "Simple as that."

For a few beats of the clock, we remain quiet. Each holding the other's gaze. Our weapons are drawn.

"That honesty could get you in trouble."

"I'm not afraid."

"And it's the only reason I'll concede to your request." Malcolm places his gun atop the desk, and I do the same. "Welcome to the Asher family, Javier."

"Gracias." I extend a hand and he takes it, giving it a hard squeeze.

"You hurt her, and I'll kill you."

"I hurt her, and I can guarantee she'll pull the trigger herself." At my words he throws his head back and laughs, shaking his head while picking up his gun and mine, handing over the latter. "Smart man."

"Now, where do I sign?"

"Your word suffices, but I do believe you're owed a signing bonus."

# 3

## Mariah

I'M IN TROUBLE.

So much trouble since the moment he walked onto my floor and knocked the very breath from my lungs. My palms are sweaty, and my chest feels tight. My knees feel weak, and the delicate slip of lace covering my mound has been rendered useless.

And all because of one man. A very self-assured and dangerous man.

"*Christ*, Mariah. Get ahold of yourself," I mumble under my breath, hand on the wall beside the elevator shaft after pressing the down button. For the next two hours, this floor will be closed to all foot traffic while they talk, and we await orders inside of a hidden room beneath the building where a selected few meet their fate.

The good.

The bad.

Their end.

The sound of his voice caresses my skin while the sound of footfalls over the marble floor follows. It's faint—melodic—and I shiver.

Goose bumps break out across my skin while I lean my head on the wall and close my eyes.

Breathe in. Breathe out. *Never show weakness.*

It's the mantra I've been reciting since the day I learned who my family is. What they are—what I'm capable of without remorse.

However, thinking and doing it are two very different things because I've never been affected by a man like this. *Not even by him.*

I've never felt the rush of excitement or the lick of heat settle low in my abdomen with such ferocity from his mere presence.

At the moment, I feel like the virgin I'm not and haven't been in years. And while I've only slept with one man, a worthless jerk no longer walking this earth, I feel unsure of myself.

Nervous. Jittery. Unable to comprehend how one devilish smirk could get under my skin with such ease. How with one look from a pair of soulful brown eyes I lost more than my composure.

His height made me feel dainty.

His muscles made me breathless.

But what's more dangerous than his looks is the slickness of his mouth and the challenge he presents. Because this man with his white, open-at-the-collar dress shirt and black slacks wasn't intimidated by me or who my family is. His cockiness was playful while his stare was a silent promise to devour his prey…

Me. I'm his prey.

The private elevator that leads to the lowest level of the Asher building opens then, and I let out a breath I didn't know I'd been holding. Each step inside is a bit shaky, and more so when the lingering scent of his cologne infiltrates my senses.

*Fuck.* It's earth and rain mixed with a hint of spice that causes my thighs to clench and another stuttered breath to escape. "He can't work here." *Malcolm will have to find someone else.* But as those words run through my mind, a pang of remorse follows. I can't help my attraction to him, even if he equally pisses me off.

If anything, it's the danger—the demand in his tone that excites me.

He's not going to *yes, ma'am* me because of my last name.

He isn't what I expected to arrive today, and I feel off my game.

The large metal door opens, and the men within greet me with a nod of their head. They're standing against the back wall, watching a man tied to a chair in a three-piece suit whose facial expression gives way to his fear and a bloody encounter with his captors.

We know why he's here, but he doesn't. We've given him the accommodation he deserves while he's returned our kindness with whining and unnecessary tears.

"Has he been given anything to eat or drink since last night?" I ask Carmelo, a trusted guard. He's standing closest to Acevedo and without the customary all-white coveralls that Malcolm demands his cleanup crew wear.

"Not—"

"Please, Miss," he interrupts Carmelo, looking at me from the one eye that isn't swollen shut. "This is a mistake. Help me out of here, and you'll be rewarded by the Colombian president."

Carmelo raises his hand to strike the idiot, but I give him a minute shake of the head and he stands down. Instead, he retakes his position of silence while biting back a chuckle.

"Will he, now?"

"Yes." Relief colors his features as he thinks I'm intrigued by the offer. He has no idea who I am. "You'll never work another day in your life."

"Never?" I keep my voice low, almost sweet and innocent. He's buying it too. "I'd be rich?"

"Beyond your comprehension, *linda*." Because calling me beautiful is supposed to win me over. *Idiot.*

"But what if my taste runs a little more—"

"Whatever you want."

"Morbid," I finish off with a glare, and his lips snap shut. His shoulders slump and eyes close, a few stray tears falling down his bruised cheek. "Why the tears, Acevedo? Why the sudden plea for mercy when you were willing to murder women and children to hurt the Lucas men?"

"What is he to you?"

"You've always been a curious one, Castro," Javier answers for me, his voice reverberating throughout every square inch of the room as he steps through the threshold, and the horror-filled expression on our guest is comical. His body shakes and a pitiful cry escapes a set of chapped lips while a breath gets caught in my throat.

My pulse races. My nipples tighten. My core clenches.

*Lord help me.*

"How? Why?" Acevedo looks to me for answers, but I merely shrug and take my place beside a silent Malcolm. My cousin's standing a bit to the left, leaving Javier to run this show, but remains within everyone's line of sight.

"Because you sold your soul to the devil and he delivered you to me." Javier steps forward while slowly undoing the buttons of his shirt and slips the garment off his shoulders. He's precise in his movements, adorable while placing the neatly folded dress shirt atop a small table close to Acevedo.

There are no weapons in sight. No way for him to exact revenge, but the prospect of what those muscles—the bulging cords of tattooed flesh—can do leave me breathless.

"Javier, I was just following commands." It leaves Acevedo in a low whisper, but the silence of the room makes it so we all hear clearly. "Quintero—"

"Fucked you without lubrication," he spits out, face contorted in rage before softening when he looks in my direction. The action is fast, and the softness that flickers in those warm orbs pulls a smile from my lips. It's brief, this moment we share, before he looks away and the killer I've heard so much about makes an entrance.

He's magnificent. Overwhelming.

*Perfect.*

"Please." Tears and snot and the faint scent of urine are unmistakable in the room. "Please don't kill me."

"You accepted the offer Quintero made."

"But I never carried it out!" Javier just smiles, walking around his form once before stopping at his right wrist. Without pause, he undoes the rope keeping Acevedo in place and then the other. Both feet are next. "Please, Javier. I didn't touch anyone; that has to mean something!"

"Stand up."

"Just listen...*fuck*!" The first strike is straight to his mouth and two teeth fly out, landing near Malcolm's feet. The next is to his neck and he chokes out a cry, bending at the waist with both hands up in an attempt to defend himself while his legs give out.

Javier doesn't let up, though. Blow after vicious blow is landed on Acevedo's upper body and the back of his head. Javier's knuckles are white and bruised. His chest is heaving, his mouth curled into a sinister grin.

He's brutally beautiful and my walls clench when he drives a knee in to the bent man's face.

"You knew exactly what you were accepting, Castro." Fisting Acevedo's hair, Javier forces the bleeding man to meet his stare from his position on his knees. There's a gash across the bridge of his nose and the swelling has already begun, but it's not enough for the assassin now working for the head of the Asher family. Bloodthirst is real, and he's given in to the need for vengeance. "I warned you once in the past, and there won't be a second chance."

With that, he lifts a leg and brings Acevedo's face down to his knee repeatedly. Over and over without pause, he breaks the man's face down to the point it's nothing but a bloody mass of cuts and broken bones.

And even then, he continues until our guest's nose caves in and all his front teeth fall out. Both men are a mess, but it's the beast standing that holds me captive—spellbound—and unable to look away as he smiles and then lands another direct strike to Acevedo's jaw.

There's a sickening crunch, a splash of red that decorates the floor, and then a body falls limply, making the most disturbing gurgling sound. Each breath becomes more shallow than the last. Each second his body struggles, you see the life drain from his eyes until there's nothing left but a broken man and the victor standing over his frame with his eyes set on me.

Around us, Malcolm's men quickly move as they begin the process of decontamination...

Water is turned on, and the floor near Javier is flushed out.

The body is removed in a large black bag.

My cousin leaves without a word.

And while the world carries on, we watch each other. Take in the rise and fall of our chests and the mirroring want that's left me breathless, a bit nervous and unsure.

"We need to talk, Muñeca." *Why do I like it so much when he calls me that?* I'm already shaking my head before he finishes, ignoring the clench in my core, and take a few steps back. There's mirth in his eyes, but he doesn't follow, choosing instead to tilt his head while licking his lips. I'm inspected from head to toe. His stare feels like a soft caress. "But not today."

That catches me off guard and I pause mid-step, my face scrunching up in confusion. "What?"

My sputter amuses him, and the jerk lets out a low, throaty chuckle. "I said, not today."

"Then why are you wasting my time," I grit out through clenched teeth, hands balled at my sides while fighting to ignore the pictures adorning his upper body, more so the black and white angel of death design that looks like the counterpart to my fallen angel. They're both Gothically haunting yet beautiful. A mated pair. *This is ridiculous, chica. Snap out of it.* "Better yet, I'll see you around. I have better things to do than—"

"I'll be picking you up tomorrow night for dinner, Mariah."

"I'm not going out with you." What kind of game is he playing?

Javier rubs a hand across his chest, spreading the fresh blood across the dark angel. "You will."

"What makes you so sure? I'm not a woman who lowers her standards."

At my words, he takes the steps between us and grips my chin. His hold isn't hard or meant to hurt, but to prove how much he affects me, and he does. I'm jittery and sensitive between my thighs, and goose bumps rise across my flesh. But more damaging to my psyche is the hungry way he watches me. Memorizes my face while cataloging each reaction with that devilish smirk across his lips.

*I'm screwed. More than.*

"Be a good girl, Muñeca. Don't fight me."

"You haven't earned the right to make demands on my time."

"I own your time, Mariah. Learn to accept that." Then the bastard lowers his head and kisses my reddening cheek, rendering me speechless. Unsettled. Angry at his cockiness.

Then on the next breath, I'm turned on by the heat in his eyes and command in his tone.

This sudden urge to test his patience and conviction is a dangerous game, and I find myself meeting his stare without an ounce of fear. Without a care for the consequences.

Because I'm not a wilting flower, and I'm ready to play if he is.

"To own me, you have to catch me first, Mr. Lucas. Are you worthy?"

"I'd kill every man in this city if you so much as asked."

Christ, those words stir something deep within me, but I walk away before impulses become problems down the road. Each step away from him is harder than the last, but I make my way back to my floor without looking back.

He doesn't follow me inside the elevator. He doesn't demand I respond, but I am aware of his heated stare and then the near suffocating presence he exudes the moment he steps onto the CEO's floor an hour later. Javier doesn't talk to me as he strides past my desk fully clothed and without a single hair out of place.

No blood. No slick remarks. Not so much as a look in my direction before slipping inside of Malcolm's office. It bothers me, this ignoring my narrowing eyes and the small huff that escapes, but more so when a few minutes later my phone rings with my cousin's extension blinking.

"Yes, boss?"

"Two coffees, please, and bring in the Bernard file."

"Right away." I'm already grabbing the folder he needs, anticipating it earlier in the day, and closing the bottom drawer before locking it. There's certain client information that can't be lost or tampered with—stolen—and I only keep on hand the bare necessities at all times.

No one knows where we store physical documents except Malcolm and me. They have no access to the hidden room with restricted access a floor below. Most never realize that this building has an entire floor blocked off and that the elevator shaft skips it.

It was designed that way. Made to appear as though the vault room downstairs was its separate floor when in fact, it connects with one small step changing the elevations.

With the file in my hand of a notorious French art smuggler worth a billion from trading in the black market, I head to the small kitchen on the other side of the wall behind me. It's not large, but it gets the job done for what we need; coffee being the main focus.

That, and pastries from a small Hungarian bakery my family loves to visit. There isn't a single house that bears the last name Asher who doesn't have a never-ending stock, and I plate a few while pressing the start button on the Keurig.

While it percolates, I make a conscious decision to let Javier use my mug. A shiny and pink and full of glitter unicorn cup that my aunt gave me after our Black Friday hunt last year.

"Good-looking jerk," I mutter under my breath, filling both cups before adding creamer, sugar, and the pastries to the tray. "Should've just...*Jesus!*" I scream, almost dropping their refreshments. "How long have you been standing there?"

My tone is accusatory, my posture defensive, but Javier only grins at me while pulling the tray from my hands and placing it on a small dinette table to his left. "Long enough."

"For what?" I'm shaking, but not from fear. His scent envelops me in a web of want.

"To hear the need in your voice."

"You mean repulsion?"

"You and I both know that's a lie." Closer, he takes the three steps separating us and grips my hips with both hands. "And the feeling is very mutual, sweetheart."

"Let go," I hiss out and then bite back my disappointment when he does. His warmth is gone. He's now by the door, holding it open with the back of his foot with the full tray in his hands. "What game are you playing at?"

"Hurry up with that file, Muñeca. Asher wants to go over it with me and I don't have all day to wait."

"You motherfu—"

"Watch the words that leave that pretty little mouth."

"Or what?"

"Or you'll find yourself praying to a different God." Then he winks before walking away, leaving me an angry, frustrated, and intrigued ball of nerves that follows a few minutes later while plotting his demise.

I'm not going to let him get one over on me.

He should be afraid. Very afraid.

# Javier

S HE'S GLORIOUS IN her indignation.

Beautiful and majestic while placing the file down atop Malcolm's desk with more force than necessary while glaring at me. *So sexy in her anger.* There's something about her that's gotten under my skin, and the more I see of her sweet lips and dangerous eyes, the more I want.

To taste. To bite. To bend her over and show her how good it could be.

Every instinct within me fights to bring her closer, to not question the why, but I hold my stance with a stoic expression on my face. Her every action draws me in, and the dare in her eyes fuels a fire I've never experienced before.

I'm not one to date and have never given a single fuck about settling down.

Not in this life. Not when your next day is never guaranteed and leaving a family behind is irresponsible. So I've kept to myself and when the need arose, I found a willing woman who understood the no-questions-asked and no-repeats rule.

Moreover, I've seen it before in my family when Alejandro's father was incarcerated for being an honest man. Women and kids suffer. Most end up repeating the cycle because that's all they'll ever know. Because they'll always be the product of what society deems to be scum.

*I'll make an exception for her, though.* That thought has been running through my mind since our little exchange earlier in the day.

"Will that be all, boss?" It leaves her on a sneer directed at me, and I bite back a smirk.

"Yes." Asher's eyes are on me, watching my reactions, while I continue to ignore anything but her. "Just make sure we're not disturbed. You can head out whenever you want."

"Wish I could, but I'm meeting someone for dinner nearby. It would be a waste of time to drive—"

"Who?"

"None of your concern, Mr. Lucas. Remember that." The glare is gone, and the sass is back. It's there in the swing of her hips as she passes by my chair on her way out and then the quick look of triumph when I reach out and stop her, my grip of her wrist firm. "Is there something you need?"

"There is." I rub my thumb along the veins of her wrist, enjoying the tiny little flutters at the pulse point. The softness that overtakes her features and an almost inaudible sigh that makes me swallow back the demand to submit and clear her calendar. *Not yet. Not here.* "Do you have regular milk for the coffee? Could you get some for me?"

"I'm not your—"

"Play nice, Mariah." It's on the tip of my tongue to tell our boss to fuck off, but I take in a deep breath and let it out slowly. "He's new and valuable."

"My pleasantries will cost extra."

"I'll remember that." She doesn't pull her hand away from me during their exchange. Instead, I notice the small step in my direction. The leaning of her hip. "We do have milk, Javier. Is two percent okay?"

"That would be fine."

"Then I'll be right back."

Neither of us moves until a throat clears and our heads turn toward an amused CEO. "Was that for today's coffee or tomorrow's?"

"My apologies." Reluctantly, I release my hold and she nods, giving me a quick smile before exiting. There was no mention of the milk I requested or if she'd be back, but I watch that door, hoping to catch another glimpse of the little demon.

"You know..." Malcolm begins, and I tilt my head so he knows I'm listening "...I thought this would be a mistake and I'd kill you before the week was over."

"That's a funny assumption."

"The dead part?"

"The part where you think I'd go down easily."

"I don't underestimate you, Javier. That's where it becomes dangerous for you." At those words, I shift my attention to him and arch a brow. "Your heart is black, and I hired you for that quality, but watching my cousin run you around will be the highlight of my days. Just don't let it interfere with work. You do, and the consequences won't be agreeable."

"Understood."

"Good." He waves a hand in the air. "Now, go get your milk because she's not coming back."

"Not necessary." Picking up my lukewarm cup of coffee, I bring it to my lips and take a large sip. "I take it black and without sugar. That was just to annoy her."

"She's not a wilting flower. Her bark is darker than her bite."

"I'm counting on that."

THE FIRST THING I notice as I exit Malcolm's office a few hours later is the lack of movement. No one's here. No noise. Nothing but the sweet lingering scent of her perfume and the temptation it causes.

It pulls me in the direction of her desk where it's stronger, where I can almost feel Mariah's fire surround me, and I sit in her chair.

A little creepy? Maybe.

Do I care? Not one bit.

The first thing I take notice of is how organized—uncluttered—her items are. Not so much as a pen is out of place and I remedy that by repaying the little beauty for making me hard all afternoon.

For each time she walked into his office with a file.

For each time she brushed past my arm, extending herself while placing an item down in front of him.

My muñeca could've walked around but chose not to. So I'm choosing to do this.

I pull out a pen with my name monogrammed and leave it in her holder. Then, I take hers. All ten of them. A simple switch that will annoy her, and so will the flipping of file placements.

What's on the left will move to the right and vice versa.

"She's going to kill you."

"More than likely." I'm scribbling a note for her to find before standing from her seat and facing an amused Malcolm. "I'm not afraid."

"Don't say I never gave you fair warning. I think I've more than done that today."

"Understood." Patting my pocket with her pens, I smirk. "Now, have a good evening."

The elevator's already waiting when I press the arrow down, and as I step through, my phone rings. It stops at the third ping and then starts again once I press the button for the lobby.

Not many people have this number, so I pull it out and answer without looking at the caller ID. "Hello?"

"Mijo!" Mom's excited voice comes through the line, wind rustling on her side. "How are you? Are you eating okay?"

"I'm good. Can't complain too much." The large metal doors close and the metal box begins to descend as I lean back. "I'm pretty settled in now and I've made the necessary moves. Have you thought about my proposal?"

"Not interested."

"Think of it as a mini-vacation." I want her out of the country for a few months. "Just enough time for you to relax, maybe cook me a meal or two—"

"I know what you're doing, and it's unnecessary." There's a hint of annoyance in her tone, that motherly don't-argue-with-me-on-this that almost makes me laugh, but I rein it in. If I go that route, I'll lose. Ida Lucas is the most stubborn woman I know. "Besides, I'm staying with your aunt Sara for now. Alejandro picked me up yesterday against my will."

"Did he, now?" The doors open and I step out, nodding at the guard beside the entrance. He has an envelope in his hand and casually slips it into mine before I cross the exit. I know what's inside: my ID for clearance, a key to a company SUV, and a monetary donation for agreeing to his terms. "When was this?"

"Did you give the order?" she counters, and I can imagine her arched brow and the drumming of nails atop the wheelchair's arm. "Am I being shipped off next, too?"

"Mamita, I had nothing to do with that. I swear." Lies. All lies, and she knows this. Her huff over the line tells me as much, but at the moment I'm left with few options. With Quintero Jr. coming into power as the next Colombian president, we're on the defensive. Their family hates ours, and the feeling is mutual. "Listen, come and visit me here and see for yourself how well I'm living. Even cook me a meal or two?"

"That's the second time you mention food."

"Just miss yours."

"No." There's a pause between us, the silence heavy right before she sighs. "I love you, Javiercito. Love you more than my own life, but I need you to accept something. I was born in Colombia and I'll die here...that family nor their hijueputa obsession with mine will send me running."

"One week?" It's a compromise. The parking garage is up ahead and I walk toward it, ignoring the passersby and the one lady in her fifties that sends me a wink.

"Three days."

Pausing at the Asher garage entrance, I look up toward the sky. "Five, and—" I'm cut off by the sudden bump to my side and the sharp pain at my hip. The hit isn't hard, but I do lose my balance and end up staring at the car's owner with my front bent over and hands splayed over the hood, phone still caught between ear and shoulder.

Her eyes dance with mirth.

Her lips quirk up into a devilish grin.

Mariah's the epitome of trouble and simply asks me to move out of her way with the flick of her wrist. The action is meant to be condescending, but I catch the sly lick of her lips when I bite my own.

I'm not mad. Not at all.

She hit me with her car, and I'm hard. Throbbing.

*Get out of my way,* she mouths, and I shake my head. She's revving the engine, and I grin.

"Javier! Mijo!" Mom's voice gets louder with each unanswered call of my name, and it's the worry in her tone that pulls me back from lustful thoughts. It's enough to make me stand and move to the side—to give the beautiful little criminal a bow as she stops and lowers her window beside me.

"You might want to take care of that. It looks painful?" She's not the least bit worried about her actions or the fact I'm going to be bruised where her sports car met my flesh. No, her eyes devour me where I stand and the heat behind her hooded stare is thrilling. More satisfying than every throat I've slit.

"I will." My voice is rough and my cock flexes behind my zipper. "You have a good night."

"You, too." Her brows furrow and lips pout at my dismissal, driving past me when I don't say anything else.

But now isn't the time. Not yet.

I'm going to confuse and overwhelm and then conquer Mariah. I'm going to own and enjoy her.

"Que fue eso?" Mom asks in my ear, and I laugh at the simple yet arduous question: *what was that?*

"That was your future daughter-in-law hitting me with her car."

She gasps, the sound a mixture of excitement and awe. "What did you say?"

"I met someone crazier than me." *And I'm infatuated after one encounter.* Crazy but true, and yet, I'm following my gut on this one. Something is driving me toward her, and I'll let it.

"Give me a month or two and I'll come."

"Now you want to come. Wait…why so long?"

"One, yes. And two, none of your business."

"What are you up to, woman? Do I need to call Alejandro?"

A loud giggle comes through her end of the line and I smile. "Quit it and send me a picture of this beautiful, crazy girl."

"I'm still calling."

"Don't ruin my small getaway with your aunt, kid. I need some relaxation near the coast."

"Two months."

"Deal, Javi. Now be the gentleman your father never was."

My face scrunches up in disgust at her insinuation. "I'm going to ignore that last statement."

"Put a ring on it first, Javier. Mother knows best."

# 5

## Mariah

"**Y**OU'RE KIDDING ME?" My friend Allison asks between fits of giggles later that night, her margarita sloshing—spilling over the rim and dirtying her white silk blouse. She's more than amused by my encounter with Javier; the certifiable she-hoe is jealous and excited. "He sounds delicious."

"He is." No point in denying it. I'm sure it's written across my face and highlighted by the lights above our table inside of our favorite taco bar. There aren't many people here tonight and I'm glad. The decibel of her gossiping battle-cry is embarrassing.

Especially since my shame surrounds me like a halo, and now that the lust-induced fog he created has receded, I'm left exposed. Open to judgment by one of the few people that know my past and the promise I made that night.

Someone who's been trying to get me to agree to a blind date for a month now. *I'll never hear the end of this.*

"Height, eye color, and to the right or left?"

The mere question makes my body flash hot from jealousy—an aggravating feeling that I fight to push back. It takes me a minute, breathing in and out slowly while forcing my expression to remain friendly. She's not buying it; her smirk only intensifies my annoyance.

"At least six foot three, warm brown, and don't ever ask me that again."

"Possessive much?" The gleam in her eyes makes me want to hit her, but I settle instead for a subtle middle finger and shrug. "Girl, I'm liking him more and more. This level of feisty looks good on you." Bringing the glass to her mouth, she takes a large sip, smiling before it turns into a petulant pout. "Now, if only Malcolm would marry me, we could double date."

"Not happening." Two voices answer, and she goes from red to white to near blue as my cousin slips into a seat beside mine, shocking her.

"You suck!"

Malcolm rolls his eyes, not sparing her outburst much thought. They've always been that way, though. Allison says something, he blows her off, and then she whines.

One day she'll get it. He's just not into her, and the man isn't subtle about it. Malcolm isn't cruel, but his disinterest shows clear as day.

*He doesn't trust women after Karina.*

The woman who catches his eye has to be near sainthood to put up with his grouchiness.

"You're crashing our dinner and you're going to ignore me?"

"Option one or two," he says, impassive eyes on mine. I know what he's asking. Life or death.

*He can't—* "Don't touch him." It leaves me through gritted teeth and clenching hands, the stem of my glass breaking. It pierces my hand, the sting surprising me while he just nods, stands, and leans down to kiss my forehead.

"Take the day off and sleep in."

"That's it?" Not telling me it's a bad idea. Not warning me about fraternizing.

"It's all I needed." For a brief second his eyes soften before he exits, Carmelo walking out behind him.

In the background, I hear Allison chirping about Malcolm and his suit and something about handsome cocky men, but I can't focus past the emotion of something happening to Javier. It's left this raw mark on me. Hurt me, and I hate it.

I feel vulnerable, something I vowed to myself to never feel for a man again.

*Walk away, Mariah. Men like him are all the same.*

"Are you even listening to me?" Alli's staring at me with a raised brow, and all I can do is down what's left of my margarita in one go, clean my hand with the nearest napkin, and ask a passing waiter for the check.

"Let's go."

"Go? Go where?" Any other time I'd find her expression comical —as if I've grown a second head and she isn't sure whether to call for help or display me like a circus attraction. "Mari, we need to—"

"Figure out my next move and take me to get stitches."

"Oh shit!"

"Indeed."

---

A SUDDEN KNOCK on my door wakes me from a nap. I've been crashed out on my large sofa with a soft afghan, ignoring the world and all my duties while trying to push the memories of the last twenty-four hours out of my mind.

His presence.

His effect on me.

The person on the other side of the door pounds louder, the rhythmic *tap tap tap* grinding my gears and I throw the blanket off, stretching my arms high and causing my back to arch and release a soothing pop. I'm a bit stiff, but it feels good to do so, and I move my neck from side to side to do the same.

A few quick cracks and I throw my legs over the edge, stumbling a bit to the door. "I'm coming!"

All noises cease and I quickly grab my Glock, the one I keep by the entrance table, and stand on the tips of my toes to look through the peephole. It's a young man with an old trucker hat and a shirt that matches the company logo. He's holding a delivery bag and I stand back, tucking the gun in the waistband of my spandex shorts.

*Maybe Malcolm sent this?*

With that thought, I open the door partway and look at the kid with a raised brow. "Can I help you?"

"Delivery for a Mariah Asher," he squeaks out, and I fight back a smile. All men are the same, and with how little I answered the door in, I'm surprised the looks-to-be high schooler hasn't drooled a bit. Because I know I'm a beautiful woman, that I turn heads, but I don't live in a land of delusion where appearances make you untouchable. I can hold my own, and I'm just as deadly as Malcolm when pushed.

"That's me. Who sent you?"

His eyes sweep down quickly over my crop top, and he swallows hard. "No name, ma'am. I was just told to deliver and—"

Whatever explanation he has dies the moment a dominating presence makes itself known. He's here, standing but a few feet from me with a handsome smile on his face, taking me in as I do him, though, when he reaches the expanse of bare skin—between my crop top and the waistband of my shorts—his expression turns predatory.

Javier's eyes narrow and he takes a step closer. Just one, and I feel him as though he'd pressed every square inch of his muscular frame against mine.

"Hello, Muñeca."

"How?" is all I manage to get past the sudden dryness of my mouth and the shaking of my limbs. He's standing there looking devilish in a pair of grey sweats and a University of Chicago hoodie with a smirk across his tempting lips.

He's wearing my alma mater. He's becoming a weakness.

There's just something about a man dressed down, comfortable, and unable to hide the muscles beneath. To hide the hardness between his legs.

It's the highlight of the cold months for women all across the world. A special treat we enjoy without being obvious, though, he seems to know where my mind is as a touch of pink grazes my cheek.

"I'm here for our date." Javier bites his bottom lip, eyes softening while perusing my figure. He pauses at my chest, then hips, before spending a little extra time on my thighs and the nonexistent gap there.

I'm curvaceous, and he likes it. More than, and his heavy-lidded eyes are a tell.

"How do you know where I live?" I ask instead, fighting my smile back at his audacity. At the hint of possessiveness in his stance. Because I can't deny to myself that his unexpected visit is a bit sexy. Pushy, yet cute. "How sure are you that I won't shoot you?"

Javier shrugs, placing a hand on the delivery boy standing a few inches from him. He doesn't look at him when turning him away. Not so much as a word when pointing toward the elevator bank down the hall, where the kid scurries off to. "I'm sure you can, but a little wound doesn't scare me."

"Wanna bet?"

"Let me in, beautiful." He takes a step forward but I hold my stance, hand on the doorknob. "Are you going to deny me this meal?"

"I'm tempted to." But I don't want to deny him. A large part of me wants to drag him inside and do something that I shouldn't. *Why?*

Why is he getting under my skin?

Why am I curious?

Why is the thought of turning him away unattractive?

"You will." Then he wrecks me. Utterly destroys my resolve by jutting his bottom lip out in a pout.

"Get in here," I hiss out, pulling the door open and stepping back. "Hurry up before I regret it."

"Gracias, Muñeca." The moment he crosses my threshold, I shiver. But more so when he stops an inch from me and lays a kiss on my forehead. "Point me in the direction of the kitchen."

"Right through there." I'm pointing behind me where an archway opens into my kitchen, but my eyes are on him. On the way he bends and picks up the bags with our food. On the way he passes by me and his scent surrounds me—hugs me while I lean over just a bit.

I slightly stumble. His chuckle pulls me from almost tripping and I close my eyes, gritting my teeth and clenching my uninjured hand. A mistake, since it causes a whimper to slip and for the man in question to rush back to my side.

It's then he notices my injured hand, the bandage a little red from the few beads of blood that seeped through the six stitches over my palm. His touch is soothing, a gentle sweep of fingers over my wound that calms and excites. Sends my nerves into overdrive.

Javier doesn't say anything, but those warm brown eyes stare into mine, gauging my reaction, and when he's happy with what he sees, I'm swept up and into strong arms. I'm cradled against his hard, warm chest. He's kissing my temple while striding back to my kitchen.

"I'm okay," I say, voice low, feeling almost shy for a second as he deposits me atop a counter stool and disarms me on my next breath. Javier takes my gun and places it beside me; I can feel his gaze as if it were a caress. "It's just a small cut."

Two fingers tip my face up, and my breath catches in my throat at the look of lust mixed with pride. His face is close to mine. His exhale is my inhale. "Still unacceptable."

"Javier, I—"

"Let me feed you, Mariah."

"Okay."

# 6

# Javier

"*O* *KAY.*"

The word sounds like heaven coming from her plump lips. She was granting me entrance into her life with it, a soft agreement that I'd be around from now on getting to know her. And if tomorrow her attitude returns and her eyes challenge me, I'm not backing down.

Not after holding her close and receiving the small smile she's giving me.

Because there's something about this fiery beauty that calls to me —that pulls me in closer with each interaction. I know it's fast and dangerous for me as I now work for her cousin, but I like tempting death and I'm unafraid of the possible repercussions.

"So what did you bring me?" Mariah's peeking at me from beneath long lashes and my cock jerks, the movement caught by her. The sweatpants do little to hide my length and girth and the little demon licks her lips, unaware of her reaction. There are goose bumps across her flesh and hard nipples pressing against the thin strap of fabric she calls a shirt, highlighting the piercings there.

My mouth waters and I swallow hard, fighting back the desire to nip each nipple. "Do you like your food spicy or mild?" There's no mistaking the hunger in my tone, nor the way I admire her body. "Anything in particular you don't like?"

"Hot." It's breathy. "Very hot."

"Good girl."

"And no onions if possible. Just not the biggest fan."

"As you wish." We're more alike than I thought, and I hide my smile because I hate the vegetable and order everything without it. It's another coincidence that I plan to take full advantage of without her knowing, like the fact we live in the same building, my unit being two floors below hers. "Is tea okay, or do you want a Coke?"

"Tea, please." So complacent. So sweet. Such a little liar.

Pulling out the first container from the Thai place I found a few days after moving here, I begin to lay them out on her counter. Because nothing in life is simple, and she'll put up a fight. It's in her nature to do so, just like it is for me. This life hardens you—family ties will hold you down—and Mariah will give me as good as I gift tenfold while smirking and taunting me with what she believes I'll never own.

It's a dare I'll accept. Be there every fucking step of the way, and when reality smacks and she's left choking for air, I'll pat her back with a grin.

There's a reason we are both here, and I won't let her stand in my way of putting together this enigma and the feelings she evokes.

"Do you like green papaya—"

"I love it! I've been known to eat an entire container all by myself." Her little squeal is so far removed from the woman I met earlier yesterday, but I like it. More than I probably should, but this is another side to her, and uncovering each is fast becoming an obsession. "This place has the best, too. Did you get any drunken noodles? And chopsticks? Can't eat this without chopsticks."

"You're beautiful when you smile." The smile drops and she eyes the gun and then me, trying to figure out who's faster if push came to shove. *Dangerous little criminal.* "I'm not taking your piece, calmate."

"What does that mean?" she asks after a minute of silence, watching me dish her meal onto paper plates I brought with me. Noodles, salad, and my newest addiction: chicken basil fried rice.

Setting her food down, I reach back into the bag and produce a few sauces and the chopsticks she needs. "It means to calm down. Now eat."

"I'm not that—" A loud growl comes from her stomach, and I raise a brow. "Fine. I'm starving...are you happy?"

"Very." Plastic fork in my hand, I grab the container of rice and dig in. No talking. No glares. We eat in silence while watching the other. I'm leaning against the counter behind me and she's perched like the queen she is in her seat, eyes happy while enjoying a little takeout with me.

*This feels right.*

"Can't use chopsticks?" Mariah asks, bringing me away from that thought. *I'm so at ease with her.* She's patting her stomach after finishing two-thirds of her plate and eyes the rest of the salad. "Are you clumsy..." Mariah picks up her iced tea and brings it to her lips, sipping while assessing me "...or a messy eater?"

Wiping my mouth with a napkin, I mock glare. "No. Just never used them."

"So, the big bad man isn't good at something."

"I'm good at plenty."

"Tell me one?"

"Ruffling your feathers." At my words, her eyes narrow. "And you? What are you good at, Ms. Asher?"

"Shooting. I have a very precise shot."

"Always with the threats." I tsk, shaking my head. "After all I've done for you."

"Done for me?" There's a curse that slips through thin lips and a twitch in her hand, but I don't back down. I'm getting to know her through each interaction. With the gestures that come naturally and not the composed heat at work. "Please enlighten me here. What exactly have you done again?"

"Saved you from a boring existence." A flush of red sweeps across her cheeks and her breathing accelerates, chest rising rapidly. It's a beautiful sight.

This woman in a simple pair of shorts and top, with her nipples hard and the barbells through them rubbing against the cotton, fuming at me while trying to dispel her truth. "Now, it's my turn to ask the second question."

"Hit me." Yeah, I'm under her skin, and she hates to crave it.

"What's your guilty pleasure?"

"Life hack videos that make no sense." Mariah takes another bite from her salad and then tilts her head to the side. "Weirdest food you've eaten?"

"I'd say fugu on a trip to Japan."

"You ate a poisonous fish?"

"Yes." At my blasé response, her eyebrows shoot up to her hairline. *Cute.* "It was quite the experience."

"How so?"

"My cousin, Emiliano, ate too much and couldn't feel his tongue and lips all night. Let's just say he drooled on himself more than once."

"Oh my God!" Snickers erupt from her, shoulders shaking while a small palm meets the countertop. "That's priceless."

"His wife didn't think so." I snort, and that only causes her to laugh harder. Full-on belly laugh. "She ran him down the street with a flip-flop after he left a trail of spit down her cheek. He went in for a quick kiss and left a nasty mess."

"That's mean," she tries to say with a straight face but fails and falls into another fit of giggles. "Why did you let him eat so much? Shouldn't you have—"

"We warned him. The chef warned him." Bringing the can of

47

soda to my lips, I take a quick drink. "But Emiliano, being the stubborn mule he is, decided that a little venom couldn't hurt and that the tingling feeling on his lips was fun. That was all on him."

"Still messed up."

"My turn."

Her amusement dies and she juts out her jaw. "Hit me."

"Favorite animal?"

"I'm a dog lover and miss owning one." Sadness flashes in her eyes, but she looks away and finds whatever is above my head fascinating. "My Frenchie passed away six months ago."

"I'm sorry to hear that, doll. My condolences—"

"And you? Favorite animal?"

"Wild? Jaguar. Domestic? Dog." Seeing we're no longer eating, I pick up our trash and clean up, storing the leftovers in her fridge. I'm thankful now to have bought two containers of the green papaya salad, not knowing it was her favorite. "I have a Doberman back home."

"Are you bringing him to the States?" Once again, those seafoam eyes meet mine and my skin prickles with electricity—this almost dominating force that makes me take a step closer. And closer. I don't stop until I'm around the counter and sitting beside her curvaceous form.

Knees touching. Arms brushing.

*Why am I so intrigued by you?*

"No. Chulo is staying with my mother in Colombia." Her expression is soft and inviting, and all I want to do is kiss her. Taste her. "I'll miss my little Parcerito, but she needs him more. He's a great dog and very protective of her."

"Chulo? That's a weird name." That teasing tone does nothing but excite me, but I don't fall into her trap, choosing instead to just roll my eyes. Something out of character for me, but that's what she's doing—breaking my normal behaviors and replacing them with childishness. *She's trouble.* "What does it mean?"

"That he's the most handsome good boy out there."

"Doesn't sound very threatening or protective."

"It's meant to be that way. Always confuse your opponent. What they see is never what you are."

"Hmmm," is her response before jumping down from her perch, the stool a little high for her, and I find the action cute. Adorable even. Walking around to her Keurig, she opens the pod holder beside it and peruses the contents. Seconds turn to minutes. Our breathing and the sound of plastic pods jiggling against each other fills the space before she huffs and turns. Green eyes on mine, she purses her lips. "Would you like some coffee?"

"No, thank you." This is my cue to leave. Mariah is a difficult woman, the few interactions we've had prove as much, but I know when to back off. When to strike. There's something hidden behind those eyes—a little wariness she fights to conceal—but I see her. All of her, and plan to erase every doubt with my actions. "I'll be heading out."

If she's surprised by my words, her expression doesn't show it, but body language never lies. Tense muscles, hands clenching, and the tapping of her right foot. I wouldn't be surprised if she's unaware of these actions, but I'm loving every single one.

Fight all she wants; I've gotten to her.

"Let me walk you out."

"No need. I know the—"

"That wasn't a request," she grits out, chin jutted out. Gorgeously defiant.

"Of course." Without waiting for her, I turn and head in the direction of the front door. And I'm almost there when she sighs, causing me to smile.

I stay silent, though. Waiting to see what she does or says.

"By the way...why a jaguar?" Mariah asks suddenly a few seconds later. Her curiosity makes me pause and look back, causing the little beauty to bump into my back. "I never asked you to stop walking."

"You asked me a question." Before she can step back, I turn and hold her close. Breathe her in. "I'm being thoughtful."

"How so?" A small shiver runs through her as my fingers grip her hips and run soothing circles over the flesh there.

"By giving you my undivided attention." Dipping my face down to hers, I lay a kiss on her cheek and then the other, loving the sudden rush of goose bumps and her stuttered breath. "And to answer your question, I love jaguars because they're deadly yet regal. Dominant over their habitat while bowing to no other predator." Another tiny peck, this time right on the tip of her nose and I turn, leaving her apartment before I bend her over the entry table and bury myself to the hilt.

This was a win.

The beginning of something that holds a wicked promise.

*I'm going to wear you down, Muñeca.*

# 7

# Javier

"**R**IGHT THIS WAY, Mr. Bennett." I step aside, and the three people I picked up this morning at the airport walk into the conference room on the executive floor. They're an affluential family from California, a Silicon Valley genius with a penchant for walking a fine line between the ethical and immoral while spoiling Mrs. Bennett. He's here with his wife and one guard, a man I've been watching from the moment they put a single foot inside the all-black SUV I drive.

His attention isn't on security or asking me what has been done to assure his boss's safety, but instead, on her. The wife. She's unaware—face pinched tight in anger while holding her husband's hand—but I saw, and by the clenching of her husband's jaw, so did he.

*What are they playing at?*

"Thank you, Javier," the wife answers, and the other two enter with nothing more than a nod in my direction. Not that I give a single fuck as the object of my frustration walks toward me with a stoic expression on her stunning face. The same expression was saved solely for me since our mini date in her apartment.

All five feet and three inches of perfection in her high-waisted black skirt, white cap-sleeved top, and red stilettos saunter in my direction with her hair down and the ends curled. With ruby lips and the sweet scent of flowers surrounding her—infiltrating my senses. Embedding itself into my DNA.

Mariah is teasing me. Avoiding me; a week of silence unless work-related and even then, the responses are minimal and to the point.

Her stubbornness doesn't deter me, though. Not one bit.

I find her adorable.

"Morning."

"Morning," she says, looking past me and toward the table where our guests will sit. "Excuse me." Before she can sweep by me, I grab her wrist and pull us back just outside the door and to the left where we are out of sight.

Mariah's back meets the wall in a soft thud, and I stand a mere inch or two from her, soaking up her decadent scent and the heat radiating from her body. Our eyes lock and breaths mingle.

A shiver rushes through her and flows through me as I lean in, lips hovering, but before they touch, I lift my face and kiss her forehead. At the contact, a stuttered breath escapes and I smile against her soft skin.

"Ignore me all you want, Muñeca. It won't change a thing."

*Ignore the pet name, Mariah.* "Move."

"One day you'll beg me to stay." With that, I push back and walk into the room. I take a seat beside Malcolm while she walks in a few seconds later, face flushed, and sits across from me with narrowed eyes.

Malcolm gives me a quick look, questioning if everything is okay, and I nod. He's not asking about his cousin, but the other people in the room.

I've already sent him my observation in a text and have the clearance to proceed as I see fit, should something occur during their stay in Chicago.

It's a trust he's given me. I might be his right hand here, something I never saw myself doing—not even for my own family—but the woman beside him has left me no choice.

I'll play my role while making sense of my sudden need for her presence in my life.

Because it's true what they say; there's more value in a single drop of your woman's come than a million pounds of gold. I want her taste in my mouth. I want to own her pleasure.

It's a compulsion I can't control and don't want to.

This game—ignoring me for seven fucking days—has done nothing to deter me.

If anything, she's poured gasoline onto this fire.

Malcolm stands, fixing his cufflink before extending a hand. "Good to see you, Kyle..." his attention then turns to the wife "...Clarissa."

"Likewise, my friend."

"It's been a long time," they answer in unison and then smile, the first one I've seen since picking the couple up, but that drops again when the manila folder in front of Asher is opened. That's when Clarissa's expression darkens and she turns her head toward her spouse, openly glaring. "This isn't necessary, Kyle. Please stop this nonsense."

"No." The response is cold. His body is tense and he's breathing harshly. "We need to make sure you're protected at all costs. Everything of mine is yours, but this makes it lawfully binding."

"Please." There's a broken plea, the tone of a woman who's hurting, and I flip my eyes to the security guard standing just behind her chair. They sit two chairs from mine with hers being the closest, and the way he hovers seems possessive, almost challenging.

Fingernails drumming on the table pull my attention, back toward the owner and Malcolm nods, the action barely perceptible, but acknowledging what I see.

"Any questions before we begin?"

"No."

"Yes."

"Go on, Clarissa," Asher says, giving her his undivided attention and I notice the guard's hands clench from the corner of my eye as I turn to look at Mrs. Bennett. "What concerns you?"

"I just see no need for this. Nothing will happen to my husband."

There's a tinge of anxiety in her tone and her husband reaches out, intertwining their fingers and placing their united hands atop the table. "It's just a precaution. Nothing else."

"Your money means nothing to me." Her face turns toward his. "I need you safe and with me."

For some reason, I look at Mariah at that moment and take in the almost wistful expression on her face. The smile curling at the corner of plump lips and the quiet sigh that escapes. As if feeling my eyes on hers, she looks over and at once, a flush of pink dances across her soft skin—from her cheeks to the very top of her chest where the silk of her top begins.

*You okay*, I mouth, and she nods quickly before turning her attention back to Malcolm's clients.

"...do this for me." I catch the end of Kyle's sentence and then watch as the woman beside him nods, but her eyes become glassy.

"Fine."

"Thank you."

"Clarissa, I understand your concerns, but let me assure you that this is a necessary step for any man in your husband's shoes. This isn't to lead him toward an impending ending, but to give him the peace of mind that you'll be taken care of no matter what." Malcolm pushes the envelope in her direction, and I move it the rest of the way, grabbing a pen from the pile at the center of the table between us.

She looks my way with a forced smile in thanks before picking up the pen. "I'm doing this for you, not because I want to."

"I know, love."

Mrs. Bennett signs her name and then closes her eyes. She takes in a deep breath and lets it out slowly before staring into his eyes. "I did that for you, but if you ever—"

She's cut off by a sudden curse from behind her and a bullet that lodges itself high on the wall across from where they sit. Her screams rend the air and so does the sound of multiple guns being cocked, but it's a missed shot, and I have her guard on the floor with my weapon drawn to his temple before anyone has time to dislodge.

My foot is on his hand with the weapon; I aim for his shoulder and then a knee. The first makes him writhe, while the second splatters the back of my leg and hip.

No one moves, but I see Clarissa's going into shock and then the appreciation on Kyle's face when I bend and knock the man unconscious with the butt of my Glock. I also notice the sudden paleness in my muñeca's face, but I can't acknowledge it right now.

I'll deal with her after the room is cleared. That flash of worry doesn't sit right with me.

"How? What the?" Bennett lifts his crying wife from her chair and walks Clarissa to the other side of the room, an arm possessively around her midsection. He's shielding her from the scene, her face buried in his chest and body shaking.

"Kyle, get her out of here. I'll meet you later."

"Yeah, we'll head back to the hotel. I'll—"

"No." Malcolm holds up two fingers. Plan B is in effect, which is the use of a backup escape for clients of this nature. "Use my penthouse. I'll have someone drive you."

"Are you sure?"

"Yes."

"Thank you, Malcolm." Asher nods at this and I send Carmelo a text, telling him to drive the Bennett's to the private condo Malcolm keeps near the office. They both begin to step out of the room, but Kyle pauses just within the threshold to look back at me. "I owe you my life, Javier. You noticed he was off right away and protected us both. Thank you."

I nod at him and they walk out, leaving the three of us standing on different sides of the table. My side has a man who's grumbling beneath my foot and bleeding.

"Tell me," Malcolm asks.

"The idiot is obsessed with Mrs. Bennett and doesn't hide his reactions well. I noticed his body language when they got in the car; hard breathing, glaring, and when Kyle kissed her cheek, his hand flexed over the gun at his waist."

"How can he keep him on his payroll? Why didn't he see this?" Mariah's talking, but her hand with the gun shakes, and without a second thought, I leave the idiot on the ground and make my way to her. I take the Glock and lay it on the table, squeezing her fingers with mine.

Her reaction isn't what I expect from her. Not from someone accustomed to our way of life.

Shit happens, but you never waver or lose composure. *What's wrong, Muñeca?*

"You okay there, cousin?"

"I am." Voice a little stronger—steadier, she pulls her hand from mine, eyes avoiding. "This just makes no sense."

"Kyle will get his chance to explain tonight. Have this idiot taken downstairs and keep two guards in the room at all times."

"Done." With a final glance in her direction, I walk out and call the team working in the cells below the bank. The phone rings twice before someone picks up and silently waits. "You have a pick-up and delivery."

"Yes, sir," the guard answers, and the dial tone follows. It takes them four minutes to reach this floor and another three to remove the semi-conscious man, now with a bag covering his head. They take a private elevator, the one used only by those who work security or the Ashers themselves, and disappear as if they've never been here.

Behind me, in the room, I can hear mutterings and a few hissed whispers, but I pay the two cousins no mind and move toward my own office beside Malcolm's. It's a decent-sized room, the view behind my chair fantastic, but it feels complete a few minutes later when an angry Mariah storms into the room.

Her chest rises and falls fast. Her lips are thinned and the looks she's giving me are cold.

"How can I help you, Ms. Asher? Is there something you need?"

"You could've been shot," she spits out, hands clenching at her sides.

"Why do you care?" I challenge, standing to match her heated stare and lean over with two hands atop my desk. Not one to back down, Mariah does the same and puts her face a few inches from mine, nostrils flaring and always challenging.

"It was reckless of you to knock him down like that, forcing his arm toward your body, while the gun was in his hand." Each word is coated with venom and is gritted out through clenched teeth. Her anger is palpable, but clearer to see is that she cares about my safety. "We don't need that kind of shitstorm. If word gets out about what happened here…"

"I know how to do my job."

"You're an egotistical idiot."

"Why do you care if I get shot?"

"I-I don't."

"Liar."

"Fuck—" she doesn't get to finish her insult as I grab the back of her neck and quickly press my lips to hers. *She's poison and fire, and I want nothing more than to be consumed by her.* The kiss is fast and heated—decadent in a sweetness uniquely hers, but I don't let her melt into me after a moan slips from her mouth to mine.

Instead, I pull back and watch her even though every cell of my DNA demands I retake those swollen lips and devour. Instead, I breathe in her intoxicating scent and lick my lips, savoring the last hint of her taste while Mariah flushes and her red lips part.

There's shock in her eyes. There's a hunger that matches mine, too.

Mariah knows I want her. Just like I know she wants me.

But more than that, there has to be a level of respect—trust—for this to work. I'm not a punching bag, and she isn't a toy. In our world, stupid reactions can be costly.

So I stand upright and level her with a blank expression. "Next time, please knock."

"Are you kidding me?"

"No. I'm not." Walking around my desk, I stride to the door and pause just within the threshold. "I don't take kindly to being questioned on both my common sense and professionalism. Don't make that mistake again."

Mariah saunters over, hand on her hip and face close to mine. Her heels giving her the height needed to reach my chin. "Or what?"

Always challenging. Always pushing.

Leaning down enough that my lips graze her ear, I exhale roughly. She shivers, and I bite back a smile. "Or I'll put you over my knee and give you the spanking you need. I'm going to enjoy reddening those sweet cheeks, Muñeca."

# 8

# Mariah

I WANT TO kill him.

I want another kiss and the feelings his lips on mine evoke.

I want what I shouldn't—the path I refuse to travel—and walk out without another word. Without another glance in his direction, no matter how much my body craves it. Craves him.

It's late enough in the morning that I stride to my desk and grab my purse, heading for the elevator without letting Malcolm know that I'm stepping out. *Screw it.* I'll deal with every missed call later, and push the down button, opening the doors. I'm thankful no one is inside and without being stopped, I make it out of the building within minutes, walking down the sidewalk and merging with the passing crowd.

I have no destination in mind, but the further I walk from the Asher building, the more my mind wanders down dangerous roads brought to the forefront by Javier's actions.

What if he got shot? What if I lost him?

Those thoughts have been plaguing me since the scuffle and for some reason, it throws me head first into my past. Down a rabbit hole that leads to a memory I've fought hard to bury even though the two men couldn't be further apart.

One is successful, determined, and proud.

The other was spoiled, unworthy, and unfit to run the family business.

*It's late when I make it home, much later than I expected I'd be when I left this morning. With Thiago Rivera arrested and the scandal over confirmed family ties to both the mob and cocaine traffickers, we've been moving information and money all day.*

*Moving to offshore accounts. Clearing all bank records. Wiping every server with information that can be traced back to them and Asher Holdings.*

*We made sure that anything unclean is no longer accessible, and not even the best hacker in the FBI can find a speck of dirt on our client.*

*And while I'm tired and hungry, I gladly do my part as a shareholder and family member.*

*Slipping my heels off, I relish the feel of the cool hardwood flooring beneath my feet before tossing my keys in a bowl atop an entry table. My purse sits beside it.*

*"Guess he went out," I mutter under my breath, undoing the top few buttons of my blouse while making my way to the kitchen. Food would be amazing, but a glass of wine will hit the spot, along with a bath.*

*However, the second I grab a glass and a bottle of Malbec from the wine cooler, the lights flicker on. "What the hell!" I scream, whirling around with a hand on my chest. I'm gasping, narrowing my eyes at Lane. "You scared the bejesus out of me."*

*"Where were you?" His tone is eerily calm, his body language tense.*

*Nothing new in that department as of late. He's changed in the last few months—demanding and possessive, but not in a way most women find sexy. This isn't an* I love you and want to keep you by my side while cherishing you *sort of way.*

*No. Not one bit.*

*After giving him my virginity, it's been a never-ending battle of wills, and I'm growing tired.*

*Fighting isn't a turn-on. Explaining my every move isn't foreplay.*

"Hey, babe." *I leave the unopened bottle and walk to him, winding my arms around his neck to placate him. It fails. My touch doesn't calm him and the feel of him gives me no comfort in return.* Maybe I should break it off already. Why am I even trying? "You didn't need to wait up for me. Did you get my text earlier?"

*His hands snake around me, one hand on my hip while the other grips my hair. He's smiling, eyes soft, and I think for a flash that he'll make this bad feeling go away when a sharp hiss escapes me. With my hair wound tight around his fist, he yanks my head back so hard that tears gather, and fear settles over my limbs.*

*Lane has never hurt me, but I'm not feeling safe anymore. I don't trust him, and that dangerous edge he's been teetering on between obsession and unhealthy sends chills down my spine.*

*One day he's sweet. The next, he treats me as though I'm an enemy. He's nothing like the man I began seeing two years ago.*

"Where the fuck were you?"

"You're hurting me." *My voice is steady, eyes on his, unwavering. Because you don't back down from an aggressor. You don't show fear or weakness.* "Let go, and get out."

*A dark chuckle leaves him, his fingers tightening, and I feel as strands of hair are pulled from their follicles. His other hand leaves my hip and sweeps across my cheek in a caress.* "You don't know what pain is, princess."

*That's when the scent of alcohol greets me—when I notice the bloodshot eyes and rumpled clothing.*

"Get out and leave. Don't force my hand," *I hiss out, heart beating fast while I walk us backward three steps. There's an empty wine glass on the counter and a gun that I keep inside the entry table; if I could just get to—*

*Blinding pain sears my right cheek and eye, the impact forcing my head to the side, but his hold only forces me back. His eyes are angry, not even a hint of the man I thought I knew and cared for.*

*Another point of contention between us:*

*He loves me, but I don't reciprocate. Those words have never passed through my lips, and it angers him.* More reason to call it quits. I should have never waited so long.

*"If I ask you again, you won't like the outcome."*

*"At work."*

*"Do you think I'm stupid?"*

*"It's the truth." I'm calm—almost chilling—as Lane lowers his face to mine, lips hovering. The stench of liquor is near nauseating, and his touch makes my skin crawl. "Ask Malcolm if you don't believe me."*

*"Malcolm," he spits out with so much venom, spittle flying over my lips and chin. "That son of a bitch would lie for his slutty little cousin. He's as much of a bitch as you are."*

Ignore the insult. *I repeat this in my head a few times, remembering all the lessons drilled into my head since the age of ten by my uncle, even though my father, his brother, didn't think it was necessary:*

*Breathe.*

*Don't underestimate your aggressor.*

*Kill without mercy.*

*Taking in a steadying breath, I let it out slowly while keeping my eyes locked on his. "You knew we had to finalize everything for the Rivera De Leon family. Why are you being like this?"*

*"Who is Ivan? Why is he sending you a gift basket?" Lane releases my hair, and I relax a bit—then choke. His fingers tighten around my throat, cutting off the air while my fingernails dig into his skin.*

*He hisses but doesn't let go. My vision gets a bit hazy behind my tears, but I don't cave. I've been groomed all my life to defend myself when the time came, and it always would.*

*You don't escape our world unscathed.*

*I take another step back and he follows, unwilling to release his hold. Another, and he brings his hand down across my other cheek, catching the corner of my mouth and breaking the skin. The metallic taste fills my mouth. The flash of pain almost makes me stumble, but I regain myself and take two more steps back.*

*And on that final move back, Lane slams me into the counter, the force knocking over the bottle and emptying its contents all around us. It breaks in half, the top slicing my arm and I grit my teeth, holding back the pain.*

*I grab the sharp glass and wrap my fingers around the unbroken opening.*

*He doesn't see it. Lane's too busy breathing hard against my neck, right below my chin where he's pressing his lips, a complete contrast to his other actions.*

*His lips part and the kiss is tender. Almost worshipping.*

I hate his touch. I don't want this.

*"Who is he, Mariah?" Teeth scrape against my skin and I shudder; I feel disgusted, and sadness fills my chest. Lane isn't giving me another out, and I close my eyes. "How long have you been fucking him behind my back?"*

*"Don't force my hand, Lane. Please leave."*

*"How fucking long!" he screams and snaps his teeth over my neck. His bite hurts. It burns as the stupid man breaks the skin.*

*"Forgive me." And on my next breath, I shove the broken, jagged glass into his neck. Push it in a little deeper before he can step back and scream out from the shock and pain.*

*Lane stumbles, his hand coming up to his chest, not paying attention to me. I kick him. With all the strength I have, I land my foot on his chest and run to the front door.*

*He's grunting; I hear him stumble and the crash of something glass. Then his footsteps come near, and it's as I make it to the entryway table and grab my Glock that he appears in my line of sight.*

*He takes a step my way and I remove the safety, pointing the barrel at his chest. "Stop." My voice is shaky, my emotions threatening to overtake me as I let the first few tears fall. "Last chance."*

*Lane laughs, the action causing blood to spurt and stain my floor. "You wouldn't."*

*"Leave."*

*"Not before I kill you." And he means it. The hate in his eyes sears me. The threat isn't without intent; his position as next in line for the Molly empire his father built makes him a dangerous man with the means to do just that.*

*It's why our union interested both his family and mine. My father to be precise.*

*The Asher's don't need them, but I won't deny that they're useful at times.*

*Then, everything happens fast. One second, I'm swallowing back a sob, and the next, I'm pulling the trigger four times. Two to the chest. Two to the stomach.*

*Lane falls back on impact, his head banging against the archway behind him and groans. Blood quickly pools, and his shirt is proof of how little time he has left.*

*The gun slips from my hand and I walk over, kneeling beside his head, and push the hair back. His eyes are still aware—wide and scared.*

*"Ivan is De Leon's youngest son, Lane. He sent a basket to everyone who worked on clearing their money and file, not just me." My tears fall on his cheek, and his expression fills with remorse. "I never cheated."*

*"I'm sorry." It's low and hoarse. Our eyes stay locked for a few minutes, but then his close and don't reopen. His chest no longer rises and falls. He's gone.*

*"I am too."*

"Are you okay?" someone says, and I snap back to the present, pushing back the thoughts I've fought to bury. Lane was my first and only boyfriend. My first kill.

Did I love him? No. Not a single part of me belonged to him—not like a woman loves her man—but regret still lingers over my actions and stupidity to stay and please others. To make him happy while I became wary and miserable.

I should've broken it off before then.

I should've seen that Lane needed help.

I should've, but didn't.

His demons had nothing to do with me, and yet, I became his focus and allowed it to go that far.

My eyes focus on the person in front of me, and I'm shocked it's Javier. "How did you find me? Are you stalking me?" The latter leaves me in an accusatory tone, which causes his brow to raise.

"No. I'm not."

"Then how..." my words trail off as I look behind him and realize where I am. I'm back outside of the Asher building, a few steps from the door, and have no recollection of how I arrived. Squinting a bit, I make out the receptionist and she's looking at me from her desk with concern stretched across her face. "*Christ*, I'm a mess today."

"Just today?" Javier jokes, his hand on my shoulder, squeezing it. I didn't realize it was there, nor do I know where I went or how long I've been standing here. "Hey, look at me."

"I'm heading back inside." I rebuff him, shrugging his hand off. His touch, no matter how small, feels good, and it's for the best I keep him at bay.

Men like him are dominant and distrustful. They come and go as they please, while the women stay behind to clean and cook—to give the world around them the illusion of perfection.

Perfect wife.

Perfect kids.

Perfect house with a large yard and a beautiful dog running around.

I've seen it from my father. And while my mother has always

remained quiet, I refuse to let anyone else hold that power over me. It's why I admire Malcolm's mom. My aunt doesn't play by those rules and refuses to let her husband or son become that sick.

Because this misogynistic idea, the illusion of a killer being a family man, gives him a reputable status. It makes him dependable and trustworthy, something that no criminal is.

I will kill anyone who crosses those I love without remorse.

And the sole reason I regret killing Lane? His mother.

The pure look of horror and devastation in that woman's eyes when Malcolm turned the body over and gave them three days to leave the country still haunts me. Gail was devastated to lose her only child, and the raw pain of her wails made me realize that I never want to be in her shoes.

To be that vulnerable.

*"No!"* Gail stands, eyes blazing in anger and despair. *"This isn't true. Tell me it's not true, Mariah!"*

*"I'm sorry,"* I answer, my voice low. A little unsteady; her pain makes my chest clench. I feel bad for her. His mother, even though she was overindulgent and turned a blind eye to Lane's bad behavior —her son's many addictions—genuinely loved him. That was her baby, her only child, that I killed. "He's gone."

*"You fucking—"*

*"Tom, I'd be very careful about how you finish that sentence."* Malcolm sits forward in his chair, hands flat atop his desk. "Disrespect her, and your wife will be burying two bodies, not one."

*"Nephew,"* my father says suddenly, hands up as if to pacify the situation. *"Leave this to me. It's my daughter at fault here and who needs to make amends to the Dermots."* That stung, a sob catching in my throat at the look of disgust he sent my way. In his eyes, I messed up. He's afraid of the Dermots for some reason. *"Mariah needs to pay for her crime. I'll make sure they're not to—"*

*"Not another word before I lose my last shred of patience with you. I'm not your brother, nor do I hold qualms over hurting one of my*

*own." At Malcolm's words, Dad steps back and sends me a murderous glare. Something my cousin catches. "Stay in your lane, and keep those eyes on the ground. She's above you and always will be."*

*"Do you not have a heart?" Lane's mother steps in front of her fuming husband, her fingernails digging into his arm, a silent plea to keep composure. There's more he wants to say, insult me, but can't. Not with Malcolm here, and more so with the six fully armed guards standing post. Their Molly operation, while quite large, only holds that power because my family has allowed them to flourish with the agreement that they know their place and pay a due, giving them rights to a certain area. I was just a bonus. "She killed our son and you—"*

*"You should thank her for being merciful."*

*Both Lane's parents and mine gasp, but it's Tom's face I focus on. He's turning red in anger. Hate. "You seem to forget that we hold power in this city, too, Asher. Chicago is—"*

*"Mine." Malcolm interrupts, standing from behind his desk, and walks toward a small storage cabinet in the room. Inside there are a few guns, a knife, a ring, and a glass used when certain business agreements are made.*

*It's an old-school tradition. You sign with blood, not ink.*

*A collective intake of breath and the glass shatters upon impact, creating a small hole where it met the wall. It's a symbolic gesture. Their accord is over.*

*"You've fooled yourself into believing you are more than what you are. All of you. It's the same mistake Lane made the night he attacked my family, in her home, intending to end her life." His back is to the room, voice controlled, and yet you feel his ire. The evil that lurks beneath the surface and his enemies cower from. "You are nothing but what I allow. One word from me, and your entire life can be burned to the ground with you inside the building. Or in your case, Uncle, the home I've allowed you to keep. I'm being more than courteous here, at Mariah's request, by letting you all live. Because*

*had he succeeded or ran, I would've made you watch me dismember him limb by limb while alive."*

*Neither set opens their mouths, but their eyes speak volumes. Fear. Almost choking panic at his words.*

*If they stay here another minute, he'd order their execution on the blatant disrespect alone.*

*"Leave." At that, all four parents snap their eyes my way. I don't give them a chance to refute my demand or negotiate. I'm saving their lives, even if they don't see it. "Take your son's body, sell what you can, and get out of the country within the next forty-eight hours. Do not look back. Do not come back."*

*"Mariah, sweetheart," Mom says, voice low and contrite. And I believe it, too. Problem is that she's a product of a male-dominated home where his word is the law and his demands reign king. She has no real backbone. "Baby, please stop this nonsense. This isn't how I brought you up."*

*"I think it's better for all involved if you two leave as well." Tears gather in her eyes, hurt, and disappointment flowing down each cheek, but I'm not moved. Not this time.*

*Lane's dad opens his mouth, the retort on his tongue sure to be coated in venom, but he's interrupted by a guard stepping inside. There's a body over this employee's shoulder, the body-bag hiding their identity, but everyone knows.*

*"Heed her warning. My cousin's more generous than I am." Malcolm snaps a finger, and the body is placed at the Dermots feet. His mother's eyes fill with tears that fall as a hurt-filled wail escapes her chest. Her husband, though, shows a little more composure. There's sadness, but overpowering the pain is hate. He's scared, but the disdain is just as powerful. "She asked me to return him to you, and now I have. So do as she bravely suggests. Leave. Don't further tempt me to break my promise."*

*"You have our word," Mr. Dermot says, and her cries grow louder. He understands that this means their entire operation must leave—every member of the family—or face the repercussions. With*

*his arms around her midsection, he turns, and they make it to the door where one of their men, a distant cousin, awaits to take Lane.*

*And when they step across the threshold, Malcolm claps once. "The clock is ticking. For you as well, uncle."*

Two steps are all he lets me take before snatching my wrist and pulling me against his strong chest. "What's wrong?"

"Let go."

"Talk to me."

"Respect my boundaries, Mr. Lucas."

"Understood." And all of a sudden, I hate that word. Despise how easily he gives in to my request. *This yo-yo'ing is going to drive me crazy.* Javier makes me want to run to him and then away, far away, because I'm not ready to let the walls down I've built around myself.

This is for the best. Has to be.

"Good." Snatching my arm from his hold, I continue toward the door. He doesn't say anything, just lets me walk away, and it confuses the hell out of me, but then a hiss meets my ears and I shiver.

*"For now."*

# 9

# Javier

MALCOLM GIVES ME a nod before entering the opulent establishment near the Asher building the next morning at ten. The Bennett meeting had to be pushed back due to medical reasons, and while I still don't believe his wife is okay after what occurred, extending this another day isn't feasible.

Not when dealing with the sentencing and execution of a man.

Mistakes can be costly. Destructive.

Walking through the lobby, I make eye contact with each man standing beside the three exits and nod. We're in the heart of the Loop, a few minutes from Malcolm's financial building, and I'm impressed with the surveillance I've seen thus far. Not that it can't be improved, but he has a solid foundation I can work with.

He owns it, provides all security for it, and only those trusted—business associates that pass through frequently—are allowed to reside within.

I had the choice of an apartment here but chose wisely without knowing.

Mariah can run but can't get far. She has no idea how close we are.

How easily this predator can reach his prey.

Because that's what this dance feels like; a game of cat and mouse I don't plan to lose.

"They're waiting and the room is ready," Mariah says from beside him, looking straight ahead while matching his steps. I'm two behind them and watching their dynamic, taking in their reactions from the moment they entered my SUV. They speak through looks and short answers, but behind the professional demeanor is respect and familial love.

"Thank you. Make sure Mr. Bennett is down in five."

"Already sent him a text, and he's downstairs." She's checking her phone, but I catch the tilt of her head and the slight look back from the corner of her eye. "The guard is also in attendance and awake."

"Perfect. That'll be all." Malcolm stops at the elevator and puts a key to the panel. "Take Javier's car and head back. I need you to work on the Frederick contract."

"Are you sure?" Now she does look back and meets my stare. I'm not hiding or avoiding. "I'm more than happy to—"

"Positive." He kisses her cheek, pulling her attention away from me, and I hate it. Loathe her looking at anyone that isn't me, but I keep my reactions at bay. This feeling—this rage-fueled jealousy—isn't something I've faced before. It makes me see red. Yearn to feel the life essence of whoever holds her gaze on my fingertips. "I want the twins in and out of my office before they start trying to sell me bullshit I neither care nor have time for."

"I know." Mariah laughs and its warmth settles around me, calms the devil within, while my expression remains blank. She sneaks another look after a minute, almost like she can't help herself, and narrows her eyes at my demeanor. *What kind of reaction are you looking for, Muñeca? Are you thinking about our kiss?* However, the longer we stare, the more I see what lurks behind those pretty orbs.

Something is bothering her. Maybe a hint of annoyance for being asked to leave. "The food has been ordered and the files are ready. We'll be using conference room two for this one."

"Will they need an escort to the office?" She doesn't respond to him, too busy trying to read me. The only things she gets from me, though, are a raised brow and a nod in her cousin's direction. "Mariah," he says, and still nada. Not even an acknowledgment of her name.

"Pay attention, Muñeca." That snaps her out of it and with a quick wave to Malcolm, she rushes out without answering. My eyes follow her the entire way. "I'll be picking them up."

"You two are becoming quite entertaining to watch." He enters the elevator and Carmelo and I follow, not another word spoken on the matter. We ascend to the sixty-eighth floor, and the doors open into a spacious living space with nothing but a large conference table at the center. The room has floor-to-ceiling windows that line the outer walls from one side to the other, the view showing us a slightly overcast day with an uninterrupted view of city landmarks and skyline.

Mr. Bennett sits at one end of the table while the guard is placed at the center, tied to a chair and gagged. His face is swollen and a tooth is missing, and while both men hold enraged expressions, one person is missing.

The wife. The victim.

"How is she?" Malcolm asks, sitting down at the other end while I take my place right across from the aggressor. "Will she be joining us?"

"No." Kyle doesn't explain further, and no one probes. Instead, we turn to look at the one person who does owe an explanation. "Speak," Bennett hisses through clenched teeth a minute later, and the man flinches a bit before composing himself. "Tell me why you earned the bullet in my gun."

Nothing. No answer.

And all it does is piss me off. More so because no matter what country you're in, it seems that disrespect is a common trait that all assholes share.

There's a paperweight at the center of the table and before anyone asks him again, I pick it up and throw it. It lands near the bridge of his nose and a gash appears, the blood rushing to the surface before falling to his lip and filling his mouth.

"The next blow, I'll aim for your eye with my knife. Answer him," I say, tone even and low.

He trembles, his fear palpable. "I love her."

"What did you just say?" Kyle stands, the chair scraping harshly against the floor. His hands come down atop the glass table, the force making it shake while his lip curls up into a snarl. "Repeat that, Douglass."

Douglass swallows hard, coughing a bit. "I fell in love with Mrs. Bennett."

"Did she reciprocate?" Malcolm asks, holding a hand up to Kyle who moves in Douglass's direction. He pauses with a minute nod and waits. We've already discussed how to handle him. Get what we want. "Or is this a gut feeling?"

"I knew the day she hired me." Douglass smiles. It's wistful, yet there's ire lingering beneath the surface. His disdain for Mr. Bennett is clear. "She's sweet and kind. Nothing like this asshole who spends more time making enemies than paying attention to his wife. I was there when he wasn't. I saw the smile slip from her face each time he canceled a dinner date or weekend away." No one misses the way Kyle flinches slightly back at that, and it further fuels Douglass. "It was me," he sneers, and I find his backbone almost comical. Any other man would've pissed his pants by now. "Always me."

"So, she led you on?" At my question, all three look at me, but my focus is on the guard. "Are you saying she's a—"

"Don't you fucking dare!" He's struggling against his bindings, the rope cutting into his skin. "Clarissa is an angel."

"How so if she's toying with your emotions?"

"She's too innocent and pure to realize I've been—"

"Planning to kill her husband, kidnap her, and then force her into a relationship while you gain access to their millions?" Silence. Utter silence. Malcolm asked me to dig and I did, finding out more than they expected. This runs deeper than a simple infatuation. "Or does the name Jorge Wendell ring a bell?"

Kyle's head snaps in my direction. "What does my business partner have to do with this, Javier?"

"Why don't you explain, Douglass? Tell him what Wendell's secretary told me for a few thousand dollars."

"She wouldn't." His voice wavers.

"She did." Carmelo steps forward then. He hands Malcolm the two files I gathered in the two hours before arriving here. "Cindy was more than willing to fax me what I needed, too."

"No!"

"What the fuck is going on?" Kyle growls out, storming toward Douglass and fisting his hair. He pulls the dark blond strands hard, forcing the guard's head back while staring at me. "Tell me."

Malcolm slides the folder over; it's open and the top page shows the forged signatures on paperwork, making it seem Mrs. Bennett is unstable and needs a guardian. That Kyle was putting Wendell in charge of everything if anything happened to him.

"The plan was to kill you via robbery gone wrong." The disdain in my voice is noticeable. I take offense to shitty criminals playing the bullshit badass role. "With you out of the picture and then the filing of this paperwork, Clarissa would've been under their thumb. Wendell gets the company and other business ventures/assets, while Douglass gets your wife and a 50/50 split of the money. The sick fuck is obsessed with her, and more so, after being ignored. Isn't that right?"

"Fuck you!"

Kyle turns his head up to the ceiling and takes in a deep breath.

He holds it for ten seconds, his hands clenching twice before his right hand pulls a gun from the back of his pants.

We don't stop him. We don't even draw our weapons.

Instead, we watch silently as he bends and puts his mouth near Douglass's ear. Kyle whispers something to him; it's too low for anyone to hear, but the guard becomes enraged just long enough for Bennett to pull the trigger and his body to go limp.

A bullet in each eye and brain matter scatters behind the body on the pristine floor.

"We'll be leaving tonight on an extended holiday," Kyle says, not looking at us but watching every drop of blood seep from the bullet wounds, a small smile on his face. "Do you need anything from us?"

"No. You're set." Malcolm gives me a nod, and I text the cleanup crew to come and eradicate all traces of this meeting. "Have a good vacation, and please send my regards to Clarissa."

"Thank you both." With that, he walks out and we stand, heading back downstairs toward Carmelo's car while the Bennett's prepare for their departure.

---

It's near nine at night by the time I make it home, and the front door hasn't fully closed before my jacket is tossed aside and my tie pulled off. I'm shrugging everything off, leaving the piles for tomorrow, while heading toward my bathroom.

I'm in need of a quick shower. A release before ending my night with a little taste and tease.

The lights flick on as I enter the large, all-white bathroom with an oversized shower that extends from one wall to the opposite. Its large subway tiles in marble cover almost every inch, from wet areas to the dry with hardware in gold to compliment the stone.

Turning the handle toward the hot water, I step back and remove my boxer briefs before stepping inside. It's been a long day; from meetings and training for Malcolm's guards to Mariah's haughty, cold shoulder.

One I returned. Then, I sat back and watched the fight to ignore me become the search for any reason to get closer. No matter where I turned, she was in my line of sight or near enough to touch.

Hair up in a messy bun.

Glasses perched on the end of her nose while biting a pen.

Giggling at something.

The coquettish minx made sure to punish me, but I held back. My not giving in caused her frustration and a few muttered curses thrown my way, but it'll be worth it soon enough.

Heat fills the room, and I step beneath the waterfall showerhead. The hot water slides down my limbs and hard cock, caressing my skin and causing a shiver to rush down my spine.

I grab my bodywash and loofah on the small alcove to my right, pouring a large drop in to the sponge before rubbing it across my chest. The suds glide lower and over my pelvis before they kiss my balls.

I'm throbbing. In pain. My hand fisting over the tight skin, knuckles strained white, before pumping once. Then again. Just knowing that she's a few floors from me...

"Fuck," I hiss out, my strokes becoming rougher with each twist down and then up. My eyes close and I throw my head back, picturing her sultry eyes and sinful smirk before leaving for the day. Mariah was bent over her desk while looking for something, giving me the perfect view of her ass and hips while talking on the phone, ignoring my presence. "Delicious little beauty."

Her skirt was mid-thigh and tight with no visible panty line, and instead, I got a peek of the soft skin between her thighs through the small slit with a pleat at the back. Perfect and round, and my mouth waters as I remember how the fabric moved with her, rising a little higher on her thighs until I groaned.

A little more, and I'd see the round cheeks I want to bite. Smack. Smear my come across.

Heat licks at my balls and with each pump of my hips, the pleasure increases, and more so when Mariah's evil grin flashes behind closed lids. She'd turned around to face me then, back slightly arched and with a hand on her hip.

*"Need something, Mr. Lucas?" Tone breathy, she looks at me from head to toe, pausing a bit at the thick bulge in my pants. My suit jacket's over the back of my office chair and I'm not hiding her effect on me. Fuck that—she caused it and I want her to see.*

*To hunger for it.*

*For her plump little mouth to water.*

*"Do you?" I counter, my voice husky. Deeper. "Need help?"*

*"I have fingers for that. No help needed."*

*"But sometimes a little assistance makes the task sweeter. Dirtier."*

*"Are you speaking from experience?" She licks her lips and my cock jerks, a bead or two of liquid rolling down the tip. "Is using your hands something you do a lot?"*

"I'm going to make you pay for that," I grunt low, tightening my grip before swiping my thumb across the sensitive head. *Christ*, that feels good and I pinch the tip, the sudden jolt of pain giving me another minute or two. My hips don't stop pumping, fucking my fist while imagining it's her tight cunt and the slap of skin is my hips slamming into parted thighs. "Slowly break you down until my cock is all you know."

*"Do you think of me when you do?"*

"Son of a bitch." That memory of her words—the look in her eye when whispering—brings me over the edge. My palm slams against the wall, holding myself up while come shoots from the tip, dribbling down the wall and to the drain below.

It takes me a minute or two to calm my breathing and for my cock to stop twitching, and I step out, wrapping a towel around myself. My bedroom's past this door and the bed is my destination, where I was smart enough to toss my phone before giving in to the need for pleasure.

"Now, I want the tease." Towel thrown aside, I get comfortable with a pillow behind my head and send the first message.

*What are you wearing?* ~

# 10

# Mariah

**HAT ARE YOU wearing? ~Unknown**

W I'm lying in bed, staring at my ceiling and thinking about the text that came in a few seconds ago. I won't deny the sender has piqued my curiosity, that gene all women have when it comes to deciphering the unknown, and my finger hovers over the screen without looking. *Do I ignore or answer?*

Because this can go one of two ways: the person is a creep, or someone is sending a little naughtiness to their other half. Moreover, I'm nosy, and trying hard to ignore the little voice inside my head that wishes this was Javier messaging me and not a random stranger.

His kiss, that quick and will-crumbling touch of his soft lips on mine, has messed with my head. With my goal and wants and the desire to stay single—unattached to any man, because I am. Javier seems to be near whenever my defenses are low and always on my mind when out working and protecting our family's interest.

He's loyal when he doesn't need to be. He isn't some nobody looking to come up.

I've read his file front to back, looked up the Lucas organization in Colombia, and I can't come up with a single plausible reason for his determination to be here. To work for the Asher's when his name is respected, feared, and admired.

*He's here because of me.* A thought I'm fighting to ignore. It's not plausible. *But what if?*

Because there's no denying our attraction, this pulsing energy that fills me when we touch. Moreover, his kiss stole every reason why this can't work and turned it into doubts on why it shouldn't. *Jesus, help a girl out here. Amen.*

Indecisiveness lasts but so long, and I'm further tempted/thankful when another ping draws my attention to the screen.

**Are you waiting for me? ~Unknown**

Definitely someone trying to reach their lover. Something I'll never have, and it makes me jealous—hate how untrusting I've become. Giving two years of my life to a man that treated me like an enemy, a cheating whore, broke something within me that turns away from any possibility for more. *Then why flirt with Javier? Why is he different?*

An answer I don't possess, or maybe I don't want to acknowledge how much the man affects me. How his indifference, the way he doesn't take my abuse, both excites and scares me.

I'm never going to be dependent on a man, but I won't deny that having someone be my equal is a yearning that Lane tampered with. The last thing I want is a controlling asshole or to be forced into a mold I neither find attractive nor need.

I'll never be arm candy. I'll never want to be the perfect little housewife.

"Even dead, the jerk ruins my fun," I grumble, typing out a quick response to the sender before tossing the device beside me.

**You have the wrong number. ~Mariah**

Their response is immediate and I furrow my brows, reaching blindly and bringing the lit-up screen to my face. I read the message once, twice—three times, and a little smile curls on my lips.

Because there are only two people in my life that keep their responses short and to the point, and my cousin wouldn't send something like this.

Malcolm's messages are solely concerning work.

And if it's family-related, I get a call, and even that only lasts long enough to be told what to expect or where to show up in as much of a loving way as the ever-present grouch can express.

**No. I don't. ~Unknown**

**Then who wants to know what I'm wearing? ~Mariah**

Stretching a bit, I let myself sink into the bed and wait. I don't know how he got this number, but a part of me is happy he did. This way I can flirt, play, and maybe get to come without everything that comes attached to the title of being his.

Because the last thing I want is another possessive man laying claims.

*Liar.*

Another ping reverberates throughout the room, and I'm beyond grateful to ignore that little voice inside my head.

**A wolf who isn't hiding his hunger. ~Unknown**

My stomach clenches and toes curl with that simple response. I also find myself typing back without hesitation, a smirk on my lips.

**Should I be afraid of the big bad wolf? ~Mariah**

A minute passes and nothing. Then another. And just when I'm ready to toss the phone aside, annoyed that he didn't respond to my taunt, a message comes in.

**I'm going to eat, bite, and make you scream my name. ~Unknown**

*Christ,* I shiver. The undisguised hunger—the unadulterated want gives me a high I've never encountered before. Not at this level. This feeling of euphoria mixed with danger that I need to chase and conquer. Push a little further no matter how wrong this could end.

*His fire might destroy me.*

**Is that a threat~ Mariah**

**It's a promise, Muñeca. ~Javier**

And then an attachment pings on my device, and I click the link like an idiot. Like the in-lust little girl I am.

The picture's a close-up of his mouth and chin with day-old stubble across a lickable, defined jaw. Then there's the way he bites his bottom lip, teeth embedded into the corner, making him smirk in a way that causes goose bumps to rise across my skin.

I feel feverish. Excited.

*I'm in trouble.*

**Can you catch me? ~Mariah**

**You'll always be within my reach. ~Javier**

---

THIS MAN IS GOING to drive me to the point of instability where people snap, and reactions have costly consequences.

Like now; this is stupid. A bad choice on my part.

The beginning of what can only be described as my fallout.

And why? Because I'm sitting on the grass against a building my cousin owns with a vast field in my direct line of sight. I'm here to watch him exactly five days from my demand to be left alone. For him to respect *my* boundaries when I didn't follow the same protocol.

I can't seem to stay away. I keep trying to find ways to get close.

During meetings. During his two p.m. coffee break.

"He's going to think I'm certifiable." *He's no saint, either.* Which is true, and his smirk while dropping a handful of Hershey's kisses atop my desk on his way to his office, Cafe Con Leche in hand, tells me as much. Javi is enjoying my indecisiveness, which aggravates me.

It's a vicious cycle of hot and cold, and I'm screwed.

He also knows I'm here; knew the very moment I sat down and my eyes wandered down his tattooed upper body. I saw the small shiver rush through him. I saw the way he tilted his head in my direction, the flex of his pecs while he addressed those here today for training.

This group is new. All men that have come with some level of vouching by associates to Malcolm.

Moreover, he's aware of my small and newly discovered fetish. Watching him put men on their knees, crying out in pain while tapping out, is something I find sexy. Extremely. Almost obsessively.

The way he stands in front of the guards, no shirt on, and demanding they follow through with the new moves he's shown them; a mixture of boxing meets mixed-martial arts, and each segment follows a new technique.

It's a little chaotic. The moves are meant to cause harm, and yet, I'm salivating as he takes the youngest in this bunch to the center where they've put a large mat over the grass and squares off.

Sweat glistens across his chest.

His muscles ripple while he waits for the other to charge forward like the idiot he is. Because fighting isn't about brawn or weight.

Anyone can be brought to their knees no matter the size. Which is what happens next.

One second, he's charging like a raging bull, and the next, the young guard is flat on the ground, facing down, while Javier locks his arm in a hold. He pulls back and the man groans, gritting his teeth while Javi continues to teach. The group surrounding them comes closer—they're hanging on his every word while Javi points out pressure points with his free hand.

I can't make out his voice from here, but I follow the movement of his lips. The way he signals the lines and position of his body and arm, the way it's tucked and crossed over his opponent in a way that's near impossible to escape.

*I could escape.*

And God, I'm tempted to challenge him. Show him just how equal we are.

"Pair off," I hear him call out and I lift my eyes to his, fighting back the urge to admire every solid inch of his physique. His brown eyes are narrowed, lips curling up into a small snarl while listening to something one of the new men to his right says.

Whatever it is, he doesn't like it.

His face contorts, and the demon behind the facade of perfect makes an appearance. Javier is glorious in his anger. His movements are precise and meant to cause more than harm.

With a quickness no one predicts, the guard flies over his back and lands harshly on the ground, away from the mat. Head bouncing, he's disoriented while Javi mounts and pins his arm with one hand and his knees in a kimura, ignoring the cry to stop and doesn't let go until breaking the forearm in two.

And as the man cries, Javi proceeds to break the other.

No one stops him. No one dares to protest.

Instead, they watch him land punch after punch on a defenseless man until he's unconscious and bloody, face swollen and rapidly bruising.

My feet carry me closer on their own accord, pausing only when his angry eyes meet mine. "Any one of you disrespect Miss Asher, and Malcolm will be the last person you should fear. I'll personally empty a clip into your skull."

*Jesus.* I shiver. My thighs clench.

White-hot desire pulses through my womb, and I step back and then again, all the way to my belongings on the grass with my eyes on him the entire time.

This, my reaction to his protectiveness and possessiveness, proves I'm weak when it comes to him. I'm a ticking time bomb.

Want. Need. Hunger.

Those three words describe me to a 'T' and he knows. Mirrors those feelings.

*How can I win a losing battle?*

---

COME MONDAY MORNING, there's a cup of coffee from my favorite little shop near the office; a quaint location owned by a lady older than dirt and run by her granddaughter. It's hipster meets old European vibes, and I can't get enough of their eclairs.

I've been known to buy half a dozen per visit, and the box in front of me holds seven with a note above in neat penmanship.

*One is for me.*
*I'll be by on my coffee break to pick it up.*
*~ Javi ~*

"STUPID ATTRACTIVE MAN." I'm smiling as I bring the cup to my lips, almost moaning as the rich cappuccino greets my caffeine-deprived body. There's a hint of almond to this one, just the right amount without overpowering, and reminds me of my mom's favorite biscotti.

The one thing we have in common is our sweet tooth.

"Do you and your coffee need a moment?" Malcolm says from beside me all of a sudden and I yell, almost dropping my coffee. There's a hint of amusement in his eyes, and I'm tempted to kick his shin or stomp his foot with my heels.

"Shut it."

"Did you bring me anything?"

"Nyet." He's eyeing the box of pastries, a frown on his face. "These are a gift, and since you were a jerk, the answer is no."

"That's not very nice."

"And neither are you," I counter, bringing the cup to my lips and taking a hearty sip of the perfect temp brew. "Not sharing."

"I can always make you go get some." He's sipping from his favorite traveling mug. It's expensive, ridiculous for what it is, but the damn thing keeps his Jamaican special blend the perfect temp for a few hours.

He does not start his day without it.

Coffee is a religion in our family.

"You're going to be that petty?" Malcolm merely raises a brow, and I huff. "Fine. Grab one and go."

"Two, and I pay for the lunch you'll be ordering for Javi."

"I'm not—"

"Liars never make it into heaven, little cousin."

"Neither do murderers and pitiful eclair extortionists."

He shrugs. Not one care is given. "I know what would make his day."

"What's that?" It slips before I can stop myself, and his grin widens. I'm starting to get annoyed with him. "Just for your amusement's sake."

"Lying is a nasty habit, Mariah." For a second, he turns serious, watching me through narrowed eyes. "You need to stop living in the past and comparing every man to Lane and his dipshit failures. He wasn't a real man, just another child hiding behind his mother's skirt while breaking every plate on the table."

"It's not that—"

"I know you. Remember that."

Nodding, I sigh, because he's right. I'd already thought to do something nice for Javi. Not today, but maybe Friday before they head out to Nevada. "Where?"

"Paisa on the green."

"I'm not even sure what that is."

"For him, a taste of home."

---

My plan to set up a lunch delivery for this week became an impossibility as a soft alert came from our FBI informant, causing protocol *blink* to go into effect. The IT department came onto the executive floor, wiping down every trace of the Frederick file.

The twins lied when Malcolm asked about possible investigations into their business.

*"Antonio, I couldn't care less about the possibilities you're claiming when nothing you've presented says the FDA backs your findings. Are you under watch? Is there any possibility of a probe at your lab?"*

The man sweats, a few beads trickle down the side of his head. *"N-no."*

*"Lying will cost you in the end. I can't move the amount you want if it's seized."* From the corner of my eye, I watch Javi stand and walk out. He comes back a minute or two later with two files that Malcolm takes from his hand. I don't know what's in those folders, and my brows furrow. *"Final chance."*

*"Malcolm,"* Mildred, the other twin, calls softly. She's sitting forward, another button on her shirt undone while her finger traces her collarbone. Pathetic and useless. *"Why the distrust? We've been friends for a year and—"*

*"Answer the question or leave."*

*"No. No investigations."* Though she doesn't meet his stare now, instead, Mildred looks at her brother through hardened eyes. *"Everything is clean and ready to be moved. We have a private account offshore in the Bahamas."*

*"And that means nothing to me."* Malcolm pushes the folders toward them, sitting back in his seat while they read through the contents. *"I chose the where, how, and when. Not you."* Mildred tries to protest, her brother shaking his head, but my cousin carries on. *"If you lie, at any point, I'll take ownership until my fee is paid. Ten million per infraction. Understood?"*

*"That's outrageous!"* she yells, standing from her seat. The rough movement causes her chair to tip back and for her brother's face to become pale. *"I'm not giving you—"*

*"We'll sign."*

*"Are you kidding me?"* Mildred glares at her brother not a full second after he agrees, face red with anger. *"We can't just give him—"*

*"Shut it and sit down, Mildred!"* Antonio's voice thunders: it's

*the angriest I've never seen him. "We need him, and I won't get fucked in the ass because you think the world should bend at your feet. I'm the president, not you."*

*"If this goes south, I'll spit on your grave," she hisses, her face turned and I hear a low sniffle that's out of character, but I don't question it. Mildred has always been off to me. Instead, I focus on the apologetic expression her brother gives Malcolm.*

*"I don't want your apologies." My cousin nods at the group of pens atop the table. "Sign before I change my mind. Those are my stipulations. Take them or leave them."*

They took, and now we overthrow after removing all traces of the contract in this country. I've sent the files out this morning via private courier to the office in Costa Rica.

"Ready to head out, Muñeca?" Javi asks from the edge of my desk, pulling my attention from the scheduling I had to adjust due to today's bull. My neck cracks as I look at him, my head throbbing a bit from hours upon hours of tracing every last chunk of info with the IT department. "You look exhausted."

"I will be in a minute. Why?"

"I'm waiting to walk you out before heading out to pick up the twins."

"They're not hiding under a rock in Utah?"

"Hiding in plain sight approximately twenty minutes from here."

Nodding, I ignore the sudden bout of butterflies at his smile. At the softness in his eyes. "Who's going? Should I prepare a statement or—"

"Not necessary, beautiful. I already put something together for you in case we're intercepted by anyone watching the place." Javi places a USB flash drive beside my pen holder that l left right where he left it and he smirks every day it stays that way. Sure, it pissed me off, but at the same time, I find his knack for finding ways to get under my skin annoyingly endearing. "They shouldn't, but it's just a precaution."

"Okay." I grab the small device, shut my computer down, and

open my purse, leaving the USB inside a small pocket. "My car's in the—"

"I've moved mine beside yours. It's not an issue."

"Thank you." *Christ,* I find him sexy when thoughtful.

"Muñeca, never thank me for taking care of you. It's my pleasure."

And damn me if I didn't blush right then. I like the sound of being his more than I should. Love the thought of him being there for me.

Not because I'm weak, but because it makes *him* happy to be near me. Because I'm his focus.

*He's going to break my walls down, and I'm starting to question if I need them.*

# 11
# Javier

I ARRIVE AT the private penthouse the Frederick twins keep in Chicago. It's in a nice area, less than half an hour from the Asher building, where they hide in plain sight. Not in Utah like they hope we'd think, burning daylight hours that could lead to their escape.

Because it's hard to find an ant in a pile where possibly millions surround the guilty one, but I have a skill many don't.

Patience.

In Colombia, I took personal care of my family's enemies. Politicians and cartel members, it made no difference and there are plenty of places to hide but give a rat confidence, and it shows its face. Security gives comfort and the feeling of untouchability; that's when I strike.

The lobby is busy when I step inside. Multiple heads turn to look —the group of women checking in begins to whisper and giggle, but I don't pause or encourage.

I'm here for the twins, with Carmelo as added encouragement if need be.

And while I'll never hit a woman, if I have to make her brother suffer so she complies, so be it. They brought this upon themselves.

"What floor?" Carmelo asks, stepping into the empty elevator cart.

"Penthouse." At my response, he presses the needed button using a pen and leans back, adjusting the two boxes in his left hand. And so do I, pulling my phone out and bringing up Mariah's number.

There's been a subtle change in her over the last few days. She's been a tiny bit softer toward me, and I love it—revel in the rosy tint that sweeps across her cheeks when I bring my daily offering of chocolate or coffee.

A bribe? Maybe.

But there's something so delicious about those innocent reactions.

So unlike her normal demeanor, and yet, Mariah is letting me in. Little by little. One interaction at a time.

**Whatcha doing, Muñeca? ~Javier**

Immediately three dots appear.

**Thinking. My mind keeps going around in a circle. ~Muñeca**
**About? ~Javier**

For a second or two no sign of her typing, but then her next words fuck with my head. My dick.

**Here I am, all alone inside of this large bath with bubbles and a glass of wine thinking about you. About the one kiss you stole and how much I liked the way you taste. ~Mariah**

*Fucking tease. Motherfucking destroyer of my will.*

A low hiss escapes, my cock swelling at the mere thought. She's going to pay for this.

That little demon knows what she's doing. This game of hot and cold—taunt and chase that she both loathes and yearns for.

With one hand she pushes me away, and on her next breath, pulls me closer.

Close enough to touch but not bend over.

*I could be back home in thirty and at her door in five more.*

A throat clears, and I look over at Carmelo. "I'm a little hungry."

"We can stop after." My response is a little strained, my thoughts jumping between my needs and responsibility. "Anything in mind?"

This mindless conversation is needed, and I focus on him and not the throbbing of my length, the pulse in my veins that's thankfully hidden behind my suit jacket.

"Dominican if you're down?" My response is a nod, and he smiles. The guy's young and ambitious, but smart and hard-working —reminds me a little of the men in my family. It's also why I've taken him under my wing; he could go places in a business like this if he remains loyal. "I hope the crying doesn't last long. This woman is too extra for me."

"Agreed," I say, nodding absentmindedly while staring at my phone's screen. Mariah sent me a picture while he interrupted me, and I wish I hadn't clicked on it. Not now, when I can't rush back and punish my Muñeca for this infraction.

The pic is of her in a large free standing tub with bubbles covering her body and just enough of her breasts, that the two tips aren't visible. *How did she manage to get such a perfect shot?* I see them, though. Can make out their dusty rose color and their slight pebbling. The way her skin has broken out in goose bumps and the smirk on her lips just below the edge of the picture where she cut the image off.

*Tonight she's going to see what I'm like when pushed too far.*

**I'll be picturing you just like this tonight when I come with your name on my lips. ~Javier**

Pocketing my phone, I close my eyes for a second. Breathe in and out through my nose—focus on why I'm here and not where I want to be.

With her.

Between her thighs.

Tasting her every moan.

My phone pings twice, but I don't look. Instead, I wait for the door to open and exit with Carmelo two steps behind while thinking of everything I find unattractive.

And my mom's seventy-year-old neighbor in a swimsuit at her birthday cookout does it. I'm soft before I'm three steps onto their floor.

There are two doors here: A and B, with the latter being our first stop. The twins each own a unit, but scum always sticks together.

Antonio will try to protect her, while Mildred will shove him in the way to save her hide. Their dynamic is a bit sick and predictable, something I'll use to my advantage.

It's why I put on a pair of gloves and press the doorbell. No fingerprints. No cameras are on; they scrambled the moment we walked in via the company's hacker.

"Hey, Ant? Can you get the door?"

"I'm on the phone!" Antonio calls back, and a shrill scream follows. Then there's the stomping of feet and a high-pitched *asshole* before the door is swung open.

She didn't look. Didn't see the added work Carmelo put in by stopping a random delivery guy and taking the two boxes of pizza, tipping the pimple-faced kid two hundred bucks to walk away.

"Oh shit." Mildred gasps, backing up with her hands shaking a second before trying to slam it closed.

The hardwood hits my shoe as I kick it back, causing it to smash against the wall, and a scream rends the air. It's full of fear. Of a pathetic attempt to get sympathy. "Please."

Mildred falls to her knees, shaking. The tears pooling in her eyes are real, but that doesn't stop her from arching her back, showing us that her fake tits are free to ogle. Tries and fails to distract me.

*Disgusting.*

"Get up," I hiss, walking in and closing the door after Carmelo enters. He drops the pizza boxes beside her legs, the sound loud but her whimper is louder. "I won't ask you again, Mildred. On your feet."

"Okay." Meek. Submissive. Bullshit.

"I'll go escort Mr. Frederick to the living room," Carmelo says, Glock in hand and safety off. He cocks it in her direction, and she jumps to her feet, rushing beside me. "You got that?"

"I do." Removing her hand from my arm, I push it off none too gently and point down the hall. "Don't touch, and walk."

"Let us explain. We can come to an—"

"Get him. I'll be there." Once he's out of sight, Mildred fingers the bottom of her top, trying to play the card of a willing tease, but stops all movements when I pull out my gun and wave it in the direction of Antonio's voice. "Walk."

The corridor isn't long, opening into a spacious, unused kitchen with access to the main living space.

"This is all a misunderstanding." *Those* words annoy me. Famous last words said by every lying asshole I've dealt with.

"Don't speak unless I ask you a question. Understood?"

"Millie!" Antonio rushes to her side, cradling her face and checking her for injuries. His concern is almost touching, a little too personal and not brotherly.

But then again...

"Your wife is fine, Mr. Frederick. Please have a seat."

He tenses while she lets out a panicked whimper, his eyes on her wide ones. "What did you say?"

"What part didn't you understand?" I take a seat on an oversized chair across from them and Carmelo does the same on another beside me. We're the picture of relaxation while understanding sets in for them. "She is your wife, no?"

"Mildred is my sister," he thunders, snapping around to face me with a false bravado that brings a smile to my face. "Who the fuck do you think...*fuck*!" His knee buckles and Antonio drops, biting his lip to the point of breaking skin from the pain.

I settle the Glock back down on my thigh. "I'll aim higher next time. Watch your tone, Mr. Frederick."

"Please don't!" Not-Mildred falls beside him, cradling his head.

"We'll give you whatever you want, no questions asked. We'll leave the country and disappear, too."

"You two have a lot of explaining to do to Mr. Asher and have an appointment within the hour. Clean up, get your emotions under control, and don't even think of drawing attention to yourselves when we exit through the garage." Hope fades from his face. I know that this penthouse goes from top to underground parking without needing to bypass the lobby or gym floors. "And if I were you, I'd pray. Beg your God to have mercy because lying is the ultimate sin."

---

FIVE PEOPLE SIT inside Malcolm's office an hour later.

Malcolm and me.

Antonio and his wife, not-Mildred.

And finally, the real Mildred herself.

No one's talking. No one has explained as of yet, but the way Mr. Frederick looks at his sister, you'd think he'd seen a ghost. That, or a mistake.

"You three have ten minutes to make me understand this mess," Malcolm says calmly, sitting back in his seat, a Desert Eagle and knife within reach atop the table while his eyes remain on the real Mildred. It's a little unnerving how much the two women look alike, from the bleach-blonde hair to their grating, high-pitched voices. Their clothing is similar, and the way they sit with one leg crossed at the knee and hands in their lap is not a coincidence.

"Antonio hired someone to kill me a little over a year ago, but the marksman failed." At the sister's words, there is no outrage or explosive defense from her sibling. His wife, though, is staring daggers at her and biting back whatever retort is on the tip of her tongue.

His fingers are gripping his wife's, and the strength used to keep them in his grasp makes them turn a purplish red from the pressure.

"Is that true?"

"Yes, Malcolm. I did." And while I give him credit for not denying, there's no remorse either. "Mildred knows the reason, too."

"I see." There are three files in front of him and he begins to read the one furthest to the left, nodding his head before flipping to the next page. This goes on for a few minutes. He's reading and the ones across from us wait, two with fear and the third a little smug.

There's something about the real Mildred Frederick that doesn't sit right with me, though.

For someone betrayed by her brother and usurped by his wife, she's cocky, not hurt.

Unafraid. A little taunting. *What are you really after here?*

"So you see, Malcolm, it's—"

"Not another word unless spoken to, Ms. Frederick," I interrupt, letting Asher finish his reading. Her eyes narrow and lips thin; I raise a brow and almost smile at the way she backs down.

He puts the first file down and then picks up the middle, ignoring the group. Malcolm doesn't see the way Antonio sweats or the way his wife's lips move in silent prayer.

Instead, he takes his time, reading the paperwork his team gathered after I found a discrepancy in Ms. Frederick's signature. I'll give them that it was a good match, but all it takes is one wrong loop to catch someone's eye. My eye.

Before taking on jobs as a hitman in Colombia, I oversaw the contracts that Alejandro signed with a fine-toothed comb.

It's a necessity when millions are on the line.

This time, though, when putting down the next folder, he doesn't pick up the third. Instead, his gaze meets Antonio a second before a shot is fired from his gun. It's a clean entry and exit with his shirt staining red at the shoulder this time.

"Explain yourself."

"He thought that—"

"I wasn't talking to you, Mildred." Malcolm flicks his eyes toward her for a second, stare hard and challenging. "Understood?"

She nods, and he goes back to Antonio. "Well, Mr. Frederick? I'm waiting."

"What she said is true. I did try to kill her for the company, and because of an issue she created two years ago."

"What issue?" Something in the way he says the words pulls my attention from the idiots across from us. There's a hint of undisguised irritation mixed with ire I didn't expect from someone who shows little to no emotion.

"My sister slept with an almost married man and the family was not happy."

"Hmmm." That's all he says before turning to the wife. "What's your gain in this?"

"He's my husband and needed help."

"Nothing else, Delia?"

"No." She looks at her husband and a tear falls. Not fake or to gain sympathy like before. This time, Delia is showing her emotions without any bullshit attached. "I simply love him and did what I had to."

"I need more than that, Mrs. Frederick. Tell me why you'd go along with such a stupid plan and try to deceive me?"

"Because when you love someone, you help them no matter the cost."

"Even if that's your life?"

"Yes." Delia's eyes close, and more tears fall while her husband watches. His expression is one of repentance. Of utter sadness, which has caught Asher's notice as well. There's more to this story than greed.

"Okay." That's all before lifting his gun a second time and firing again, this time hitting Antonio's ear and blowing the body part clean off. Blood spurts out, staining his wife's clothes and skin. "You forfeited your life the moment you signed those papers inside my office, and I plan to collect my pound of flesh. Mildred," he calls the woman without taking his eyes off a frantic Delia putting her hands on the head wound, trying to slow the bleeding, "choose her punishment, and I'll carry out the sentence. You have three minutes to decide."

The couple is horror-stricken by this, a whimper escaping the wife while Mildred tries to hide her glee. But I saw the look that flashed in her eyes before she took on a more stoic expression. She's enjoying this.

Most in her position would show hurt and betrayal. Would demand a better explanation, instead of glaring when Delia began to talk—the contempt and threat behind the heated look made the other woman a bit nervous.

After a minute, Mildred gives Asher a pleading look from beneath her over-mascaraed eyes. "They're my family, and I should be the one to—"

"Don't test my patience, Ms. Frederick. I've been compliant enough."

"Maybe we can come to a better agreement? I'll watch?"

"No."

"Malcolm, you're being difficult for no reason."

"Time's up. Javi, have them removed and transferred to a holding cell until I decide."

"Done." I stand from my seat and step out the door where Carmelo is waiting, talking with another two guards working at the bank this evening. "Take Antonio and his wife downstairs. We'll be down in a minute."

"Together or separate?"

"Keep them together for now, and no further injuries during transport. Understood?" All three men nod and walk inside, helping Antonio—nearly carrying him—while Delia follows amid sobs, body-shaking cries for leniency that no one reacts to.

Once they exit, I retake my seat and then take the last file, which Malcolm holds out for me.

"Please be reasonable," Mildred tries again, a whine in her tone. "What they did to me deserves retribution. Taking my life—my company—to make his wife happy deserves death. I'm only alive to tell my tale because of incompetence on their part."

"How did you survive a so-called hitman?" I ask, keeping my voice neutral when I'm anything but. Her audacity knows no bounds after sleeping with an almost married man, Mariah's ex to be exact.

Inside, I'm fuming as I meet her cold stare. Beyond irate.

My beautiful little criminal almost married this asshole, Lane Dermot, while he cheated. Lied. Put my girl at risk.

There isn't much of an explanation in this file. The one sheet only holds a few words, but they're enough to make my finger twitch.

I could kill her so easily.

But I don't. That pleasure will only be Mariah's. My beauty deserves the right to tell me her story—for me to earn her trust—and I'll wait because there's no doubt in my mind she's worth it.

"Since when does the help intervene in your business dealings, Mr. Asher?"

"Since he's family, Ms. Frederick."

Her plastic nose wrinkles at that while appraising me. "How are you related again?"

"One, you never asked, and I never explained. Two, he's Mariah's other half."

I'm not surprised by his words. His mind is working out logistics like mine.

Connecting dots she'd rather stay hidden.

"She's married?" Voice low and bitter, Mildred looks away, but I see her hands clench into tight fists.

"Answer my earlier question, Mildred." After putting the file face down atop the table, I rub two fingers across my bottom lip. "How did you survive?"

"I caught him cutting the brake lines of my car and staged an accident with the help of friends." Monotone. A rehearsed line and a lie. Most hitman will go for a personal approach and cutting lines is too far removed, a cop-out. "It was best to lay low after that and not tempt fate twice."

"Makes sense." Malcolm taps his fingers on the glass top, nodding to himself. "Smart move on our behalf."

"Now, about my company and my brother's betrayal..."

"What about it?" he asks with an amused chuckle at the end.

"How much will it cost to have the rights returned and—"

"Not a dime."

"Really?" Mildred smiles. Too cheery. Too easy to pick apart. "That's great, even though I am more than willing to pay with my flesh if you so inquire."

"Not interested in either your money or flesh. The company stays in my possession and so does your family. I'll execute and return the cadavers once I'm ready. You may see yourself out now."

"You're an—"

"Out." Her eyes narrow at my command, but the cocked gun makes her storm out a second later. She's muttering curses through gritting teeth. Demanding that whoever is still outside gets out of her way while the clacking of heels disappears down the hall.

"You saw what I saw, Lucas?"

"I did." My eyes narrow at the folder he gave me. "She's dirty and has help."

"So, the next question is: kill her now or let her hang herself?' At this, I meet his eyes. Malcolm doesn't realize that while I've never hurt a woman physically, if it relates to Mariah and her safety, I'd strangle one without a single ounce of remorse.

"Let her hang herself." There's an understanding between us. "The entire situation is fucked up—full of holes, and I'd rather know all the players involved than shoot blindly."

"Agreed."

"There's also the matter of Mariah's connection. She needs to know." This is something I won't back down from. I give exactly two fucks about his position in this family. When it comes to her, all bets are off. I'm protective of the woman to the point of blind madness if it ever came to that.

"Tell her." Asher stands and removes his suit jacket, then takes off his tie. "I'll handle the two downstairs in the meantime."

I follow his lead and type a message to Carmelo to bring the car around. Owing him dinner gives me the perfect excuse to pick up some dessert and personally deliver it to my muñeca later tonight. She has a sweet tooth I'll exploit if it gives me more time with her.

That, and I can explain today's event.

"They know something we don't."

"Not for long."

# 12

## Mariah

I'VE BEEN HOME for less than three hours and the place is clean, the laundry that's been inside of the dryer for two days is now folded, and I have a pan of chicken enchiladas in salsa verde bubbling in the oven.

I've also taken a bath and played a game of *teasing the killer* that brought me more pleasure than the orgasm that followed. Not because it wasn't good, but because I wanted *his* hands on me. *His* fingers pumping in and out slowly, edging me, until I fell apart in his arms.

It's getting harder and harder to deny this uncontrollable attraction. To pretend my body doesn't call out for his.

Because there's something about this man—Javier's mere presence—that undoes me and leaves behind a mass of need willing to forget promises made to herself. To forget her past and want *more.*

Of him. Of us. Of a future together.

"I'm on a roll tonight," I mutter low, the hint of sarcasm heavy, and it's because I'm still restless for some reason. Two orgasms didn't quell my inkling churning within that something is wrong.

My mind won't stop. Keeps dissecting Antonio and Mildred's behavior and then bounces to Javier and his last message.

***I'll be picturing you just like that tonight when I come with your name on my lips. ~Javier***

A shiver rushes through me and I shake my head, trying to rid myself of the images I used to come.

Javier on a bed. Cock in a tight first. His head thrown back while groaning my name.

"Oh God," I whimper low, thighs clenching—the pulse between my legs racing. *Christ, Mariah! Focus. We need to focus.*

Right. I need to think. Clear my mind.

It takes a few deep breaths for my body to relax, and I recall the twins' visit. Their mannerisms were the same: over-the-top rich and expectant. Nothing stood out. Nothing that could raise a red flag.

Those two aren't the best actors and it makes no sense. None.

Because even at their most narcissistic, faking documents and getting into unapproved—illegal human testing—isn't their deal. They've never shown this level of criminality, their specialty being seizing federal grants for what they claim will be breakthrough testing that funds their expensive taste while doing minimal effort and research.

Are they overindulgent assholes? Yes.

Are they obnoxious? No doubt.

Feeling unaccomplished and more than a little stuck, I refill my glass of wine and walk to the living room, taking a seat facing my floor-to-ceiling windows. The buildings surrounding mine are lit up, and the evening sky has begun to turn dark.

It's beautiful. Peaceful.

I take a sip and then another. My knees are bouncing and finger-tips drumming against the glass in my hold.

*Why can't I control this restlessness brewing inside of me?*

Like I know something is wrong.

Or maybe it's the confusion Javi creates. Maybe it's the electricity that shocks my senses and warms my bones when we touch. Maybe it's his persistence, that longing that matches my own.

But however I look at it, it all starts and ends with him.

I worry about him when he's out with Malcolm.

I look forward to the daily coffees and the flirty looks.

How do I fight something that I feel is inevitable? *You don't.*

I've been tempting him—pushing him to take and break the last of my walls down. A truth that is both hard to swallow and freeing. With his possessiveness and slick grin, Javier has infiltrated every corner of my mind and heart until the two became needy for his presence.

"Girl, you need to stuff your face and finish that bottle before you do something stupid. Calling him is no bueno in this state." I'm even nodding to myself, which further cements how crazy Javier Lucas makes me. "Especially since you're looking for issues with the Fredericks past the federal investigation. Remember that clear heads don't make mistakes."

I can deal with Javi and my feelings after. Much later.

A knock at my door pulls my attention and I stand, appreciative of the distraction even though I'm not expecting anyone. But what's worse is the sudden giddiness that hits my chest at the thought that maybe it's Javi. *So much for wanting to delay?*

Ignoring my subconscious, I look down at my body and I'm glad I chose the small sleep shorts and ribbed tank in a mint color. It's soft and looks sweet, but the lace edging and thin material give the like-second-skin fabric a sheer quality.

Another knock, and I fluff my hair. "Coming!" I yell out, and no other taps on my door are heard. Moreover, I don't look through the peephole or check the security camera, pulling the doorknob and opening it fully. "What the?"

No one is here. No sign of life down the corridor either.

However, what I do find is a bouquet of all-black roses in a large glass vase with no note. Picking up the large arrangement, I bring it inside and place it atop my entry table, digging through the stems for anything that tells me where it came from.

Yet there isn't anything.

"Must be a mistake." It's the only plausible explanation because no one is stupid enough to send me flowers that symbolize death or new beginnings. Because the two are tied together.

For every death, there is a birth.

For every ending, there's a start awaiting the chance to commence.

I close the door and take the flowers with me to the kitchen where I turn the oven off, pour another glass of wine, and sit while my food cools off a bit. And while I wait, I watch the flowers.

They're not helping my earlier thoughts. It's the opposite. They further unsettle me.

*Who left them outside my door? Why?*

Maybe a neighbor lost a family member? I know the lady three doors down has an elderly mother, but still, while the flowers themselves are beautiful, the meaning isn't loving or comforting.

So while I eat, I stare at them. While I wash my dishes and set them on the mat to dry, I stare at them. They don't leave my line of sight through my fourth glass of wine, and I'm so lost in my thoughts that when the ringer chimes, I jump in my seat.

At once I jump down from my barstool and rush to the door, not caring about my lack of clothing or the untamed mass of curls—the two long spirals that continually fall over my right eye now that it's dry.

It's one of the reasons I never leave my hair in its natural state. Too untamed. Wild.

"Should've straightened—" My whining is interrupted by three quick raps against my door, and I flick my eyes to the clock on the wall. *Jesus*, how did I lose two hours? It's late. A little past nine-thirty, and I pull the door open in hopes of catching...

"Fuck, Muñeca."

# 13

# Javier

S HE'S TRYING TO kill me.

Destroy what little patience I have left, and before the threadbare cord snaps, I'm on her, pushing her back and slamming the door closed with my foot. The loud sound makes her jump, but my lips swallow the delicious gasp.

"Motherfuck, baby. You drive me insane." The bag with dessert is somewhere on the floor, the thud barely registering as my arms bring her closer. "Need to feel you. Taste you."

She's nodding against my mouth while her chest rubs against mine, the two stiff peaks and their piercings making me shiver. The feel of her makes me forget what I came to talk to her about. It makes me forget the little punishment I'd planned for her teasing earlier.

"Javi, please," leaves her on the sweetest little whimper, a needy sound that settles on the tip of my cock. I'm pulsing. Throbbing behind the zipper of my slacks. "Just please!"

"Tell me what you need and it's yours," I say into the kiss, twining my tongue with hers again and flip us around. Mariah's back meets the door while my right hand wanders, caressing the soft skin where her thin tank has risen, and I pull back just long enough to catch the sight of her like this.

Swollen lips and hooded eyes.

Chest heaving.

Hair natural and wild, a perfect mass of curls to wrap around my fist.

The bare skin just above her indecent sleep shorts exposes the start of a tattoo I didn't know was there.

*Fuck.* What she does to me.

The hand not exploring her hip and skimming lower tangles in her hair and I angle her head back, tilting it to my liking. I savor the challenge still present in her eyes and the parting of those bee-stung lips, but more than that, is that she's letting me take control.

Mariah doesn't fight my possessive hold or dominating touch. If anything, my muñeca melts into me as I slant my lips over hers, growling in satisfaction.

The sound is animalistic. Hungry. Thankful for her trust.

Lips hovering, sweeping softly, I stare into those gorgeous sea-foam eyes. "Tell me, Mariah. Just ask and it's yours."

"Touch me." Two simple words, and they wreck any semblance of rationality I have left. She's all I see, smell, and feel, and on her next exhale, I grip her hips a little tighter.

My nails dig in right before I lift that tight body, bringing her warmth to just above my cock and her legs around my waist. I flex and she shivers, her small fingers embedding themselves into the hair at my nape while her perfectly white teeth bite down on my lip.

The action is one of aggression, a fight against my domination that I counter with a thrust of my hips, pinning her and enjoying the sweet heat seeping through those almost nonexistent shorts. Her nails scratch my neck, and I can feel the skin break as pleasure rips through me.

"Make me bleed, Muñeca. I'll just make you pay for it with tears later on." Another flex and she shivers; tightening those thighs, I drop my hand to the right leg, squeezing the skin there.

Mariah is perfect in my eyes.

Supple yet lithe, toned yet curvaceous, and I follow the curve of flesh until her bare cheek meets my fingertips. I caress her, palming it roughly before delivering the first of many smacks.

"Oh, *Christ.*"

"Javier, *Muñeca.*" Another spank, this time a little harder. And fuck me if she doesn't moan. Arching her body in a way that presses her cheek deeper into my palm. "My needy girl only moans for me. My name."

"I—"

"Say it. Cry out for me."

She doesn't comply. Instead, she throws her head back with her eyes closed. Denying me what's rightfully mine.

Her. All of her.

*Punishment it is, then.*

Before she can protest, I have her legs on the ground and her body facing the door. She shakes, goose bumps rising across her skin, and I use my nose to push aside a few curls and expose her neck.

Her scent is sweet against the sweep of my lips, and her hips roll as my teeth sink in, leaving behind the perfect indentation of my mouth.

"What're you...*fuck,*" Mariah cries out when I dig a little deeper and my hands traverse her front from her flat stomach to her breasts, cupping one in each hand.

I squeeze them. Feel their weight.

And when she whines at my slowness, I slap each tip with a bit of force. The metal of her piercings beneath the thin shirt makes my mouth water and I swallow hard, forcing myself to stay on course and not play a little longer.

I'll beg her to feed me each little tip later.

*Much later.*

Instead, I rake my teeth down to the center of her back between her shoulder blades and pause, ripping the offending top down the middle. And as the tattered pieces fall to the ground, so do my knees.

Immediately I take in the two dimples right above her ass and I kiss each, licking a path from right to left, and then I drag my tongue lower, right beneath the shorts that are both a blessing and a curse.

"Javi." It leaves her on a sacred whisper. The perfect combination of fear and desire. Of giving in to your wants and needs while handing over the control.

"You're always safe with me." It's a vow. The truth.

"I know."

"Good girl." One hard tug, and the tiny shorts covering her pool at her feet. Then it's my turn to groan when I take in the lack of underwear, just a thin little string between her cheeks, and the scent of her arousal. "*Motherfuck.*"

Sliding my hands up her calves, I follow the path my fingertips take and memorize every inch of bare skin I touch. I revel in the sigh of my name and the gyration of her hips when she presses her thighs together, looking for a small reprieve from the throbbing between them.

She's wet for me. Swollen, and I confirm this a second later when one hand doesn't pause at her inner thighs and cups her pussy through the lace of her G-string.

The soft material is soaked, clinging to her mound.

Slick heat. So soft.

"We should...I need..." with the tips of my fingers I rub tight little circles over her clit and stop "...more. Just more."

"As you wish." Sitting back on my haunches, I remove my hands from her body and admire her just like this. At my mercy. So beautiful and mine.

"What? No," she whines, a petulant sound that makes me smile. "Why are you stopping?"

"Spread your legs and bend over. Hands on the wall." One of her hands slips down and between her thighs, the tips of her fingers barely visible from where I sit. *Bad girl.* I don't say anything, but quickly land a harsh smack to the top of her right asscheek. Blood rushes to the surface as the sound of flesh meeting flesh reverberates throughout the room. "Don't make me repeat myself, Muñeca. Spread them." Mariah bends and spreads, but I want more. I want her asshole and pussy on display and legs shaking from anticipation. "Wider."

Perfection. She's an absolute wet dream become reality, and I lean forward when the two holes I plan to worship meet my line of sight. I trace a finger over the heated flesh where my palm print adorns her skin and travel down, slowly, learning her every moan and sigh as I meet the area where ass meets thigh and then walk my fingertips to the dip at the center.

Heat sears my skin and her wetness coats me as I caress each inner thigh and then pause at the entrance to my heaven. She's clenching, body shaking, and I've barely touched her.

"This changes everything," I say, tone harsher than I intend, but having her like this—at my mercy—is more than a heady feeling. I'm entranced. Owned just as much as I own her. "Tell me you understand this."

"Javier, we should talk—"

"Tell me you understand, Mariah. No more running or avoiding." I kiss each cheek and then lay one right over her puckered hole, flicking my tongue across the sensitive skin twice before waiting for a response. A hard shiver runs through her, her body swaying above me, and I grip her waist with one hand to steady her. She's aroused and needy and ready for more, but my words take away her docility — she wants to fight me or anything that demands her trust. Stubbornness is something we share, and I'll fight just as hard and dirty to possess her. "Say it, or I walk."

"Then I'll take care of myself," she grits out, trying weakly to push back against my hold. "You can leave...*Javi!*"

"Louder." The pathetic string she calls underwear is in my fist, the front digging into the sopping, swollen flesh of her cunt. One rough tug, and it snaps. "Let everyone in this building know I'm the one making you scream."

"No."

"Don't deny me, beautiful."

"Make me." Two words. They tell her truth, expose the push she needs from me, and yet they're the wrong words to tell a man barely hanging on to sanity and I land another smack to the round globes mere inches from my face. Then another, I leave her skin hot and body undulating, seeking the release only I'll give her.

Mariah tries to close her thighs, but before they touch, I palm and push them apart. The sight before me is almost obscene. Depravedly exquisite.

"You wanted this. Just remember that."

I don't give her a chance to answer, to further ignite me with her sharp tongue, and I bury my face between the two rosy cheeks. My tongue tastes her, flicking against the soft rosebud in a silent promise to be back before descending lower.

She's sweet and slick, soaking my lips and chin.

I lick her from back to front, pausing briefly at her pussy's entrance—dipping my tongue inside—before sliding down to her clit. The tiny bundle of nerves throbs against my tongue, coming out of its hood to greet my growls against the swollen flesh.

I become a savage for her. Take without care because she's woven her brujeria and I'm a proud slave for her.

With her clit between my lips, I bring a finger to her flexing hole and dip it inside to the first knuckle. Her walls pulse, hole fluttering around my finger to pull me in deeper, and I give my girl just that.

*Son of a bitch* she's tight. So soft.

I pull the digit out coated in her sweetness and slam it back in, pumping it a few times before adding a second.

The slam of her hand on the wall is loud, and the way she rises onto the tips of her toes, both wanting to escape my touch while grinding against my face is a privilege to experience.

"Oh my God!" she cries out suddenly, and I chuckle against her clit before raking my teeth once again down the hood, adding a little more pressure before pulling back and admiring the view of her slick thighs, flexing rosebud, and the vice-like grip on my fingers.

"You always call out to me." It's a hiss, my fingers slipping out long enough to slap the length of her pussy, fingertips landing over the throbbing bundle. The barely contained snarl, the undisguised hunger in my tone causes a rush of wetness to spill into my palm and down my wrist, a few drops marking the floor. *The little demon.* "Do you like it rough? Do you like to beg?"

Before she can open her mouth in protest, I'm gripping her hips and flipping her around to face me. Our eyes meet, my hungry ones on her heavy-lidded ones, and I slowly make my way back to her pussy, spreading her labia with my tongue as her lips part. She's panting, chest rising rapidly while I suck the first then second lip into my mouth, starving for more of the wetness coating her bare skin.

So pretty and pink. So mine.

"Motherfucking answer me, Muñeca. Are you testing my patience?"

"Please, Javi." *Christ,* her voice is all soft with a hint of desperation that pierces my gut and further stiffens my cock. I'm so fucking hard. Throbbing, I raise her right thigh over my shoulder with one hand while releasing myself with the other.

The cold air meets the swollen, angry head and I hiss, bringing two fingers to her opening and push them inside—pumping them in and out rapidly and I'm rewarded with a rush of wetness that I use to lube my cock.

With my fingers soaked in her, I bring my face once again against her core and breathe her in, rubbing my nose over her clit.

Above me she's whining, arching her back and pulling on her nipples while my tongue follows the same path, using the flat of my tongue to catch every drop and bring her closer to the edge.

"I'm so close."

"Give me what's mine." My voice doesn't drown out the sound of my hips meeting my hand, cock piercing through the tight fist as I forget about anything but her. Her taste. Her scent. Her scream as I bite down on her clit hard enough to make her come. "Good girl."

*There's nothing I find sexier than your trust.*

"..." Her lips part but no words escape. She's lost to her pleasure, riding my tongue while I continue to fuck my fist.

I'm so close. Just need...

Mariah grips my hair hard, a few strands breaking as she pulls me closer—holds me to her while a second orgasm rips through her lithe frame.

"Fucking hell, Muñeca," I growl, tightening my hold to almost the point of pain, and come overflows my palm and lands on the floor below.

At the same time, her legs give out and she slides down into my lap, letting me wrap her in my arms.

We sit there for a while. Just breathing. Calming racing hearts when the bag with dessert catches my attention and hers.

It doesn't look ruined, the container and bag not broken, and I clear my throat. "We need to talk."

# Mariah

"**W**HAT ARE YOU thinking about, beautiful?" Javier asks, and I'm pulled back from my thoughts. Everything he's said, the giant mess created by the twins, spins in my mind. Sadly, this makes more sense than the behavior displayed by who I now know isn't Mildred.

Because while she remained aloof this time, there wasn't the usual glare or underhanded comment she passed as a compliment in the hallway after I showed them out. A behavior that I'd roll my eyes at in the past, I found the lack of strange.

Mildred and I never spent time together outside of the necessary business meetings, but the woman has always been unpleasant. Always miserable in my presence.

However, I get it now. Mildred was nothing but the bitter other woman.

Lane couldn't leave me, not without dealing with consequences his parents couldn't spare him from. Christ, he made me the fool of the story, and even with that, this delusional bitch had the gall to be angry with me as if I'd taken something from her.

*You killed him.* I did. And would again to protect myself.

"Just thinking," I answer truthfully, giving him a small shrug before taking a sip from my lukewarm coffee. We're in my living room and dressed somewhat; I'm wearing his shirt while Javi remains bare-chested and tempting.

There's no awkwardness. No regret. No self-reproach when I've fought so hard to keep him at bay.

Instead, I feel at peace even though the situation with the Fredericks leaves a sour taste in my mouth—ire in my veins—but it's contained with him by my side. Not even the memory of my parents betrayal and the disdain on the Dermots face make my heart clench like before. Instead, I find myself thinking rationally, not acting on impulse while enjoying the view in the seat across from mine.

Javier's tan muscles and the small amount of chest hair across his pecs are on display, and I'm memorizing each. My gaze travels lower and across beautiful tattoos, unashamed, and I count each indentation that leads to a delicious 'V' I want to run my tongue across.

He's a bit of a distraction, but I like it. Secretly love the fact he refuses to let me be.

A throat clears and once again I meet his eyes, feeling the slight heat sweep across my face. I've never been a person who blushes, but this man has that effect on me. He makes me lose my train of thought and the ability to send him to hell.

*He has no idea he's already won.*

"Be specific, Mariah. You've been silent for twenty minutes, and your facial expressions range from lust to anger. And before you answer, that lust better be for me."

"And if it isn't?" I challenge back, loving the way his nostrils flare and jaw clenches. Testing his patience is a turn-on, and the earlier result was worth every minute we've fought so far. Subtly, I rub my thighs together, but he catches the act and raises a brow, smirk in place. "Answer me, Muñeca," he croons, and goose bumps rise, a stuttered breath caught in my throat as I choke back a groan. He has me with that nickname. The effect is always the same as liquid heat rushes through my veins and settles in my core. *The day he realizes this, I am screwed.* "If I parted those thick little thighs and ran a finger down your folds, I'd find you wet. More than eager." *Abort. Abort before you climb into his lap and ride that beautiful thickness you watched him abuse.* "And while God knows how badly I want you on my tongue again, I'm concerned with your reaction to the Mildred situation. You're being too passive for the fiery woman I know."

His expression is one of sincere concern and I offer a small smile back, a different feeling taking over me. It flutters, feels like a thousand and one butterflies dancing within, and I melt back into my seat. Not just because of the magnificent orgasm he gave me, but because he came here with the intent to talk—keep total honesty between us—and that's something I appreciate.

He's proving day by day to be everything his reputation preceeds and so much more. Javier Lucas is everything I find attractive, and my walls crumble with each look, that gentle way his eyes sweep over me with affection so sweet I can't fight against it.

After a few beats of silence, I give him the same honesty back. "It's a lot to take in, Javi."

"Are you upset about the nature of their relationship?" There's a hint of jealousy there, some tensing of his muscles, but I won't call him out on it.

"Not in the least." There's no hesitation from me and he nods, relaxing back a bit. "But I am curious here…"

"That's all I know, Mariah. Do I have the file? Yes." Figured as much. Getting information on anyone is just a matter of time and connections. "However, I haven't read it. I'm waiting for you to fill in the blanks."

"Thank you."

"You deserve my respect."

Again, my heart thumps harshly at his words. My smile widens. "Then my next question is how much time do you have to give?"

His scent surrounds me, his shirt keeping me warm and I inhale deeply, taking him into my lungs and holding it there. There's a yearning within me that I can't control. He makes me forget the past and live for the present.

Really live. Want the *more* I've been running from.

"My entire life."

My eyes close at those three simple words and the heavy implication behind them. "That's a long time, Javi. Are you sure?"

"I am." Now he is the one without hesitation. His conviction makes me happy until I remember the topic of conversation and the earlier surprise left outside my door. My brows furrow as my mind runs and coincidences don't seem so innocent. *Mildred.* "What is it?"

Something tells me what I'm about to say will piss him off, but if he's honest with me, then I'll always return the favor.

"Earlier tonight, I received a bouquet of roses." Javier's hands clench at my words, but he nods for me to carry on. I meet his stare and keep it there. "They were left outside the door, black from the flowers to the vase, and without a note."

"Hijueputa," he grits out, and I won't deny that hearing him swear in Spanish is a turn-on. Javier doesn't do it often, speak in his native tongue, but I wish he would. It also makes me want to find ways to provoke it.

*Bend me over and call me your little doll.*

And had someone else spoken to me the way he does, I'd have knocked out a tooth or ten by now, but with him, it's not demeaning. It feels warm. Full of this sweetness that makes my core clench whenever he calls me his *Muñeca.*

"Are you paying attention, Muñeca?"

The always-present tingles spread, and I fight the need to whimper. I'm still sensitive. Feel the slight burn from his five o'clock shadow on my inner thighs.

*Dear God, please help me get it together. This isn't the time to give in to temptation. Amen.*

"What was the question?"

He tsks, but there's no real annoyance in his features. Instead, there's a hint of a smirk. As if he knows where my mind has been. "When did the flowers appear, Mariah?"

With a sheepish grin, I shrug. No denying it. "A little before I pulled my dinner from the oven. I was sitting right where you are now, looking at the early evening sky when a knock came. They didn't ring the doorbell but knocked hard instead."

"So it should be on the doorbell recorder?"

"It should." Why didn't I think of that? *Hard to think with his mouth between your thighs.* "Let me grab my phone. Be right back." I'm rushing to the kitchen before the words finish leaving my lips. I need a moment to collect myself. To gain a bit of decorum.

This isn't the time to be anything but what I am: an Asher.

Opening the faucet, I grab a paper towel and dip it under the water before squeezing off the excess and running the dampness over my heated neck, my cheeks, and lower across the top of my breasts. The coolness feels good, but his shirt on me smells of him and it isn't helping me control my libido.

He's woodsy scents mixed with a hint of cigar and heavy liquor. He's sex and danger, and I'm sniffing the collar and abandoning the paper towel, closing my eyes to enjoy the moment. The thoughts and images running through my mind are of him on his knees—worshipping me—but the reel quickly morphs to another fantasy.

I'm praying at *his* temple. Tasting what is mine.

"I need to change."

"You okay in there?" Javi calls out from the other room and I squeak, the embarrassing sound bringing me back to the situation at hand. Wearing this shirt isn't a smart choice. It's disastrous for my common sense, and I walk out sans phone.

"Be right back." My answer comes out high-pitched while

walking toward my room. The plan is to lose the shirt and get myself together before further embarrassing myself.

And I make it inside without issue. I begin undoing the buttons and notice his lack of response, but it's as I get to the last button that two hands come up from behind and stop me, a deep rumble leaving his chest in displeasure.

"No." His face appears next to mine a second later, his cheek rubbing against mine. "Don't take it off."

"But I can't think straight." It leaves me before I can stop it, and I'm embarrassed. This isn't who I am, but with him, my defenses are nonexistent—an afterthought.

"I don't want you to think straight." Javi's hands leave mine and he begins to put each button back through a hole, lingering a little longer when he reaches the one between my exposed breasts. "Lord knows I'm unstable in your presence. Completely fucked by a slip of a girl that threatens daily to shoot me while the mere image makes me hard as fuck."

A harsh shiver rocks me, his nose skimming the length of my neck, causing goose bumps to rise across my flesh. I know I'm supposed to be looking at the video, talking about the discrepancies found in the twins' file and the possibility of who their donor could be, but when his lips follow the path back up to my jaw and he nips the skin, I lose composure.

That tiny spark of pleasurable pain makes me the aggressor. I'm the one who's salivating for a taste.

With his shirt on and a bold little grin, I turn around and drop to my knees. His eyes turn nearly black—dilated and hungry—as he watches me undo two of the buttons he closed.

My mouth waters as the bulge in his pants expands, twitches beneath my gaze. That's the only part of him that moves; he's stone still as I open his pants and lower the zipper, the angry, purple head greeting me while a drop of pre-come slips down the thick shaft.

"Hands behind your back and don't move," I breathe out, voice just above a whisper as I sweep a finger across the deep V, following the sharp indent from right to left and then back again.

"Muñeca," he groans, the pain in his voice causing my eyes to snap up to his. *Christ*, he's beautiful and masculine and complying with my wishes without a single complaint. Instead, his eyes are reverent. Hold so much affection. "Baby, I can't promise to give you full control, but I'll try. For as long as I can, I'll do what you ask."

# 15

# Mariah

**M**Y RESPONSE IS a small kiss on his right hip and then left, traversing the skin with the tip of my tongue before going lower. There, I leave an open-mouthed kiss at the base of his cock and another up the length, laving the tight skin until my parted lips caress the engorged head.

The bead at the slit glides across my lips and I can't stop myself from licking his essence, getting my first taste, and I hum. He's salty-sweet with a hint of earth, igniting my hunger in a way I've never experienced before.

"Don't. Move." The unrestrained yearning in my voice makes him shiver, but he doesn't move. Doesn't grab me when I take the first two inches into my mouth and let his weight settle on my tongue.

He's silky smooth, angry veins desperate for my touch. He's tense muscles and gritted teeth, watching me behind dilated eyes as a rumble builds in his chest.

I feel vibrations straight down to my core.

I'm wet and throbbing and my lack of underwear—the cool air in the room over my slick thighs gives away my desire to do this.

I need to taste him.

To have him lose control and take. To let him fuck my mouth.

Another inch and his thighs tense, the pants sitting just below his ass stretching, and I rake the blunt of my nails down his skin, pulling them down to his feet as my mouth takes him in deeper. I don't pull off to catch a breath or to tease her with a little teeth; instead, I slowly take him down to the back of my throat and swallow, not pausing until my nose touches the base.

"*Fuck.*" Javi hisses, eyes on mine as I touch the edge of his balls with the tip of my tongue. Spit rolls down his shaft and sack. It pools on the floor right in front of his shoes and I hollow my cheeks, pulling back slowly until the only thing that connects us is a string of spit. "God, you're perfect. Made for me."

Large hands twitch and I raise a brow, blowing a little on the bulbous tip. "I said don't move."

"You have five minutes, sweet girl." The deep vibration of his voice carries throughout the room, and I feel a rush of wetness coat my lips at the threat in his words. He excites me. "Four and a half."

Swiping a finger across the slit at the tip, I bring it to my mouth and hum. "Can you make it that long, Javi?"

"Do your worst."

"I plan to." *I'm going to use every single trick I've watched porn actresses do.* Gripping the bottom of his shirt, I rip the buttons off and leave the two sides open, exposing my perky breasts to his eyes. The piercings glint in the room's low lighting, my chest heaving as I put half his length back into my mouth and hollow my cheeks. I bob my head while my hands wander my body, from my collarbone to the edge of my mound and back again, pausing to cup a tit in each hand.

I squeeze them, and he grunts.

I pull the piercings, tugging hard enough to make me groan around his length, and a curse bellows from him.

"Son of a bitch, Muñeca. God, baby...just a little deeper." He's shaking, body fighting to grab me and take, but he needs that extra push. "Open that sweet little throat for me."

A large part of me wants to do just that, but I don't. Instead, I slow down and pull off, keeping just the head between my lips while I pinch a nipple and bring the other hand between my thighs. I also slide closer and lean back, the tip of his shoe sitting just below my pussy.

I'm hot and swollen. Soaked, and as I slip a finger through my soft lips, his hand fists my hair and tips my head back. Angry eyes meet my excited ones, and his lip curls up into a sneer. "That wasn't nice, linda."

"Are you going to punish me?"

"No."

"Then what?"

"I'm going to watch you come as I use your pretty little mouth." Pulling away, he bends at the waist and gives me a kiss that curls my toes and sets my blood on fire. It's fast and perfectly messy, but it's over too soon and then I find myself choking on his cock on my next breath.

Javi's stroke is near punishing, and with my hair wrapped around his fingers, I'm held still while he strokes in deep. He holds still when his balls meet my chin, tapping two fingers against the bulge in my throat and I swallow hard, breathing through my nose and ignoring the urge to gag.

I'm at his mercy. Being used by him.

I love it more than I should, but I can't help and rub my clit a little harder while he stares down my body and begins to thrust in time with my fingers. "Faster, Mariah. Get yourself off while sucking my cock." The two fingers on my throat become his hand and he wraps it tight, moaning each time he strokes in and feels himself expand my throat.

"I'm close," I whimper around his shaft, spit dribbling down the side of my mouth and he wipes up the mess, pushing his thumb inside my mouth, further stretching me. I'm full. His taste dances on my tongue, but it's when he pumps his thumb twice and then drags the glistening digit to my left nipple and pulls the piercing that I come.

I scream around him, eyes closed, and rubbing my clit faster as my orgasm takes me over. Pleasure grips me out of nowhere, the hold nearly painful as the pulsing wave consumes me until becoming a throb, and my body feels as if I've been electrocuted by a thousand pinpricks. But that's when I start coming back to my senses and the guttural groans above me become clear.

Javi's fucking my mouth with wild abandon. No stopping. No concern, he strokes in and out at a rapid pace while bottoming out each time, using my hair to guide my mouth.

He feels larger, his growls harsher, and when our eyes connect again, he stills. "Motherfuck."

Spurt after spurt glides down my throat and I swallow fast, making sure to not spill a single drop.

---

WE'RE SITTING in my bed an hour later, naked and with our legs crossed at the ankles. He's to my left and quiet, humming now and then some tune I don't recognize, and eating his slice of tiramisu while my phone lies between us. No shame. Not a care as his dick twitches each time my eyes wander lower.

And they do. A lot.

He's muscles and control and danger.

He's tattoos and a few scars that only serve the purpose of raping my psyche.

And while I've fought this thing between us, I know that here, like this, was inevitable. Javier Lucas didn't take my no at face value and pushed and pushed until my will gave in. He's been persistent enough for the both of us and while I still have a few reservations, I'm at peace with what's happened.

Happy. Excited.

Is this fast? Yes.

Does my attraction to a man like him make sense after what happened before? No.

Moreover, he's never given me a reason to doubt his word. He's a man of integrity.

"I'm not a piece of meat, you know." Javi's rough voice breaks my appraisal, and I blush when the words hit me. I look away and toward my turned-off TV hoping for a miracle to break the now heated flush that covers down to the tops of my breast. "Not that I usually mind when it comes to you, but you promised an explanation and a search through your front door security feed."

"You suck," is my mature reply and he snorts, hand on my knee while his body shakes beside mine. "I do." His hand sweeps higher, pausing just at the edge of my core and squeezes, grip firm. "And I'll be more than happy to remind you after."

A hard shiver rushes through me at the same time I slap his arm. "Maybe I don't want you to show me."

"You do."

"So cocky."

"I see no point in denying that." Placing his now empty plate on the nightstand with his unoccupied hand, he shifts to face me a little, a subtle turn of hips that pushes those long, calloused fingers against my still-sensitive clit. "We both know who we are and where we stand; the only thing I need clarification on is the murder of Lane Dermot."

"You swing without lubing me up first."

His chuckle warms me even when I should be annoyed. "Always aim to please."

"All right, dork. How much do you know?"

All traces of amusement die and he's back to being the stone-faced killer I met weeks ago. "Nothing but what I told you. Please fill in the blanks."

"Okay. But first…" I put my plate down and reach for the large afghan I keep on my bed at all times, pulling it over my naked body "…for distractions' sake."

"I'd rather you don't."

"I'd rather a few things as well, but they're not conducive to this conversation." Javi grunts but doesn't pull my blanket away. Instead, he gives me his attention and waits with patience for me to begin. "Lane and I met years ago when I was still in high school, and we became friends. You know, the kids of affluent families that didn't fully abide by the law and run in the same social circles, we bumped into each other a lot. He was older than me, a jerk to most and spoiled, but never disrespectful toward me."

"How long did you date?"

"Two years, and no, I didn't love him then or now." For some reason, I'm ashamed to admit my faults to this man. To let him see me as anything but a smart, fierce, and independent woman. "My reality now isn't what it was back then, Javi. I made bad choices. Let others dictate my life."

"Malcolm?" There's venom in his tone, and while I still don't meet his eyes, I grab his hand and intertwine our fingers. Squeeze them. "Did he force you?"

"No. He hated Lane."

"Then who?"

"My parents."

"I haven't met them." Not a question, although his raised brow and pursed lips show displeasure. He's demanding an explanation without uttering the words, but I read those warm brown eyes, and the anger in them isn't directed at me.

"And you more than likely won't for a long time." Sighing, I reach over to the bedside table and pick up my bottle of water, twisting the cap off and taking a long pull. It gives me a small reprieve, the moment needed to explain the dynamic he isn't aware of. "They've been exiled to Europe for the foreseeable future by Malcolm for their role and the audacity to try and pin the incident on me."

"Incident?"

"I killed Lane the night he attacked me in this apartment two years ago. A few days before our anniversary/engagement dinner was to be held."

# 16

# Javier

P RIDE SURGES THROUGH my chest at her words.

She put the dog down with mercy because had he still been alive today—breathing and walking this earth—I'd have hunted him down and left his entrails for Mildred to find.

"Do you threaten all the men you meet?" I say, and she giggles a bit, the tension in her shoulders dropping. *Is she worried I'd think differently of her?* Because if anything, I'm in awe of her and fuming at her parents.

How could they sell their child out this way?

"Are your parents active members on the Asher board?" Because if they are, I'll talk to Malcolm and make the bounty on their heads worthy of his acquiesce. Not that it will stop me, but I don't want Mariah to lose anyone she cares about.

"No." A wayward curl glides across her shoulder and I bring my hand up to her face, turning to fully face her and push it back, tucking the loose strand behind her ear. She shivers, and I see the two hard little tips beneath the blanket. "After going behind Malcolm's back and making a deal to expand territories—overthrow two other families that deal in the city in exchange for helping my father claim my cousin's rightful place, everything was taken. Money, properties, and access to all Asher dealings and buildings around the globe. They've been left with a small monthly allowance to live off and that's it."

"Do you talk to them?" Sadness flashes in those seafoam eyes briefly, but just as fast it's gone. "Miss them?"

"Not since my last birthday seven months ago." Mariah pulls her hand from mine and stands, the blanket tightly wrapped around her lithe frame, and walks toward the bathroom. Her foot is over the threshold when she pauses and turns her head slightly, just enough for me to see the pain that lingers from their actions, and I vow at that moment to take it all away. To give her the life she deserves with a faithful man at her side. "That's the day I buried them after being blamed for destroying their lives. They rather I'd died instead of the asshole who nearly choked me to death."

My muñeca slips inside the bathroom with the door closed, and I give her the time she needs. No matter how much my body wants to follow her inside the running shower or pull her close, I pick up our plates instead and run them to the kitchen.

While she's soaping up and touching what is mine, I bring us a bottle of water each, find her bottle of ibuprofen, and fix the sheets and covers. She's upset. I know there's more that needs to be discussed—the flowers and Mildred—but for tonight, I'll hold her and make sure she understands that no matter what...

I'm here.

And twenty minutes later when she comes back into the now pitch-black room and slips under the covers, I mold my body around hers. Keep her warm and kiss the crown of her head, humming a song that reminds me of her. Her beauty.

Moreover, when her breathing evens out and body melts into mine, I follow. Allowing my eyes to close and sleep to claim me.

"WHY ARE you staring at me, Muñeca?" My eyes are closed, but I feel hers on me. Like a heated caress, they've been traveling from my face to chest and lower, while tiny fingers walk up each indentation of my abdomen.

She's been counting the six over and over. Skipping, sliding—tapping my skin softly with the pad of her fingertips. She moves away, and immediately I miss her warmth and the horny little hums of approval that follow.

I've been awake for a while, since before dawn, enjoying the bit of quiet that surrounds us. Reveling in her touch.

It's my favorite time of day. The few hours between sunrise and my alarm blaring when the world stills and I can think—dissect and plan—and today is no different.

Our conversation still weighs heavily on my mind. Her taste and touch still linger on my flesh.

"Christ, Javier! You scared me."

"You're the one being sneaky, not me. Very inappropriate, linda." Turning my head in her direction, I pucker my lips but still don't open my eyes. "Morning."

It takes her a few minutes, but she pecks my lips, grazing her teeth down my bottom lip. "Buenos dias."

I can't stop the smile that spreads across my lips as my eyes greet her bashful ones. Mariah's without makeup, her hair a mess of curls, and she's wearing nothing but a thin silk slip. She's fresh-faced and sleep-rumpled, but God, she's beautiful.

My other half. Mine.

"*Fuck*, you're perfect," I groan, gripping the back of her neck and pulling her down to my lips. The kiss is softer than the others we've shared, yet deeper, and I find myself turning until I'm fully lying on top of her, my hips cradled by her thighs.

There's no rush. No desperate touches as if the other person would vanish. Instead, we savor and explore. Caress and moan as I press the blunt head of my cock against her clit. The tip glides smoothly across, her wetness mixing with my pre-come, and if I shift a little lower, there's no stopping me from snapping my hips and claiming what's mine.

And I want to. Fuck, I do.

But not yet. Not until we put everything on the table because this beautiful criminal beneath me isn't a one night stand. She's not a quick fuck.

Mariah has quickly become my everything, and I'm not fighting the craziness that consumes—obliterates rationality.

Fuck it being too fast.

Fuck the way she fights me.

Fuck everything, because, in the end, it'll be worth it. She is worth it.

I care about her. *More than.*

"We need to stop," I grit out, flexing against her one last time, and sit back when her tiny hands move to grab me. "There's somewhere we need to be within the next hour."

There's a pout on her lips, and those seafoam orbs narrow. "Where? Nothing's going on until after two, and Malcolm gave us the morning off."

It's my turn to narrow my eyes. "I was never told this."

Not that I'm giving her much of a notice on my plans, but there's something I need to see just as bad. For my peace of mind. For her safety.

"That's because I told him we'd be late last night before my shower." Rising from the bed, a strap of her gown slipping down her shoulder, Mariah grips my jaw. "And I'm not done kissing you, Javi. Not yet."

*Christ,* this beautifully dangerous woman tempts every single cell in my body. Knows what to say. Knows how to light me on fire with the faintest of touches.

*We have plans for her. She's more than a fuck.*

"I'll give you all the kisses you want after my surprise."

"What's it going to cost me?"

"Two hours in a ring with me."

I thought she'd protest, but I'm dead wrong. Her eyes light up and her body vibrates with excitement as she scrambles off the bed, pushing me over in her haste. And all I can do is laugh. She's certifiably adorable, and when she comes back thirty minutes later showered and dressed in a pair of lavender-colored yoga pants and a sports bra, I rethink these plans.

How the fuck am I supposed to test her fighting skills when all I can picture is bending her over and plowing deep?

---

"AGAIN. HARDER THIS TIME." I'm moving around her, ducking my arms, holding the focus mitts just out of her reach. She's breathing hard and sweaty, the few tendrils that slipped from her bun plastered to the side of her face and neck. An elegant neck where a few drops of perspiration glide down to the edge of her...

Her fist connects with my chin, and it stings. She's caught me off guard and looks smug. Her grin is cocky. "I think you need to focus, Javi. Or do I need to find another trainer?"

Thank God the gym used by Malcolm's employees is empty and no one is allowed inside until I give the okay. All cameras are off and the lights are dimmed, leaving just enough brightness where we can see the other move. *No one sees her like this but me.*

"I'm going to make you pay for that," I hiss, ducking her next punch and tapping her right thigh when she stumbles a bit, losing her footing while chasing me. "Think you can handle me?"

"Bring it, pretty boy."

"Noted." Holding a hand up, I take the mitts off and toss them aside along with my shirt a few seconds after. She wants to play, then so be it. "You can throw a decent punch, princess, but can you dodge them?"

Something about what I said doesn't sit right with her. Darkness overtakes her features, hate and ire her stance.

She's stiff, chest heaving in a way that worries me. "Never call me that again, Lucas."

"What that, *princess*?" Her reaction is the same: anger. A sudden blinding rage that makes me pause. I'm not going to call her out, not now, but I'll push because whatever just overcame her mind is dangerous.

Mistakes cost lives. And it's unacceptable that anything should happen to this woman.

"Don't." It's a hiss. A warning. Nodding, I slip off my sneakers and tuck the strings of my joggers inside the waistband, taking away anything that could get caught in the fight she's bringing my way. Her chest heaves, eyes bore into mine, but Mariah isn't seeing me.

I still don't have the full story of her history with Lane, but something tells me this has to do with him or her parents—their role and involvement with him is what's setting her off. I'm also wondering if she's ever truly dealt with her anger toward the assholes.

"Or what?" At my response, her nostrils flare and eyes narrow. "Something you want to say?"

"Quit it, Javi. This isn't a box you want to open."

"I'm not afraid, Muñeca." I circle her, knocking her left hand from her hip on purpose. "You want to vent, do it. You want to strike, do it."

"Back off." Two words spit out through clenched teeth.

"Get it off your chest." Rather now than during a dangerous situation. Mildred, in my eyes, is a threat, a weak one, but stupid people cannot be discounted. They're careless. Ballsy. "Why do you hate the word—"

"Fuck you." And she reacts without thinking, charging me with all her strength and I let her, taking the brunt of our fall and cradling her close. Mariah's angry, eyes a bit red-rimmed while landing an elbow across my chin, knocking my face to the side. "Never call me what those pieces of shit did. Not you. Never you."

"Why?" Before she can land another blow, I have her hand in mine and roll her off me. She's on her back when I stand, eyes following me, and I wave her up. "Again. Don't let your emotions rule you."

"Maybe we should stop for today."

"Get up. Don't make me be an asshole this early."

"Why do you care?" The ire from a few minutes ago has cleared a bit but still lingers.

"Because I'd rather you get pissed at me than make a costly mistake out there." Her features soften at that, and I nudge her shin with the tip of my sock-covered foot. "Now, get up or I'll mount you." Cheeks flushing a bit, she does as I ask and gets into a fighter's stance, leaning most of her weight on the right leg. Another mistake. You don't favor one side more than the other, and I sweep Mariah's feet out from under her.

"What the hell?" She lands with a thud, but there's a hint of a smile on those sweet lips.

"No one outside these walls will grant you mercy, baby." I take two steps back and crook a finger. "Up."

"You're going to pay for that, Javi." And there's my girl. Focusing on me. On what's important. Grinning like the Cheshire Cat, Mariah brings her two hands up to block my attack while balancing her core, feet planted firmly on the ground. *Much better.*

But there's still an opening on her left and I strike toward her thigh, not giving her the full force of my blow but enough to cause her to stumble back. She catches herself, arms never lowering and when I go for the right rib area, she counters and lands her punch.

My stomach contracts, but I keep a proud smile on my lips. "Think you can knock me down?"

"Bet you two hundred bucks I can."

"I won't go easy on you."

"I'd be pissed if you did." This time when she charges, Mariah changes position at the last second and kicks the back of my knee.

My weight drops, but before she can get me down I return the favor, chuckling as her leg buckles.

"That was good, but not enough."

"You're a jerk."

Before she can continue to berate me, I tackle the brat and cover her body with mine. "Never claimed to be anything but an asshole, sweetness."

"That's what you want others to think, Javi, but I see you." Those words pause me, and she takes the distraction as her opening, flipping our position with a hard buck of her hips, turning us so I'm on my back and looking up. I'm left marveling at the cheeky grin and the bright eyes of this incredible woman. "No one else has bothered to make me talk about shit I hate. No one else pushes me to deal with what I feel when ignorance is an easier solution."

"Muñeca, I—"

"I know you pay attention. I know you care." Mariah lowers her face to mine and kisses the tip of my nose, then each cheek before pecking my lips. "You're so much more than what I thought, Javier. Thank you."

Bringing a hand up, I cup the back of her neck, keeping her lips hovering over mine. "For what?"

"For doing more for me than those who were supposed to love me. Those who called me *princess*," she spits the word out with so much venom and tears in her eyes. This is her letting me fully in. A beautiful olive branch. "That was Dad's nickname for me growing up, and Lane adopted it. It wasn't meant to be loving, more demeaning as he thinks all women are beneath the men in their lives."

"I'm not them."

"I know." Another soft smile. A sweet sigh. "You have the possibility to be my everything, and that scares me."

"I'd never hurt you."

"And I don't think I'd recover if you ever did."

# Mariah

"**W**HAT TIME ARE you getting off?" Javi asks, pulling into the Asher building parking structure a few minutes before two in the afternoon. I'm in the passenger seat and fighting back a giggle, keeping my face neutral after the semi-argument we had outside of the women's shower where he all but demanded to drive us in today. An exchange I lost after the jerk jutted his bottom lip out while sweaty, chest glistening and those damn joggers hanging low.

I could make out the outline of his thick cock, and it made getting my point across a near impossibility. Couldn't think straight when he twitched and grew, and I had to yell out a *yes* before disappearing inside to take a cold shower.

Turning the ignition off, he sits quietly and I follow suit. His spot is next to my empty one and two down from the ones Malcolm keeps for certain clientele. We never host more than one family at a time, and no more than four members of their organization are allowed upstairs together.

A precaution for them. For us.

"Should be out by five. I left everything he'd need today on his desk before logging off last night."

"Any plans?"

"No."

"You do now," he says simply. Just like peppering the weather into any conversation.

But more comical is that I nod and inspect my nail polish. The one nail that I chipped a corner of. "What are you in the mood for? I can stop on my way home and—"

"I'm asking you out on a date, Muñeca."

My heart flutters inside my chest and I smile, turning my face toward him. "A date?"

"Si." His grin matches mine and he holds his palm up to me. I place mine atop his, and it's only when our fingers intertwine that he fully relaxes. "How does a nice dinner with you and me and alcohol mixed in sound? And to sweeten the pot, there will also be some witty banter and a lot of sexual innuendos."

"You piqued my interest. Booze is muy important."

"You're adorable when sprinkling Spanish into our conversations." Before I can respond, Javi lets my hand go and exits the SUV, coming around to my door. He opens it and leans in, lips a hair's breadth from mine. "It's one of the reasons I adore you. Everything you do to me is precious."

*He's killing me here.* "Thank you."

"That blush is also delicious." His voice is deeper. Husky.

"And about that dinner?" Because the sweet nothings are making it difficult to breathe and the urge to pull him into the back seat is becoming maddening. "Seven okay, or—"

Javier places his keys into my hand and brings the closed fist to his lips, nipping each knuckle. "Take the car and be ready at seven."

"Okay." My expensive schooling has flown out the window.

"Good girl." Another bite before kissing the slight mark. "I'll see you in a few hours."

It's then I notice another black car parked just behind us with dark tints. It's my cousin's car, and before slipping inside the passenger side, Javier looks back at me and winks.

They drive off, and I'm still sitting here contemplating life.

The taillights are out of sight, and I shake my head.

That man was made to disrupt my life.

---

"AFTERNOON," I say, stepping off the elevator and onto a floor below Malcolm's office. There are three people here today, which surprises me, and a network of computers as they run scans for anything we might've missed. *But why three of them?* "Everything okay?"

"Morning, Ms. Asher," the youngest of the trio answers. He's a recent college grad with hacking skills coveted by the government, but he's protected under Malcolm's employ as a security expert. It's keeping them back for the time being in hopes he comes willingly, but there are other plans already in the works for an unfortunate disappearance. Erik takes a sip from his Starbucks cup before turning back to the largest of the eight monitors and hits three keys, the keyboard on his lap almost slipping off but he catches it and then turns to fully face me. He's a punk, a bit of a smartass at times, but dependable and has earned our trust. "Just going over video footage I swiped from the Fredericks laboratory in Utah dating two years back. Mr. Asher approved this."

He seems a bit nervous, and I arch a brow. "You found something?"

"You can say that." Without looking at the screen, he presses a combination of keys and the video changes to a cropped one. The length of time reads just over five minutes with a date stamp of two years ago, and when he hits play, I understand why he's a bit tense.

Lane is walking into the building with his arm around Mildred and my father to his left. They walk past the security guard all smiles, as if this is a normal occurrence, and my blood boils within my veins.

Not for Lane, but because of my father.

Another betrayal. Another example of how little I mean to him.

"Did Malcolm see this?" My voice is hollow. Monotone.

"Getting the disc ready now." Again he presses a few keys, and another short clip begins. The date is after Lane's death and my father is there with Mildred, and it's his arm around her waist, her lips he kisses. *Sick bastard.* At once my stomach churns, bile rising to my throat, but I swallow it back and pretend as if I'm not affected. *Can't show weakness.*

"Burn two copies. I want one."

"Of course, Ms. Asher." The other two don't say a word and shrink back a bit when I turn to walk over to the elevator. It's best I exit now and not after I discover someone else from my side of the family is in on this clusterfuck. "Do I take it upstairs?"

With my hand on the up button, I look back at Erik from over my shoulder. "Please."

"You got it, boss."

"Thank you." The doors close behind me as I slip inside, and I allow a single tear to fall. My father being involved is not a coincidence, and the Fredericks have been doing more than testing at that lab. I bet money on it.

But the question now remains on each key player's purpose?

How many more people are involved?

*Why use me?*

---

My reflection in the mirror later that evening doesn't represent what's going on inside of me. The things that make the most sense hurt after I watched the burned copy Erik made me.

My father's involvement. Mildred's hate toward me.

I'm angry. I feel betrayed. There are more questions than answers now.

And yet, as I watch the girl in the mirror pass the straightener through another stray auburn curl, I don't recognize her. She's here, but not. She's aware, yet a part of her hungers for the one thing that will sever all ties to those who brought her into this world.

Revenge. Blood. Peace.

All these years, I believed my father to be harsh and at times a sexist jerk, but this goes beyond that. He made me a pawn—a movable piece in a game I wasn't aware of playing.

Another pass, and I twist my wrist when reaching the end, giving the bottom of the strand a bit of wave. It swishes into place when I release it, joining the others as the wild girl from this morning that Javier admired is put away and Mariah Asher takes center stage.

This woman looking back at me is everything she's been taught to be, but behind the ire is a shine in her eyes that hasn't been there before. For the first time in a long time, she doesn't feel alone and the small curl to her lips and hint of a blush destroys all notion of the persona she's let herself hide behind for fear of:

Love.

A four-letter word that can destroy even the strongest. That if she embraces, will end *her*.

"It's just dinner with him. Doesn't need to be anything more." A lie. Even to myself I lie, and it's pathetic because a second later when the doorbell rings and I look through the phone app to see who's at my door, my heart races and that tiny smile grows at the sight of him.

I know this is fast.

I know things won't be perfect.

It's a somersault of emotions running rampant through me—a battle between my heart and mind where both agree that no matter the leap, things could end badly and leave me with a broken heart.

However, I trust the man on the other side of the door wearing a bowtie and a smirk more than those of my flesh and blood. Deep down I know—feel it in my bones—that he wouldn't deceive nor put me in danger and right now, that's good enough for me.

With him, it's the opposite. Javier would avenge me even against Malcolm if it ever came to that.

*Give him an honest chance.* Taking in a deep, cleansing breath, I press the green button on the screen and wait for the crackle to talk. "Be right out. Give me five."

"You get three and a half, Muñeca. Not a second more."

# 18

# Javier

S HE LOOKS STUNNING and nothing like the happy girl I
left a few hours ago. Something is off. The softness I've
come to crave as much as I love the snark that rolls off her
tongue with venomous ease—gone.

Mariah's sitting across from me inside of a riverfront restaurant
enjoying a glass of Malbec while we wait for our starters to arrive: a
crab and corn chowder for her, and bacon-wrapped scallops for me.
We've made conversation, admired the interior of the steakhouse, but
still, I sense that she's holding back, and I don't like it.

I don't like the lack of eye contact and how the Chicago river
outside these windows holds her attention. How she looks at me for a
second or two and then turns to find something random to
comment on.

"Those lamps are from...what?" my girl asks with her face
scrunched up in false confusion while pretending I'm the one with
the issue.

"I'm waiting for you to tell me." At my words, she looks away briefly and those rosy pink lips purse. "Talk to me."

"Nothing is—"

"Don't." The low hiss makes her look back, and the expression on her face is contrite. Guilty. "There's nothing I hate more than a liar, Muñeca. Please, just don't."

"Can we talk about it later?"

"No." Reaching across the table, I take her hand and entwine our fingers. "Talk to me. What's eating you up?"

Emotions fly across her face: contentment, anger, hurt, and the last…confusion. "To be honest, I don't know where to start, and I also don't want to ruin our date."

"The only thing that could ruin my night is you walking away, Mariah." And there's the sweetness I've been missing. The way her eyes become soft and her cheeks pull up slightly while those eyes, those beautiful seafoam orbs look at me as if I'm her salvation.

It's humbling. Makes me feel like a king.

"Thank you," she says lowly, the delicate fingers between mine giving a small squeeze. She's looking at them, her smile a bit wistful. "Can we talk after dinner, though? All I need right now is to pretend that everything is okay and that decisions with no turning back don't need to be made."

"Mariah."

Her head pops up, eyes meeting mine. "Yeah?"

"You're not alone, beautiful. Whatever it is, we'll face it together." Suddenly, Mariah stands from her seat and before I can ask what's wrong, she's in my arms sitting astride my lap. We're in a private corner with the perfect outside view, and I feel complete when her arms squeeze me to her. The reaction is the complete opposite of what I know of her thus far, but I welcome it and hold her tighter. Give her the comfort she needs without question. "I got you, sweetheart. Whatever it is."

"Then I say start sharpening your knives because it seems I have enemies."

"Say the word and I'll kill them all. Lay their corpses at your feet."

"I know," she whispers and lays a tiny kiss just below my Adam's apple. "You're so different than what I thought you'd be, and I've never been happier to be wrong." Another kiss and then nip to my chin. "Please don't ever prove me right."

"You have my word." That pleases her, and she hums a cute little sound at the back of her throat before laying the next kiss on my lips. It's small. Nothing inappropriate, although I want nothing more than to devour her. To take until there's nothing left but my imprint on her soul.

"Thank you."

"Never thank me for taking care of what I consider mine." A throat clears and we look up, finding the waiter holding a large tray with our starters and salad. He smiles at us and I pat her thigh to stand, but before she moves to the opposite side, I pull her chair beside mine with my shoe. "That's better."

Mariah sits, but her amusement is clear and I'm thankful the darkness clouding her has receded. It's not gone, but she's getting a reprieve from whatever put her there. "You, Mr. Lucas, are a cheeseball."

I wink, and she giggles a bit. "Take that back, Muñeca."

"Can't, Javi."

"Why not?"

"You asked me to never lie."

And what's worse, my glare doesn't affect her at all. Instead, I'm gifted a cheeky grin full of defiance. "You're a brat."

"Are you complaining?" No. Never. I prefer her happy and at ease; unafraid to call me out and give back just as hard as she receives. My silence is her answer, and she blows me a kiss before grabbing the spoon beside the small bowl now in front of her, dipping it into the creamy soup and bringing some of it to her mouth. The second she closes her lips around the spoon and moans, my pants tighten—cock painfully pressing against the zipper of my slacks. "This is amazing."

I'm thankful for the long linens covering me, and I reach below to adjust myself. "Enjoy, beautiful."

"Want to try?"

"No," I say, and my voice comes out husky, hunger palpable in the one-word response.

"Behave, Javier. We're in public."

"My lack of decorum is your fault. Not mine."

A small snort escapes her then, and I can't hold in my laughter either. "We have issues."

"Normal is boring." Cutting a piece of my scallop, I bring it to my lips and pause. "Now eat, Muñeca."

Her brows furrow then, and I raise a brow in question. "Umm, have you noticed we haven't put our dinner orders in?"

"That's because I called ahead and ordered for the two of us."

"You don't know—"

"Mariah, I am nothing if not prepared." I cut another piece of the scallop and offer it to her which she takes, a low moan escaping at the taste. "I've planned this for a few days, and a little birdy informed me of your likes and dislikes. I also got her blessing."

"Who?" The perplexed expression is adorable.

"Someone with baby pictures of you and a love for gossip."

"You met my aunt?" A delicious blush spreads across her cheeks and lower, causing me to bite back a groan.

"Maybe."

"Whatever she said is a lie."

"Eat, baby girl. You have all the time in the world to prove that you're not a closeted romantic."

---

IT'S ten p.m. by the time we make it back to our building, and she looks exhausted. More than, and I know things are weighing heavy on her mind—the truths being uncovered are cutting deep, but she's not alone and I'll gladly bear the brunt of her pain. Of her madness.

Moreover, when I told her tonight she wasn't alone, I meant it.

The good. The bad. The insanity.

I want it all.

To help her welcome the rage I see simmering beneath the surface and embrace every emotion tearing her apart. Because if she doesn't, it will consume her. Eat her from the inside out, and I'll be fucked before I let that happen.

Moving to this country, I never expected to meet a woman like her. To care as deeply as I do.

But I do. This heartbroken woman I'll put back together owns me.

Our eyes meet once I'm parked. Her gaze is questioning while mine is expectant, needing her to ask. "It's late, Javi."

"It is."

"Then why don't you use one of my parking spaces? The owner could come back and—"

"Hush." Getting out, I come around to her side and pull her out the second the door is open. Then, we're chest to chest and lips hovering; her scent embeds itself into my DNA while those sinful lips match my grin, a tiny coquettish smirk that says everything we don't.

We are crazy.

She's my person.

Insanity feels right.

Mariah leans in closer and pecks my lips once. "Are you going to walk me up or stay?"

Goose bumps arise where my fingers touch her warm skin, rubbing soothing circles on her hip where the dress she wore has a small cutout. "It's getting harder and harder to leave each night."

"Then don't."

"That's a very tempting offer." My fingers tighten on her hip, and she giggles. "A dangerous one."

"I'm not afraid."

"That word shouldn't exist in your vocabulary."

Mariah shrugs, her smile fading a bit. "The world is an ugly place."

"And yet, you're the beauty in mine." At my words, heat rises to her cheeks, and her eyelids flutter closed. "You're making letting you walk a near impossibility."

"Then let me take you home tonight. Let me wake up with you in my arms tomorrow."

"Yes." With the tip of two fingers, she pushes me back and makes the move to slip back into my car, but I press the key fob, locking the door. Her gaze is questioning, but instead of voicing them, she simply places her hand in mine and waits. "Ready when you are."

"Thank you." No further words are exchanged as I pull us inside and head straight toward the elevator. I can feel her stare, wondering why I'm pressing the number two floors down from hers as we ascend, and then more so when it dings a minute later when reaching our destination.

She's compliant, though. Putting things together without any signs of outward rage.

And when I stop at the number that reads 1522 down the hall and to the left of the elevator, the hand not holding mine smacks my arm. "Why doesn't this surprise me."

Not a question, and I don't treat it as such either. Instead, I smile down at her. "Because you believe in fate as much as I do."

Cheeky little criminal arches a brow, lip twitching. "Do I? Or are you just my stalker?"

"Yes, you—" I'm cut off by a phone ringing inside my pocket, and I freeze. No one in this country knows this number, and those who do in Colombia would only use it if something went wrong.

"Javi, are you okay?"

"Take my keys and make yourself comfortable. I need to take this." Whatever she sees in my face has Mariah nodding and letting us in, not mentioning or questioning my sudden change in demeanor. "I'll be right back."

There's a balcony across the living room, and I don't pause my steps until the door is wide open and I'm leaning against the veranda, hitting the redial button. It rings twice and I hear the commotion, the yells in the background of anger and pain.

"Hola? Javier?" I've never heard my cousin sound anything but in control, but right now, he's angry—hurting—and dread fills my bones.

"Alejandro, what's going—"

"Primo, I need you back on a plane tonight. Your mom—"

"What happened?" I hiss through clenched teeth, my grip so tight on the plastic in my hand it groans. "Just spit it out."

"I'm sorry." I can just make out the words my aunt screams, and my world crumbles. Blinding pain overtakes my chest and the phone slips, landing on the floor a second before I feel Mariah wrap her warm arms around me. Holding me as the words I heard set in.

"Talk to me. What's wrong, baby?" Any other day the term of endearment would've made me smile—call out the beauty beside me —but I don't. Can't.

Instead, I repeat the four words that help her understand.

"My mother's been shot."

# Mariah

**H**E'S BEEN GONE seventy-two hours, and I miss him. It's a foreign feeling, this urgency that pushes me out of bed at eight a.m. on a Sunday and toward my closet with only one goal in mind...

*Go to him.*

Javier needs me. I know he does.

I can feel it. This oppressive force sitting atop my chest that demands I comply and follow my heart.

It's been there since yesterday's phone call. His news broke my heart. His sadness nearly bowled me over as the longing to hold him grew with each hurt-filled word out of his mouth.

*"Javi, baby? How are you? How's your—"*

*"She passed early this morning of complications from a blood clot in her lungs." His words are monotone, lifeless, and tears prick at my eyes. I can feel his pain as if it were my own. "She's resting now, Muñeca, and that's all that matters. I'm just sad she never got to meet you and love..." Javier pauses, and I can hear the shud-*

*dering breath escape him, the near desperate sigh he allows to slip through. "I'll call you later. We're heading to the funeral home now and then meeting with—"*

*"Don't worry about me. I'll be here when you're ready."*

*"I miss you, beautiful."*

The second the line disconnected, I was hit with every emotion in the span of seconds. From anger to sadness to despair to giddiness at him missing me, and then loss. Javier's mother is dead, and it tore me in two for different reasons: selfishness and understanding.

Selfishness because I'll never meet the woman that made him who he is today.

Understanding because I've been where he is now with someone I loved deeply.

My grandmother was taken from us out of pure selfishness, a hit gone wrong against Malcolm's dad not knowing that the passenger in the car was old and here for a simple visit.

One bullet and my Mimi was gone, leaving us here to grieve and later demand the blood of every person involved. From the financial institution's owner—a competitor trying to force us to sell—to the hired shooter: they paid with their lives and that piece-of-shit company.

"Alexa, call Malcolm!" I yell out, grabbing items in a rush before stuffing them in my bag. I'm not even sure what's making the cut, but my goal isn't organization here; it's speed.

The first ring barely finishes when an audible click follows. "What time is your flight?" he says in greeting, not sounding surprised in the least. Not upset either.

"Haven't booked it yet." I grab my passport from a small safe I keep in my closet along with two guns and other important papers. "I'm packing now and just heading—"

"The jet will be ready when you are. Do you need a ride?"

My eyes narrow at the speaker. "Why are you being so easy about this?"

"Because he needs you more than I do at the moment, little

cousin." My eyes tear up, but I blink back those tears. Very few people ever see the softer side to this man, but those closest to him have the privilege. Malcolm shows he cares with actions, and this right here is his way of accepting Javier as family.

Not just as an employee. Not just as someone I'm casually dating.

*Are we dating? Is he my boyfriend?* The title doesn't sit right with me. Doesn't describe his place in my life adequately.

"I'll still be available for scheduling and meetings through Skype. Refreshments can be catered and—"

"No."

"What do you mean, *no?*" I pause mid-zip of the carryon luggage, my eyebrows scrunching up in confusion. "You know we can't have a temp in there. People are nosy, and I'd hate to go to jail this close to my birthday for killing a snitch."

"Mom's covering." *Thank you, Jesus!* She held the position before me, helping her husband run Asher Holdings until the day he stepped down. "We've already discussed the upcoming week and moved a few things around." The sound of papers being shuffled comes through the line, followed by the creak of a chair. "So don't worry about anything."

"But when—"

"Not another word about work."

"Thank you," I breathe out, letting the worry about work melt away. If anyone can run that office better than me, it's his mother.

"Just make sure he's okay and knows we're here if needed." With that, he hangs up and I smile. His acceptance of Javier makes me feel at ease—comforted by the knowledge that someone I admire finds him worthy.

———

"WELCOME TO COLOMBIA," a man greets me with an outstretched hand the second I exit the airport. He's smiling, dressed all in black while a younger, female version of him stands against a black F350, studying me closely. No smile. No frown. "How was the flight?"

"Emiliano or Alejandro?" I ask, remembering a photo Javier showed me of his cousins one day while scrolling through his phone. They'd sent it to him and after I accused him of being stuck-up, I was shut down with the snapshot in question. All three were standing side by side with goofy drunk grins, but I was too busy staring at Javi to understand who was whom. He'd been younger in the photograph, but still just as handsome while wearing that grin I hate to love.

"Emiliano, Miss—"

"Mariah. Just Mariah." His grip is firm before dropping my hand and grabbing my bag, motioning with his free hand to get inside. "You want the front or back?" I ask the girl, but she doesn't answer, choosing instead to climb into the second row and buckling up.

I know who she is and why she's upset.

It's hard to lose someone you love—watch them take their final breath—while another close relative moves away without plans for a return. So many changes for a girl still in her teens surrounded by blood and carnage—her life path paved by the choices of others.

She's a victim in this. A survivor of a night that killed one and left the young woman with a scar she'll forever carry.

I see so much of myself in her.

And while my father didn't directly pull triggers or slice throats, he did lead many toward their demise.

Our last name is a blessing and a curse. A weight we carry and a stigma we can never escape.

"The drive is about two hours." Emiliano slips into the driver's seat and presses the keyless start beside the steering wheel. He's not looking at me. Instead, he's frowning at Lourdes through the rearview mirror. "Do you need to stop for anything?"

"No." At my curt response, he looks over with a questioning look, but I shake my head at him. "Does he know I'm here?"

"Are you okay?" *Christ*, men can be dense at times. It's obvious his sister is uncomfortable and doesn't trust me—she doesn't know me—and shouldn't be expected to open her arms easily. Not in our world. "You seem upset, Mariah."

"Please answer the question, Emiliano."

"Can you answer mine?" His expression is one of a lost puppy, but before I can respond, Lourdes takes her seatbelt off and leans forward.

"Oh, dear God!" she grits out, her head is closer to mine than his, and I see the moment her glare turns to tears. "She's just saying lay off with the reprimanding looks my way. I'm not talking because I dislike her, but because I don't have the energy. It's all too much..." Her hiccuping pause is filled with pain and before the first tear falls, I'm jumping from the front to the back and hugging her tight. *Thank God I'm small and flexible.* A shuddering breath escapes her, and the small hands clenched at my sides open and grip; she's holding on to me while letting go of what's eating her inside.

"Lourdes, please. Not now, sis." Emiliano pulls out from the curb, his voice tense as are his shoulders. "Just keep it together until—"

"Just drive. I'll handle her." If he's inclined to argue, I don't know. He simply zips his lips and nods. However, a few minutes later I catch the thankful expression at a red light when he turns to look at us.

His eyes soften when he sees his little sister's tears and the way my arms embrace her. *Thank you,* he mouths, and I know at that moment I've made a friend in him.

After a while, when the sobs turn into sniffles, Lourdes tries to move back. Her face is blotchy, expression embarrassed. "My apologies. I don't know what—"

"Stop." Gently, I wipe my fingers under her eyes. "You have every right to be upset. Javi told me what happened, and I'm so sorry for what you've gone through." At the mention of his name, another round of tears fall. Her chest heaves and her tiny frame trembles, and it breaks my heart. "Breathe, Lourdes. No one is upset with you."

"I should've done more to save Mama Ida." It's low, a whisper full of recrimination and pain that leaves her exposed. Lourdes blames herself because she's here and my Javi's mother isn't.

"How?" Tipping her face up to meet my eyes, I raise a brow. "Sweetie, they sent men there with high-round capacity weapons and one goal. There was nothing you could've done, and it's a blessing you weren't harmed."

"But Javi won't even look at me!"

"Because he feels guilty for not being here." That makes her pause. Her watery eyes are stunned and mouth open, as if to speak. She doesn't, though. For the next few minutes, nothing comes out except the occasional sniffle and I leave her alone to dissect my words.

In all her guilt, Lourdes never paused to analyze what others might think, and she just accepted the worst. Especially about her cousin. A cousin, who in my understanding, is sometimes closer to her than her brothers.

"Does he really?" she asks after a while, leaning into me, and I wrap my arm around her shoulders, hugging her tight. My response is a sad smile, and her brows scrunch up. "But that makes no sense. How can he protect us when we were ambushed and—"

"Apply that same explanation to your situation, kiddo. You did nothing wrong." Lourdes gives me a minute nod. "Good. Now rest up until we get there. Javi needs us to be strong and give him space when needed."

"You're good for him."

"I hope I'll be."

"You will." Her conviction warms my heart, and the sucker gives a harsh thump in agreement. This—us—is crazy and unpredictable and dangerous, but I wouldn't change a single thing about it. In not making sense, we fit. In not being afraid to be who we are, we become stronger.

That man has become my person.

Mine.

"Thank you," I say, and we both close our eyes after. She's lost within her thoughts, and I vow to let him know how I feel soon.

Because I love him. Completely and unequivocally, I'm head over heels for that murderous sweetheart.

---

I'M shaken awake by a hand on my arm. The movement jostles me, pulling me from the nap the car's movements lulled me into and my eyes snap open.

"Morning, sleepyhead," Lourdes smiles, and it's genuine and she looks sweet. Nothing like the hurt girl from a little while ago. "Are you ready to see him, or want to freshen up first?"

"What has you in a sudden good mood?" I ask, stretching a bit before stepping out in front of a beautiful two-story home where armed guards stand at every corner with rifles strapped across their chests. "It's a good look on you."

"He's going to flip when he sees you."

"And that makes you happy?"

"I know he misses you." She flicks her eyes behind us before leaning over conspiratorially. "Javier's mentioned you at least fifty times a day since arriving and looks at his phone twice as much. You're the half of his soul keeping him together."

# 20

# Javier

MY MIND IS a dangerous place to be, and losing myself within is taking its toll. I'm angry and hurting and still not able to fully process that the woman who brought me into this world is now gone.

That I wasn't here to protect her as a good son should.

That Ida Lucas was taken from us by a selfish son of a bitch wanting revenge over the death of a thieving asshole I killed a few months back. The same thieving asshole that left her in a wheelchair.

Two brothers. Each stole from her things that could never be replaced:

Her ability to walk. Her life.

"We'll find him, Javi," Alejandro vows, the hand on my shoulder squeezing tight. "I swear on my life that we'll find him."

"Rats never stay hidden for long." He nods and I pick up my glass, throwing back the last of the Aguardiente before standing. "Call Tito and up the reward through the surrounding barrios. I want his head on a spike within twenty-four hours."

"Listo."

"I'll be in my room. Let me know if..." *Fuck*, my heart thumps and palms sweat at the sight of her. My beautiful little criminal with a coquettish smile and warm eyes is standing just inside the doorway to the study watching me. *How did she get here? How did she know I needed her?*

Mariah's looking a bit nervous, a little rumpled from what I guess is traveling, but here. She's here, and it hits me then just how much I've been yearning for.

Her. Just her.

"Hi." Mariah's voice is soft, and I let it surround me. Soothe me. "Miss me?"

"Come here." My voice is rough with the sudden emotions rushing through me. I'm holding a hand out for her and every finger shakes, arm muscles twitching until her dainty hand wraps around my rough one.

Then it's calm, and I breathe.

No words are exchanged as I lose myself in her seafoam eyes, letting her presence give me the one thing I've been missing since Alejandro's call: peace. A small semblance of what I've had with her these last few weeks, and right now, I feel blessed to have her standing in front of me.

"You never answered my question, Javi." There's a playful tsk that comes from the back of her throat, a mock glare, but it's the twitch of her glossy lips that pulls a chuckle from me. "Making me wait is unacceptable."

"It is." I lift her hand and kiss each knuckle. "I've more than missed you, sweetheart. I've been a little lost without you."

It's the truth, and I'm not ashamed to admit it.

There are times in our lives where showing weakness is a strength, and being honest with the woman that's come to own my soul is one of them. So I let her see me. See the pain that's settled into my heart and I can't deal with alone.

"That's because we don't work well without the other." Rising to the tips of her toes, Mariah kisses my chin and then pulls back, releasing my hand. "It's why I'm here, Javi. I'm here for you...whatever you need."

Without waiting for my reply, she looks over at a silent Alejandro and walks over, giving the usually serious man a quick hug. She says something to him—it's too low for me to hear, but he smiles and walks toward the room's entrance with a knowing expression on his face.

And when he's right beside me, my cousin pauses his steps. "She's one of the good ones, Javier. Treat her right."

"I know."

"Good."

Then it's just the two of us, and the tension rises for a completely different reason. My missing her goes deeper than just the physical. It goes past carnal hunger or the way we challenge each other.

"Show me your room." Hips sway toward me and I follow the movement, admiring how beautiful she is in a simple pair of jeans and an old Spice Girl's shirt. "You look like you need some rest."

"Let me show you around first. You have to be starving—" Her finger over my lips shuts me up, and I raise a brow.

"Room. Now." Then the naughty little thing mimics my stance, brow, and all. This makes me want to bite her. "Comprende?"

"You're lucky I like you."

"And you're just lucky I'm a saint."

"Saint, my ass." With that, I toss her over my shoulder and walk out of the room with her whisper-cursing me all the way to the master bedroom at the top of the stairs with the large double doors. No one stops me or asks who she is, but I catch the smile on Lourdes's face and Emiliano smirking. Even their mother looks amused during a time when sadness is all we've felt.

"I'm going to whoop you, Javi. Put me down."

"No." I kick the door closed with my foot and march over to the bed.

"Javier Lucas, I swear to all that...shit!"

I'm looking down on her breathless form now atop my bed, her eyes bright. "You were saying, Muñeca?"

Tiny fingers wave. "Hi."

"Hi." Lowering my body to hers, I nuzzle my nose to hers and peck those sweet lips. "I'm happy you're here."

"There's nowhere else I'd rather be." Voice low and breathy, Mariah slips her arms around my neck and tugs on the hair at my nape. "I've missed you."

"Missed you too." I skim my lips across hers, slowly, softly, while taking her upper lip between my own. A soft bite. A little lick. Mariah releases a tiny whimper then, exhaling against my mouth, and deepens the kiss.

She's hungry. As desperate as I am, she pulls back a few seconds later and rests her forehead against mine. The soft look on her face makes my chest feel tight, and my heart beats wildly for her.

"I'm so sorry I didn't come sooner, Javi." Seafoam eyes turn watery, and I shake my head. Her tears are something I can't handle at the moment and she sees that, fighting back her own emotions for me. I know how she feels without her uttering a single word. Can read her even when she hides behind a persona that's cold and distant when Mariah is anything but.

"You're here now, and that's all that matters to me. To my family."

A different kind of need settles in the room then and I let her wrap those small, yet strong arms around me and pull me close. There are no more words. No need to express.

For the first time since coming back to my country, I let myself sink into the bed and gratefully take comfort in my Muñeca. And as her fingers run through my hair, tugging a bit near the ends, I rest.

Fall asleep in her arms with her heart beating beneath my ear. *I love you.*

THE NEXT TIME my eyes open, the room is dark and yet, I know it's early. There's a rooster somewhere on the property greeting the sun while annoying everyone here. There's a heaviness that settles in my chest knowing what the following hours will bring, but a soft sigh to my left calms me.

Soothes and comforts my soul.

Motherfuck, she's beautiful. Mariah's asleep while wearing an old soccer shirt from my teenage days she pilfered from one of my drawers with a bedsheet carelessly strewn across the back of her thighs. *It seems I hogged the comforter.* There's also the matter of a leg bent at the knee and an arm wrestling the pillow beneath her head in a serious choke-hold from my viewpoint, and I've never been more jealous of a sack of cotton in my life.

I want my chest to be where she rests her head. I want to be who she seeks for comfort.

*I love you.* Three little words that slam back to the forefront of my mind as her arrival replays in my mind:

Seeing her standing at the entrance to my study here.

The feel of her lithe body against my harsher planes.

Hearing those words just before falling asleep, the way she lulled me with gentle touches and the soft scent of her favorite lotion.

*My beautiful little Muñeca.* "I love you, too."

A soft knock on the door pulls my attention toward the bedroom door. "Javi?" Lourdes calls, her voice low. "You up?"

Mariah stirs on the bed, her eyebrows scrunching up, but they relax when I lean over and kiss her forehead. "Go back to sleep, sweetheart. There are still a few hours before we leave." She doesn't answer; instead, she snuggles deeper into the covers I place over her.

"If you're sleeping, cough, primo." Lourdes taps her fingernails on the door. "One cough and I'll——" The door opens before she finishes, and I chuckle at the small squeak she emits. "That's rude!"

"Hush, kid. Let's not wake her up yet." Closing the door softly, I walk past her and down the stairs, heading straight for the kitchen. My little cousin follows silently, heading straight for the fridge to pull out the creamer and milk before turning to grab our mugs. We've done this a time or a hundred, and I'm surprised she didn't seek me out before today. Her feelings of guilt are written all over her face and actions—she's haunted by memories that break my heart. "Now or after?"

"After. I'm still trying to gather my thoughts."

"Okay." Alejandro is a true coffee snob, and every family member has a setup that rivals the most expensive coffee houses around the world. The blends are rich while mine is a darker roast than what the others prefer, but I'll need the caffeine today more than other days. "Are you drinking from mine?"

"Not if I want to live." Lourdes snorts, reaching inside a small drawer next to the Keurig my mother wanted and that I bought last Christmas. She pulls out a pod of the mild stuff and preps her cup while I make mine, meeting at the coffee island a few minutes later where she pours the cream into mine and I cut us a slice of pound cake to dip.

Taking a sip from my coffee, I wait for her to start, but she doesn't. Instead, she fidgets and looks past me to the clock on the microwave. "Talk to me, Lourdes."

A heavy sigh escapes her, but her sad eyes meet mine. Tears gathered at the corners. "I'm so sorry, Javi. So sorry for not protecting, Mamita Ida." My mouth opens to refute her, to explain it's not her fault, but Lourdes shakes her head while holding a hand up. This is what she needs. To get this off her chest. "Rationally, I know I'm not at fault, but the fact I'm here and she's not isn't easy to swallow. She saved me that night. She pushed me down and fought with me to stay hidden at all costs and I...I should've done more. Dragged her out of the house if it came to that." Tears fall freely from her face and her lips tremble, but I let her get it all out. Lourdes needs this. "I failed you, Javi. Please don't hate me."

"No, you didn't."

"Yes, I—" Before the stubborn girl can finish her idiotic thought, I pull her into a hug and let her sob it out. Her body shakes and cries fill the room, and when Alejandro walks in to see what's going on, I shake my head and he leaves. This has been bottling up inside her, and I feel like utter shit because thoughts like these should never have crossed her mind.

A teenager doesn't stand a chance against high-caliber weapons and a group of men sent to kill. If anything, the men working security that night—two out of the three—who decided to head out for food instead of standing watch, are responsible. As accountable as the man who gave the order to kill an innocent woman.

Once her bawling turns to low sniffles, I pull back and take a seat. Lourdes does the same after I move her stool with my foot, and then she looks at me. "I could never hate you, bug. Never."

"I'm so sorry."

"Stop apologizing for something you had no control over. You didn't pull the trigger."

"I should have—"

"You did what my mother told you to do, and I'm thankful you listened." Picking up my mug, I take a sip of coffee and grimace. She put way too much sugar in this, but I swallow with a small smile. The last thing I want is to hurt her feelings. "What happened is horrible and God knows I'd give my life to have been able to save hers, but I was elsewhere and that's my burden to carry. I should've been here for you both and—"

"Don't you dare apologize!" Lourdes hisses, face hard, and I'm surprised by this sudden flip in her mood. "Mariah told me you'd feel guilty, that you were probably holding stuff in for my benefit, but dammit, this isn't on you. My brothers didn't know. Our security messed up. It's just one giant mess, and that woman upstairs is amazing."

Teenage girls are hard to follow. We went from crying to angry to now a small giggle.

*Lord, please don't repay my sins with daughters.*

"What did my Muñeca say?" This for some reason fills me with guilt. This beautiful, selfless, and utterly perfect-for-me-woman flew here to be my support, and I fell asleep on her. *When did they talk? What happened while I was knocked out?*

"The same thing you just did, but in a more eloquent way." Lourdes takes a sip from her mug and immediately adds more sugar. A lot more sugar. "She's smart and so sweet, Javi. Don't mess it up."

"I won't."

"He won't," we answer in unison, and my body turns in her direction. Mariah's sleep-rumpled and still wearing my shirt, just with a pair of tights beneath. "Got any more coffee? I woke up with a minor headache."

"Let me find you something for that. Be right back." Lourdes gets up and turns to rush out but stops and hugs me instead. It's a quick one, but I feel her relief and I kiss her forehead before nudging her toward the door.

"Mom's bathroom should have something for that."

"Okay." She brushes by Mariah and surprises us both by giving her a quick kiss on the cheek. "Thank you, new cousin."

My girl's shocked, but I'm not. She's too lovable for her own good.

I've been powerless against her after her threat to shoot me the day we met.

"Hi."

"Morning, linda." A hint of a blush crosses her cheeks, and she shuffles closer when I crook a finger, pulling her between my parted legs at the counter. Her warmth seeps into my skin. Her touch sets my heart ablaze. "How bad is it?"

"Mild. Don't worry." Her hands cup my face, thumbs sweeping beneath my eyes. "You sleep okay?"

"Like the dead."

"You snored like it, too." A sweet little snort escapes her, and I grip her hips, digging my fingers in when it turns into giggles. "Stop it."

"Take that back."

"Never."

"Then I'll never stop."

"Is this your way of saying you want to keep me?"

Letting go of her side, I bring my right hand to the back of her neck and hold her to me. Lips against lips. Breathing each other in. "I plan to do more than keep you, Mariah. I'm going to love you until the day I die, and even death won't stop or diminish what I feel for you."

"Good." She nibbles my bottom lip and then pulls back. "Because we will be revisiting these words in a few days."

"They won't change."

"And I won't leave your side."

# 29

# Mariah

H E'S BEEN HOLED up in his study for the last twenty-four hours.

Alone and hurting. Needing space after lowering his mother to the ground, while the rest of the house—his family—entertains me. They don't need to, but they do, and I stifle a laugh when his aunt Sara brings out another photo album dedicated to the Lucas men in their baby years.

"And here's Javier running from Ida after he decided to redecorate their living room at the time with finger paints." The little boy in the picture couldn't be older than six and had a shitty grin on his face as his mother ran behind him with a flip-flop in her hand. "Can you believe he paused for ten seconds, hand on his hip, while I took the picture and his mom closed in? Ida wanted to kill him, while I laughed my butt off." She pauses for a moment, an innocent expression on her face when Alejandro sits across from us on the lanai. "Everything all right, mijo?"

"How many has she subjected you to, Mariah?" I hold up three fingers in response and she smacks my shoulder, a mock-outraged gasp coming from her place beside me. Chulo's on the floor beside my feet and looks up then, his eyes connecting with mine as if to say *they are all crazy*, then plops down. He's been by my side since we met the night I arrived.

Sweetest good boy you'll ever meet.

*"And he's the rascal of the family, Chulo." Lourdes stops in front of a large dog bed that looks like a sofa and is fit for royalty. It's huge and looks soft, and I'm almost jealous of how comfortable the large Doberman seems to be. After Javi went to sleep and my confession, the small slip of the tongue right after his eyes closed, I became restless. Hungry. And the knock at the door from Lourdes saved me from waking the lightly snoring man. "He's a sweetheart, but be careful until he gets to know you. He's protective of the family and was hurt trying to protect Mamita Ida."*

*Not listening to her, I kneel in front of the sweet boy and hold my hand out. Chulo looks at it, his teeth showing for a few seconds before there's a soft lick, and then another. His tail wags the more he's allowed to greet me—make a new friend—before nudging my hand to give him a good old-fashioned head scratch.*

*"Aren't you the cutest thing, Chulo? Such a good boy." The dog gives me the sweetest look and I melt, as completely owned by the dog as I am the owner. And because I can't help myself, I bend over and kiss the top of his head. "I'm so going to want to take you home with me."*

*"You truly are one of us."*

*At this I look up, head tilted to the side. "What do you mean?"*

*"We aren't the easiest bunch."*

*"My family will give yours a run for its money." Chulo crawls closer, setting his head atop my lap for more scratches. "But then again, crazy embraces lunacy without question."*

*"Don't I know it." Leaning down, she runs her fingers through Chulo's back. "It's why I think you two were meant to be. You understand him, and he gets you."*

"Shame on you, Madre. Just, shame." Alejandro's voice pulls me away from the memory, and I look between the mother and son duo. He's serious, while she's outspoken and sweet.

"Zip it, Alejandro." Sara nudges my shoulder after turning the page, a younger version of the man across from us in black and white. He's dressed like a cowboy, boots and all while cheesing it at the camera beside Emiliano. The older brother's wearing a horse costume, the head in his hand, and it's large and goofy. "How cute were they? My boys—"

"Are going to dig up the old family albums my mother kept hidden in her closet." Everyone turns to look at Javier at the entrance to the back terrace. He's smiling a bit but looks exhausted and as if he's had more than a drink or two, and yet, his eyes are sharp when they settle on me and his dog's proximity. "You ready for that kind of smoke, Aunt Sara?"

"You wouldn't dare!"

"Try me." I'm amused by their banter, and my shoulders shake when she slams the book shut and hides it behind her. "That's better. Don't embarrass me in front of my Muñeca."

"I thought it was adorable," I say, and all eyes turn my way. The men have their eyes narrowed while Sara's glisten with tears. "The Lucas men as kids were total badasses."

"Is she mocking us, primo?" Alejandro asks, sitting forward with an evil smirk on his face.

"I think she is." Javi walks closer, stopping a few feet from me and his dog quickly takes a stance in front of me. "And look at this; she's stolen my best friend too."

"Total disrespect." Alejandro tsks while his mom shakes her head, a few tears falling, and my heart clenches because I know this is hard. It was her sister we put to rest yesterday and her daughter that could've been killed, and yet, she's here and entertaining me as if I'm the most important person here. *She's doing what Ida would've done had I been blessed with meeting her.*

"We should teach her a lesson." Javi comes a little closer and my eyes narrow, lip curls into a mock-sneer. "Lucas men are to be respected at all times."

"Really?" Taking her hand in mine, I squeeze it while Sara rolls her eyes. She wipes away the fallen tears discreetly while Javi focuses on his pet, silently commanding Chulo to pick his side. *God bless the women of this family with endless patience.* "My threat from the first day still stands, Javier, and I'll extend it if I must."

"What threat?" Lourdes walks out holding a tray with coffee and my newest addiction: pan de Bono. It's always to be eaten a few minutes out of the oven and is soft, the bread and cheese combination melting in your mouth, and I can't get enough of these. Placing the tray on the coffee table between the seats, she hands me my cup first and then Javier's, her mother and brother grabbing their own. "I feel like this is a story that needs to be told."

"Quit being nosy, kid."

"Don't ruin our fun, nephew," Sara says, but her attention is on me. "What threat are you talking about, Mariah?"

"You want to do the honors?" I ask and he shakes his head, smiling at me in that boyish way that makes my heart flutter. However, it's his eyes that captivate me. There's sadness in them, a pain he can't escape, but a sliver of love remains and it's directed at me. As if I'm what's holding him together and it's a heady feeling, to know that my being here gives him a semblance of peace—comfort. "Are you sure? I'm giving you a chance to look good here."

"Go on." He waves a hand around us. "Tell them how horrible you've been to me."

My glare makes his family grin. "Threatening to shoot you isn't the worst thing I could've done."

"You did what?" Lourdes screams, laughing at the annoyed look on her cousin's face. "That's priceless."

"I need all the details." That came from Sara.

"You've gone soft, primo." Alejandro had to add his two cents in.

I shrug, taking a sip from my cup. "Not the first or last time, either. It's almost a daily occurrence and a bit of foreplay for him," I mumble the last part under my breath, but they heard and coupled with my slight embarrassment at the slip, they all crack up. And it's worth it because for that brief moment they're not thinking of death and violence or retribution.

Moreover, I'd gladly become a comedian to watch him let go even if it's just for a moment.

---

"Good morning, Muñeca," he whispers from behind me, his arm and leg thrown over my body. I'm almost pinned in place by Javier —the little spoon to his giant one—and the vibrations from his chest when he speaks cause goose bumps to rise across my flesh. "You ready to start the day?"

"No." I'm being honest. Being here has been amazing the last week, but I am exhausted and in need of more than the seven hours of sleep I got last night. Javier's home where we are all staying is grand and beautiful, sitting on almost thirty acres of farmland that needs tending to.

He has horses and pigs and chickens—crops of marijuana that he and Alejandro cultivate and then test the strains before any sales occur.

Then, there is his mother's house near the large stream that runs along the back end of the property. Where she was killed, and Lourdes terrorized. He's had it demolished in the last few days after a day spent taking out what he wanted to keep, and what his aunt wanted as mementos.

It was a grueling day. The women cried and the men comforted, but it was in my arms that night that Javier truly let go.

He allowed himself the few tears that fell before rage took root instead. And I embraced it; his anger and need for revenge.

*"What are you thinking, Javi?" I cup his face, needing to keep his troubled eyes on mine. "Quit worrying about anything but what you need. Tell me, and we'll find a way."*

*"Let it go. I'm fine."*

*"Bullshit." I'm pushing him. Have been doing it since he came out of isolation, and after the emotional days he's had, Javier will snap if he doesn't accept—confront his emotions. "And we're not leaving this room until you're honest with me. Nothing you say will make me see you differently or leave; I'm here for the long haul."*

*"I'm hanging by a thread, sweet girl, and don't want you to—"*

*"I accept all of you."*

*"Thank you." His eyes soften, the slightly, red-rimmed edges crinkling when he smiles. A genuine one, and not the fake/forced one he puts on for the women of this family. Not because they need to be coddled, but because he cares and wants to shoulder their pain.*

*"Let me help and then thank me."*

*"Help with what?"*

*"I want the bloodied bodies of those responsible at your feet."*

His laughter shakes us both while fingers explore across my chest and down, not stopping until removing his leg and slipping a finger beneath the edge of my panties. "You can always sleep for a bit in the car. We have about a three-hour car ride from here to my surprise."

"A surprise?" I whimper out when he slides down to just above my clit, tapping the sensitive area to the beat of a song only he knows the notes to. "Where are we—"

"No questions." This time he slaps my flesh with three fingers, his hand stretching the delicate lace. "I want you to nod and give me a kiss before getting ready with the clothes I left out for you yesterday." Lips just below my ear, he nips the skin there and then soothes the sting with a flick of his tongue. "Can you do that for me, Ms. Asher?"

"Yes." I'm rewarded with tight circles on my clit. They range from soft to rough—a vicious cycle that brings me to the edge sooner than I thought possible. Just the tip of two fingers are touching me, circling the throbbing bundle of nerves while his mouth attacks my neck with bites and licks.

I'm moaning for him. Fighting to turn around and kiss him—touch him—but his hold on me doesn't allow anything but *his* control. One of his hands is on my hip while the other strums my clit, I'm powerless, unable to do more than cry out in pleasure each time he brings me to the edge.

"You're perfect for me, Mariah," he groans against my neck, his breathing harsh and cock hard against my backside. "Mine."

"Javi," I mewl on a breathless whisper, clinging to his forearm as the first wave of bliss knocks into me. For a second or two, I can't breathe and cling to him, undulating as he wrings every last drop of pleasure and then when there's nothing left, Javi dips below and pumps his fingers inside me twice.

They're glistening when he brings them to his lips, inhaling deep before sucking each until no trace of my wetness is left. "Fuck, baby girl. So sweet." My core clenches and he grips my chin with the same fingers, turning my face toward his. I smell myself on his lips and fingers. I can feel a small trail of wetness on my ass just above where the head of his cock flexes. "I'm going to enjoy you today, Mariah. All of you, before you leave tomorrow."

"Please." It's all I can manage past the sudden dryness of my mouth, the heat of my skin.

"Good girl." Another clench and he smiles as if he knows my body is crying out for him. To feel him buried deep. "Now, go get dressed for me, and no panties. I want access to your body all day."

# 22

# Javier

"W E'RE HERE, MARIAH," I say, softly stroking her cheek while the beautiful girl beside me stirs, arching her back while beginning to stretch. My eyes roam down her body, admiring her every curve and dip displayed in the simple cotton dress I've put her in.

It's soft against her skin; a light pink number with small pearl buttons down the middle of her chest flares a bit at her hips and ends just above her mid-thighs. And she wears the simplicity so well.

The two stiff points adorned by the nipple shield—I can make out the jeweled circular ring around each tip and my mouth waters. I also can't stop myself and lower my hand from her face, brushing my knuckles down the right and then left breast, smiling when she sighs and those seafoam eyes open.

She's looking at me with hunger. Mirroring my need.

"Where are we?" Her voice is husky, tinged with the last dregs of sleep. Warm eyes look around and her head tilts, wondering why we're out in the middle of nowhere with a large waterfall behind us that crests over a large lake. There's also a modest home, not lacking in luxury but the size is meant for intimacy and not hosting people.

It's a place I come when needing to regroup. To calm the raging ire that at times consumes me, but today, I'm here to share it with her. To show her more of who I am.

"This place belongs to me."

"Really?" Her question isn't because she doubts the money I have, but more of why the seclusion. "Are you here to kill me and dump the body?" Mariah lets out a cute giggle, the movement causing her breasts to jiggle and my knuckles to press a little harder over each tip.

Her laugh turns into a moan; the sound sends a shiver down my spine. Makes my cock throb.

"I'm here to eat you, Muñeca."

"Should I be afraid?"

"For my sanity? Absolutely." With a single sharp slap over her right tit, I cup her face and bring her closer, almost touching my lips before I stand, and just like I knew she would, Mariah follows. I'm barely touching her, but she's following my body further away from the car, walking closer and closer to the water's edge.

A mist greets our legs and I pause, groaning when her body doesn't stop. Instead, my beauty presses the length of her short frame against my harsher planes and then rises onto the tips of her toes, lips right where they belong.

On mine. Touching. Licking the seam when I don't part them for her.

"Kiss me."

"No." Fire flashes in her orbs, the challenge I've needed making itself present. And I push. Yank the proverbial chain of her pleasure with my denial. "We're here to have lunch and nothing more."

Frustrations sparks. Confusion.

But today is about her. What I know she needs.

Mariah is so used to having control that losing the tight leash around her neck—stepping out of the mold she's been forced into by other's careless mistakes—scares her. But she craves it. Silently, she wants to let go and not worry about the consequences, nor the opinion of others about who she should be.

I'm going to gift her what she's freely given me by just being here when I needed her the most. My Muñeca isn't meant to be controlled but cherished. She's meant to fly.

And I'm going to unleash and welcome the craziness with open arms because I am her home. Her peace. Her love.

"You're serious?" Confusion mars her features for a second—she doesn't understand my putting on the brakes, but I'm doing it for her. Apart from enjoying the day just the two of us, I want her to relax and enjoy herself. To yearn for and enjoy my touch as the hours pass. "But aren't you the one that asked for easy access?"

"I did."

"Then why—"

"Because I enjoy having free access to that lightly tanned flesh and the wetness that coats your inner thighs." Mariah inhales sharply, chest heaving. "Because when I touch you, I'm not going to ask for permission or deal with obstacles delaying the inevitable."

"And what's that?"

Lowering my face down to Mariah, I bypass her pouting lips and kiss the shell of her ear. "My cock buried deep inside that tight little cunt while your screams of pleasure disturb the peace of every beast that roams this jungle. I'm going to take you, baby. Fuck you. But first, I'll prove that you're my queen first and whore after."

Then, I walk away. Give her a moment to collect her thoughts and calm the shivers.

----

MARIAH ENTERS the house an hour later, and she's calm. A little too calm.

I smile when her small body sits beside me on the couch, relaxing into my side while slipping beneath my arm. Hugging herself to my bare chest. She's collected, and her body isn't showing outward signs of arousal, but fuck, I can smell it. This sweet little whisper of *her* that infiltrates my senses as if she's touched what's mine—

Bringing her delicate hand to my lips, I leave open-mouthed kisses over each tip and catch the hint of her taste. *Bad girl.* "Are you hungry, Mariah?"

"A little." Voice low and a bit meek, she looks up at me from beneath long lashes with a wisp of contriteness in her expression. *You know I know.* "Is there anything you'd like me to make?"

"No need." And because I can, I wrap my lips around her middle and pointer fingers, sucking once and pull back. Mariah's orbs become heavy-lidded and body rigid, and then her nipples poke through again. *Christ, they're perfect.* "I'm here to cater to you, sweetheart."

"I don't mind, though. We can cook together and—"

"You've done enough." My girl's smart enough to not argue—deny— her theft and then nods. "Why don't you rest for a bit."

"Can I take a shower or a bath?"

"No."

"Why?"

"Are you uncomfortable?" At my question, she squirms a bit and I smirk. "You touched yourself and will now sit there in your wetness and wait. No complaining. No begging."

"I can always take a dip in the lake." Not a threat, but a statement. Pushing to see if I snap and give her the one thing she needs. Craves.

Me. My touch. My cock.

"Go ahead. See what happens if you do."

No response. No pushing me away.

Instead, Mariah purses her lips and tries to relax back into my arms. She can't, though.

My denial makes her wet. More than the pathetic orgasm she might've had a few minutes prior.

"I didn't come," she says this low, so low I almost missed it, but I can't deny the fire that rushes through my veins at her confession. "Just couldn't finish."

"Why?"

"Because I need you." On her next intake of breath, Mariah finds herself on her back, looking up at me with wide excited eyes. "Hi," she says and it's breathless, her chest expanding, and every inhale rubs the two pointy tips on her chest against mine. For me to feel the metal surrounding each nipple.

"You love to tease and push, baby girl." I'm throbbing, my cock pressed tightly against her mound. "I hope you're prepared to deal with the consequences of this disrespect."

"Please." One word, and the last thread of patience left in me snaps. "Take what is yours."

Closing my eyes, I nod and breathe in deep.

I had plans for us. I wanted to cook and spoil and make love to her slowly.

"I'm going to ask for your forgiveness now." My voice is rough and my body shakes, but I keep my eyes soft when I look down at her. She's everything to me, and I need her to understand this—know that no one comes before her. "Because once I'm inside of you, there will be nothing in this world that can pull me away."

"Javi, I trust you. I—"

"I love you more than my own life, Mariah."

A warm hand cups my jaw, and she pulls me down to her, my lips just touching hers. "I love you, too. In an almost obsessive crazy way and without control. All I want is you. All I think about is you."

"Motherfuck." It's a rough exhale. A harsh shiver that runs from the top of my head and settles on my swelling cock. I'm throbbing— pulsing within the warmth of my girl's parted thighs.

She makes me lose touch with reality.

With the regime I've followed since the day I made my first kill.

I'm hers to do with as she pleases, and when she kisses me again, I give in. Lose myself in her touch and scent, in the way her plump lips feel against my own. *Jesus*, she's sweet and soft and explores my mouth with a keening mewl—almost begging for more of me. My touch. My cock.

"I'm going to spend the rest of my life spoiling you, beautiful. I'll live for you." Her hips undulate at that, and the thin fabric of her dress slips over her hips, exposing her cunt to the cool air. She hisses and I pull my lips from hers, looking down to the soft pink flesh. "So fucking pretty."

"Please."

"What do you need?" I'm rewarded with another horny little sound, but right now I need more. "Use your words."

"Kiss me. Touch me."

"Like this." With the tip of two fingers, I part her labia at the same time I retake her lips. I swallow her moans. Taste her need. She's wet and pliant, her noises filling the room with a symphony that I wish to spend the rest of my life listening to. "Or like this?"

"All of it as long as it's with you."

"Til death do us part." I slip a finger inside and pump it a few times. Then add another. Mariah's tight, walls clenching, and I smile against her mouth, deepening the kiss—her tongue battles mine for dominance, but gives in when I bite her lips.

We're a brutal explosion of lust and hunger, this raw, uncontrollable yearning that I call home. She's my reason and purpose.

"Javi," she moans, a reverent sound when I nip her chin and down the path to her neck. Her skin flushes under my ministration, her nipples hard, and I bite one while slipping from her small hole. Wetness coats my fingers and I rub her clit with the pad of my middle finger. "More."

Tight circles. Pressing down hard.

"Take your tits out," I hiss out, giving each tip a lick over the cotton and pull back. Shaky hands do as I say and undo the top three buttons slowly, teasing me, but I'm past the point of patience.

I smack her clit, and she opens the next two a little faster. *This won't do.*

Grabbing the bit of undone fabric in my hands, I rip it down the middle.

Buttons scatter. A gasp escapes her.

The look in her eyes is intoxicating, and I take a moment to look at her just like this:

She's on her back and looking up at me with hooded eyes, tits on display and her pussy lips wet with desire. This woman is my heaven. My weakness. Mine.

"You're so fucking beautiful, Muñeca."

"And you're perfect for me," she whimpers, spreading her thighs wider on my couch. "I love you."

"I love you, too." Kneeling between her parted thighs, I place a finger at her mouth and dip it between wet lips. Her breath is warm and her tongue soft. Her throat bobs and I trace a path down to the center of her chest before cupping a tit, my fingernail flicking the metal adorning the pebbled tip, and then the other before taking it between my lips, my tongue lapping at the sensitive flesh.

"More." One of her hands embeds itself into my hair and tugs me closer, holding me against her breast. And I suck harder, flipping between the two tips until her free hand slips between us and pulls at the drawstring of my shorts, pushing the waistband low enough that the engorged head slips out. "No foreplay. I want you just like this."

I can feel her heat. If I snap my hips, I'd be buried deep.

Mariah traces the head while her thighs try to push the basketball shorts lower. They don't move much, but just enough to rub the first few inches over her clit before I bite down on the flesh between her breasts.

She screams and I pull back, admiring the perfect indentation of my teeth.

I want her body littered with these. With my mark.

My cock throbs, and I look down in time to catch the sight of a little pre-come falling onto her skin. *So fucking beautiful.*

"I'll love you slowly later." I take my hands from her body long enough to remove my shorts and then toss them aside somewhere, could care less where they land. Her dress is torn. It hangs on either side of her body and I plan to frame the fabric after. I'll carry a piece of it in my wallet wherever I go.

That's how obsessed with her I am. No shame, either.

"And I'll let you baby me all you want."

"Good girl." Rubbing the head of my cock from clit to slit twice, I pause at her entrance. A whimper escapes her, thighs spreading wider—she's gorgeously indecent. "Now, hold on."

I'm inside her in one fluid motion, buried to the hilt as her fingernails dig into my arm. She's arching and bucking against the intrusion while I pull out and slam back in.

No pause. No waiting for her to adjust.

My baby takes my cock so prettily with a cry on her lips and her wetness dripping down to my balls. Her eyes roll back, neck pushing against the cushions. She's shaking. Breaths labored.

"Baby," Mariah moans, pulling me down until our chests are flushed and I anchor her to the couch with my hips. Fucking her with hard strokes, and when she clenches, I slip a hand beneath and grip an asscheek.

"You feel so good, Muñeca. So tight." I flex my hips and then pull out slowly, dragging my cock against her walls before slamming back in. A delicious clench comes from her core, nearly choking my girth. "Again. Do that again."

My pace is near punishing and every thrust pulls from her a cry of pleasurable pain that hits me in the chest like a sledgehammer. I'll live the rest of my life worshipping her just to hear those sounds again and again.

She's my reward. My fucking life.

"Kiss me, Javi. I'm so close." The nails on my arm move down to my back and the blunt tips rake down to my ass. She grips me, forcing my hips to pound deeper—harder—until those perfect thighs shake. They tremble and squeeze my sides. "Need them."

And I comply because this woman owns me.

I kiss her with every bit of the passion and love and hunger I hold for her. Mariah's tongue is soft and she makes a whiny noise at the back of her throat when our tongues twine. She tries to fight for dominance, to control the kiss, but one sharp bite to her bottom lip and two things happen:

She clenches around me and screams into my mouth; I swallow each cry as the sound of her pleasure grows and juices soak my cock. My balls are heavy and the slap of skin on skin is loud, but it's the way she closes her eyes and smiles that breaks me.

Every muscle in my body coils tight, but I never stop pounding into her, pulling out every last drop of come. Her pleasure comes before mine, and I revel in each spasm. Own her with each snap of my hip.

But when those seafoam-sated eyes focus on me again, a groan escapes and I lose control.

"Motherfuck, Mariah. So tight. So wet." I slam in a final time and hold myself deep inside, filling her with ropes of come. The euphoric peak knocks the breath from my chest, and I bury my face in her neck, kissing every bit of skin I can reach.

We stay that way for a while. My body on hers and her arms holding me tight.

There's no rush. No thoughts of her impending flight tomorrow morning where I'm not joining her.

She'll be in Chicago, and I'll be here hunting.

Painting the streets with blood.

*I'm going to miss you, Muñeca.*

# 23
## Mariah

I NEVER THOUGHT leaving him would be this hard, but it is, and I can't fight back the tears that spring to my eyes. I can't help but hold him a little tighter while around us the world carries on without pause; the people walking through this large terminal are either looking for food and drink, or a wall plug to charge their electronics. Because no matter what airport or country you're in, it's always the same, except this one time when it feels as though my chest is caving in.

I'm going to miss him. I'm going to need him to come back.

This stubborn, beautiful man that's swept me off my feet and I've been unwilling to fight off as he took possession of my being. I love him. Completely and without pause, my heart belongs to Javier Lucas.

"I'll be back before you know it, Muñeca." His arms tighten around me and his lips press to the crown of my head. "Trust me, you'll be back to kicking me out—begging me to leave Chicago again within a week."

"Or I kick your ass." It's mumbled against his shirt, but the deep rumble of his laugh lets me know he heard. "Promise."

Javi pulls back just enough to tip my chin up with two fingers, his soft eyes staring deep into mine. "I love you, Mariah Asher. I love and need you and can't breathe right when you're not near. Nothing can stop me...not even God himself, from coming back to you. Trust me."

"I do." My reply is without hesitation, and it earns me one of those cocky smirks that I adore. "Find them, Javier."

"We already—"

He stops talking when I shake my head and pull him down low enough that I can reach the shell of his ear. "You're not understanding me." I take a moment then to just breathe him in, soothe my soul with his touch, before exhaling against his skin. "Baby..." Javi's fingers tighten their hold; they dig into the bruises from last night and I whimper, the sound just as needy as I am, but now is not the time. When I leave, go back to Chicago, I need him to focus on my request. To carry it out before coming back to me. "Baby, I need you to find them and kill each slowly. I need you to make them suffer, dismember them limb by limb until there's nothing left but the horror-filled expression on their faces before taking their last breath. And when it's done, and the country knows to never cross a Lucas again...come *home*."

He releases a shuddering breath, but I don't stay to hear his confirmation. Instead, I extricate myself from his hold and walk toward the boarding area and wait to be called. It doesn't take long, and just when I cross the entrance to the tunnel, I look back and immediately find his eyes.

Javier's been watching. He's giving me a look full of promise.

But more than that is the subtle nod. It's his agreement to my terms.

A WEEK HAS COME and gone without news from Colombia.

No local coverage of violence abroad. No Spanish-speaking networks discussing political unrest of affluent families with ties to criminal activities.

Not a damn thing, and I was losing my mind with worry.

This is also why I didn't notice the large bouquet of black roses sitting just outside my door after work. Again, there wasn't a note or a card from the shop making the delivery, but it's now clear to see this isn't a mistake.

Someone wants my attention, and the first person that crosses my mind is Mildred.

She slept with Lane and possibly my father. She's still roaming around according to Malcolm, and while I'm sure in part it has to do with her twin still being alive, my gut tells me there's more.

That *I'm* that more.

Pulling out my phone, I dial Malcolm, but it goes straight to voicemail. *Crap, he's still probably in the meeting with the Jameson family.* The customary bland and impersonal message comes through the line followed by a beep to respond.

"Call me when you get this. I just got another delivery." He'll know what I'm talking about and I hang up, looking down at the screen again with this uncontrollable urge to call Javier. My finger swipes down the contact list, hovering just above the call button beside his name. "Screw it."

It rings after a few seconds. And rings three more times.

No answer. Nothing.

All I receive is a generic instruction to call back because his inbox is full.

"Guess not, then." With the bottom of my foot, I nudge the arrangement inside and leave it on the floor beside the entrance. I'm sure Malcolm will send someone later to pick it up, and I'd rather not get my fingerprints on it. "Hopefully he'll call later."

Without pause, I toe off my slingbacks and leave them there as well, walking barefoot toward my room. My phone is still in my hand and my attention is garbage, which explains why after changing and heating some leftover spaghetti, I pick up the video call without checking the caller ID first.

Dad's face is the last one I want to see, but there he is, smiling. "Why were you out of the country, Mariah? Where have you been?"

"That's none of your concern."

He bristles at my detached tone. "You will always be my concern, daughter of mine."

"You forfeited that right two years ago. I have nothing else to say on the matter."

"Watch your tone," he hisses through clenched teeth, glaring at me with so much hatred and disappointment. "You seem to have forgotten your place, Mariah. You are my daughter, and you will respect me."

"Respect is earned." A text from Malcolm blinks on the screen and I hit ignore. "Now, what do you want? Calling isn't something you do and when it occurs, it's because you need something from me."

"Why were you in Colombia with Javier Lucas?"

My blood runs cold at that. *How the hell...*

"Are you having me watched?" His lack of a response gives me the answer I need, and while inside I'm fuming—wanting to strangle the man—my expression remains unemotional. Cold. "I guess this is a trait passed down from generation to generation."

"Are you fucking that—"

"Where is my mother?" Dad doesn't like that I interrupted nor my line of questioning, but I couldn't care less and match his icy glare. "What did you do to her?"

"She isn't of your concern."

"And my life isn't of yours."

"Mariah," he spits out, but his attention isn't on me but someone on the other side of the phone. It's a woman's voice, speaking low, but I catch part of their reflection in the windowpane behind my father. She's familiar. Someone I'll be paying a visit to soon.

"Get to the point." Walking to the fridge, I pull it open and take out a can of pop. "Some of us would like to eat dinner in peace."

His eyes snap back to mine and the woman turns her face, but I do catch a better look. *Mildred, you stupid bitch.* "I'm not above hurting my daughter and you're pushing me, sweetheart. Back down and do as you're told if you want to see your mother again."

Popping the top, I take a large sip. Noisily, which I know annoys him. "What is this going to cost me?"

"Malcolm is currently holding control of the Frederick's laboratory in Utah. Get me the—"

"No."

"The fuck did you just say?"

"I said no." Then I take another sip and smile. "Mom isn't dead, and I will find her."

"The hospital will never release her without my signature."

"Maybe, but you just signed your death warrant." Disconnecting the call, I quickly press the number for Malcolm and wait. It rings twice before there's an audible click.

"Did he call you?"

"He did. Much sooner than I expected."

"Was anyone with him?" His ire matches my own. A familial betrayal cuts deep and the punishment is served without mercy, something I am okay with.

"Mildred."

"Okay. See you tomorrow." We hang up and I go on with my evening. Within the last week, we've watched videos, gone through endless files, and started the search for my mother. Mildred Frederick and my father have been corroborating for the last few years on unapproved medical testing for a few viral strands that have been slowly growing overseas but haven't hit the States, and yet, their end goal is a worldwide bidding war.

That's their goal, but I have mine.

I want their blood on my hands.

"THANK YOU FOR YOUR TIME." For the sixth time today, I hang up the phone and close my eyes. It's taken me a few days to narrow down my mother's location after Dad's video call, and she isn't in a mental institution. She isn't in Europe either.

Looking down my list, I cross off another women's shelter in Indiana and sigh.

For some reason, she's back in her home state and hiding. Using cash and prepaid cards, but facial recognition has come a long way and Erik found a video clip of her at the aquarium with a group of kids no older than eight.

My mother wasn't dressed as the society queen she once was. In a pair of dark-wash jeans and cream-colored blouse, she walked with the group from exhibit to exhibit while answering what she could—helping this one little girl in particular that seemed too small to play with the others.

"Why hasn't he called me?" I ask aloud, rubbing my temples when footsteps approach. They're heels, the clacking loud within the open space, and I look up in time to watch Mildred try and sneak past my desk. "Take another step and adhere to the consequences."

Mildred's head snaps in my direction, face pinched tight in anger. "What did you say?"

"Are you deaf?" Shuffling the list of numbers in Indiana under a financial report, I raise a brow. "Well?"

Crossing her arms over her chest, she turns to fully face me. "No. I'm not."

"Then you know I both find both irritating and disgusting," I sneer, catching Malcolm's imposing figure standing just within the entrance to his office. "Leave."

"You have balls for a secretary."

"And we both know you spread those legs for anyone, my father being one of them." Standing from my seat, I open the drawer to my right and pull out a gun with two bullets. "Married men. Engaged men. Do you sleep with family members too?"

Her face goes from furious to near ghostly white. Fake tears gather at the corner of her eyes. "How could you say something like that to me? I'm a respected member of—"

"Please cut the bull, Mildred. We both know what cloth you are cut from." Picking up my Glock, I pull the clip out and insert the two bullets before resetting with the safety off. "Why are you here? And don't give me some line about an appointment because you don't have one. You have two minutes to explain."

She fidgets, eyeing the weapon in my hand. "Malcolm called me to go over our merger. We've come to an understanding."

"Lie. Try again."

"It's the truth, Mariah. Call him and ask."

"Again, that's a lie. One more chance." I raise my hand and point toward her chest.

Mildred shakes, but her eyes are full of hate. Her animosity is palpable and so is her greed. "I came to talk to Malcolm about *my* brother and company. We need to come to an amicable agreement."

"Is that so?" My cousin steps forward now, a smile on his face and Mildred calms immediately.

"Yes." Her response is low and meek, and he's the epitome of gracious when holding a hand out. "I'm very sorry for showing up without a prior appointment, but please, I need—"

"No worries, Ms. Frederick." His eyes snap to mine and harden a bit for her benefit. "Put the gun away and show some respect, Mariah. She is a customer and must be treated as such. Understood?"

"Of course, Mr. Asher."

She's smiling at his reprimand. She enjoys me being put in my place.

Stupid fucking woman.

Mildred is pushing her luck with me, and if she catches me on the wrong day, I'll be the one putting a bullet between her eyes.

# 24

## Javier

"**H**AVE YOU HAD any news on his whereabouts?" I ask Malcolm, holding the phone between my ear and shoulder while Alejandro and Emiliano hold a meeting inside the family compound. We've been here for the past two weeks, smoking out those responsible for my mother's death, while they try and hide.

I know where the three men are:

The shooter. The enabler. The general of Colombia's army.

They've been lying low and I haven't. The country—the president—wants me for my crimes but don't have a shred of possibility without cause and evidence. You can't be proven guilty of words alone, and the citizens demand proof of the murders committed.

"Her father is in Athens, Georgia."

"And the whore?" Because I'm well aware of the second set of roses Mariah received, even though the stubborn woman hasn't spoken of the incident. Nor did she tell me of her encounter with

Mildred a few days ago. I might not be there, but I have ways of keeping tabs. "Has she left the state?"

"According to Mildred, she was heading home last night to Utah. She's put her home on the market and there's been an offer." He chuckles, the sound of papers shifting coming through the line. "Her plane landed two hours ago in Atlanta where she rented a sports car, and she is on her way to see my uncle."

"How many are tailing her?"

"Three, and two on him." At his response, I hum, scratching the five-day-old stubble on my chin. "They're too cocky and reckless. Antonio was honest in what he's shared so far."

"He's been useful," I admit. "Has his sister asked for the body again?"

"No. My word that he's dead sufficed."

"And the Dermots?" Both Lane's mother and father were killed last week—an unfortunate incident at their vacation home in Italy. House fires are a dangerous thing, and unfortunately for them, I traveled to the Italian countryside to play with matches. "Does Mariah know? Are the other two making any moves?"

"Negative, but her brother did warn us before you left. They're staying quiet as all avenues begin to close."

*"Evening, gentleman." Malcolm steps into the room, nodding at the guards standing watch. "Antonio. Delia."*

*"Boss," his men answer in unison while I grab a chair and take a seat, keeping my eyes on the bloody man in front of me. He fidgets. She whimpers.*

*"The food has been ordered as Mr. Lucas requested." Carmelo hands over the credit card I'd given him and I pocket the plastic square, not taking my eyes off Antonio and Delia. These two know more than they let on, and I'm not taking any chances with Mariah's safety.*

*"Thank you, kid."*

*Malcolm drags a chair beside mine and we wait. And wait. No* one in the room says a word until Mrs. Frederick breaks the silence. *"Is there any scenario in this where we don't lose our lives?"*

An honest question, and Malcolm nods. *"There's always an open option, but the outcome lies solely at your feet."*

*"What do you need?"* she asks, gripping her husband's hand tightly in hers. *"Name the price and it's done."*

*"The truth,"* I answer for him after having discussed this development. *"We want the full story, Antonio. Why did you try to kill Mildred and then turn your wife into her replica?"*

The male twin sighs, rubbing a hand down his face, wincing from the pain of Malcolm's bullet. *"My sister was sleeping with Lane Dermot and working with his family on a shady contract with an overseas investor. The laboratory was being used as their personal tester, playing with viral agents that we've yet to encounter as a society—creating and testing—for a profit. This wasn't about the betterment of the world, but a fat profit. One she was going to use to order Mariah's death."*

Every muscle in my body locks down and beside me, Malcolm is just as angry. Fire burns through my veins while the need for vengeance—her blood—grows. *"What else? Who else is involved?"*

*"Her father."*

*"That son of a bitch,"* Malcolm hisses, fingers twitching on the gun sitting atop his thigh. *"Why did you do it? Jealousy or anger?"*

*"Fear."* Antonio looks over at his wife and his expression softens. It's full of so much remorse. *"I was afraid that if the Ashers caught wind, we'd go down with her sinking boat. It was only a matter of time before the shit hit the fan, but I never thought I'd be the catalyst."*

*"Which brings me to my next question..."* Asher sits forward, eyes hard on the couple *"...why try to move money through me if you're being investigated? What kind of game are you playing?"*

*"I'm not."* Antonio shakes his head rapidly, sweat dotting his upper lip. His wife isn't any better; her body's shaking and leg bouncing. *"I came to you because we had to keep up the appear-*

*ances of nothing being wrong. Had we gone with a different financial institution; more flags would've been raised. You would have asked around or demanded to know the why."*

"And the federal investigations?"

*"Mildred." Delia spits out the name with so much venom. "She sent them to the lab, even though we stopped all experiments the day I switched into this role. He screwed us on the records we kept in boxes down in the basement, but no active work was being done at the time."*

*"But trust me, my sister is cunning. And when push comes to shove, she'll hide to save herself.*

Alejandro snaps his fingers and I look up, pulled from the memory of a few weeks back. My hunch about Mildred Frederick was on point, and the woman didn't disappoint. Rats never stay hidden for long, and I know she's digging around. Looking for payback.

"Parce, look at the screen." Emiliano points, and I pay attention to the footage playing on the giant TV screen. It's of a small, worn-down home a half an hour from the Presidential palace, inside of a community owned by the central bank of Colombia's owner. He hasn't remodeled it since the purchase, nor do people reside within the subdivision's gates. The home on the screen is large, and in its prime, I'm sure cost a pretty penny, but that's not my focus.

There are four cars parked outside, but not all seem occupied as the drivers begin to step out.

"What the hell is going on?" I ask, and on his end of the line, Malcolm's gone silent so I can understand my cousins.

"Three bodies inside." Alejandro takes a sip from his water, eyeing the screen.

"What's the fastest ETA?" I ask them while the man behind the wheel of a black Hummer gets down, his eyes darting around. More-over, it's when he knocks on the door that the camera angle changes. This is a live feed from a front-door transmission, and I smile.

We have the shooter on the screen.

Then the enabler opens the door.

And I hear the clear voice of the General coming up from behind my mother's killer.

Alejandro hums, fingers typing on his phone. "Taking back roads and avoiding the expressway, I say twenty minutes at the most."

"Suit up." They nod at my command and empty the room, going in search of what we'll need for this. We won't take security or have these three picked up; I'll take my pound of flesh without pause the second I enter that home.

"My guess is you're heading out to play a game of catch?" Malcolm chuckles, and the clink of a glass follows the question. "Alone or with a team?"

"Absolutely, Asher. It's my favorite pastime. My cousins enjoy it as well."

He chuckles and then sighs. "Be careful and keep a cool head."

"Always." I know he's not being intrusive or trying to tell me how to handle myself. I've gotten to know him on a personal level while here; our phone calls and worry over Mariah has created a bond that we both appreciate. He's family to me. He cares about everyone who bears my last name since I signed the contract, but more so since my mother's passing. "Besides, I can't give your cousin a reason to shoot me. I'm planning to grow old and grey with her."

"Good."

"What? No warnings to slow down and—"

"Come home and marry the woman, Javi. She's not letting you go."

"And I was never leaving. I'll text you later." With that, I hang up and pull up her contact.

**I love you with all my heart, Muñeca. I'll be home soon. ~Javi**

THE GATE to the community has two armed guards standing out front and they're busy talking when we pull up. They're laughing, the one to the left throwing a punch to the arm of his friend after a joke, and completely oblivious of the three men stepping out of their cars until Alejandro slams the door.

Then two sets of eyes are on us, weapons pointing our way. "Who are you? This is private property and—" Two bullets and they hit the ground, a hole in each forehead. The silencer from my gun doesn't make much noise, and the hard cement cradles the impact of their corpses.

"Right or left?" Emiliano asks, and I tilt my head toward the right, following the sound of Vallenato playing loudly. The beat pulses as the male singer declares his love for a woman who he's never so much as kissed, while the off-key voice of a heavy smoker follows.

The sound of splashing water comes from a home three down from where we stand, and it's quickly followed by laughter. Female giggles and male chuckles as someone shrieks. And begs.

"Please stop this! I don't want to get in!"

"Don't be such a spoilsport, Luisa." It's one of the men, his speech a bit slurred. "It's just water. Nothing will happen to your hair."

"Take me home."

"No."

We share a look before taking account of the car with two guards sitting inside. This old, black beater wasn't in the video earlier, but I recognize the uniform and its military. They're young, more than likely just following orders, but it doesn't stop Alejandro from killing the two with a single shot that travels from one head to the other, a straight shot through the ear.

Their heads slump forward, and I nod, impressed. "Nice one."

"I'm an environmentalist." He shrugs, and I chuckle. Asshole.

"Front door or back?" Emiliano asks, and I point toward the main entrance. And we find it unlocked when entering the home a few minutes later. The music is louder from here and the place is trashed, dirty, but the men seem to be enjoying themselves.

It's a straight shot from the front door to the sliding glass that leads out back, and I step out first amidst empty liquor bottles. It's disgusting, the stale stench a little nauseating, but I'm smiling as I shoot the enabler from my place just over the threshold. He falls forward and into the pool, his blood spreading out.

The women scream. The two still alive scramble for a weapon.

"You four need to get the fuck out of here." Alejandro points the end of his Colt at the group of college-age women panicking on the pool's steps. "You have two minutes to gather your shit and run." They don't move and he sends out another shot. This time it hits the cheap speakers beside the drink table. "Hagale."

They try to rush past us, not taking a single item with them, and Emiliano takes their phones. "The keys to the Hummer are on the kitchen counter. Grab them and go. Understood?"

"Si, and we won't say anything," a small brunette answers and the girls leave without further prompting, leaving the two assholes in nothing but their boxers outside. They have guns, but their hands shake. They're scared, but don't have enough common sense to try and escape through the back door a few feet from them.

It makes sense when I look around and find a table with cocaine and a few cut lines on a mirror. *Fucking idiots.* "Please have a seat."

"What's the meaning of this?" General Gustavo Mijares asks, his hand flailing. "Do you know who I am? What I can do to you without repercussion?"

Emiliano pulls a knife from his back pocket and grabs it from the tip; a flick of the wrist and it embeds itself into the military man's arm. His scream rends the air while the man beside him seems to have gone mute. "Watch the tone."

"Gentlemen, can't we talk this out?" Gino asks, his hands up. "Let's all relax and have a drink. No need for violence."

"I'll accept your drink, but it comes with a condition." I walk over and pull up a chair right across from him. "Everything in life comes with a price."

"Of course, but first we drink."

"Do we drink to Francis or my mother?" Both men pale, but Gino's hand on the bottle tightens, knuckles turning white. "A loving woman or a piece-of-shit thief?"

"Javier, we've both lost." A shot is poured, and he pushes it in my direction. "It's time to let go and move on. We're even."

"Did you hear, primos? We're even."

"We heard." They each follow my lead and take a seat, weapons now atop the table. "Seems worthy of a celebration...don't you think, Gustavo?"

"Yes." His tone is nervous. He doesn't trust us.

"Great!" Gino picks up a small mirror beside him and without pause does another line, wiping his hand across his nose to dust off the excess. "Do you two want a shot?"

"We do." Then they empty every single bullet inside of Gustavo. Two guns. One clip each. And as the general begins to fall face forward, I lean across the table and fist his hair in my hands.

He's breathing is near nonexistent. Gustavo's body is heavy as his last seconds draw close, and I take the blade on the table, holding the sharp end to his neck, and slice it across. One quick pull from right to left and his neck is open, nearly chopped-off, as the blood rushes out from the large wound.

"Say hello to the devil for me." His eyes are wide with horror. His lips are bloody, a trickle of red sliding down the corner of his mouth before there's an infinite nothing.

The general is dead, and his accomplice pisses his pants. "Please don't." *Pathetic.*

"I think it's time I collect my favor."

"W-what can I do for you?" he stutters, body shaking so hard his teeth rattle as the reality sets in. As his fear begins to dominate.

"We're going for a ride."

THE ROAD we're driving down an hour later is deserted. Barren. And I spend my time just watching Gino; the way tears roll down his cheeks and his chin quivers. The low prayer that slips past his lips and burns my skin.

A man who killed an innocent woman will never receive the pardon he begs for.

He's unworthy of forgiveness.

We're in his car, an older model full-sized van with two captain's chairs and a large sliding door beside my seat. The vehicle is spacious. Somewhat clean.

"Javier, please. Let's be reasonable." His hands are clenching, body racking with sobs. "We both made mistakes here. Let's forgive and forget."

"Silence."

"Come on, parce—"

"Fucking idiot." I kick him in the mouth, my combat boot knocking out a few front teeth and I rub the sole against his mouth, making him swallow back the red substance. "Die with dignity."

"I don't want to die!" He wails, now fighting me. His weak attempts only make this sweeter.

"Did you know my mother was supposed to fly out in two weeks to Chicago? We'd planned it, but it'd become difficult when she caught a small cold and we decided to push it back." This time my foot kicks his chest and he falls over, trying to breathe through the burn. "She was supposed to meet my girl and love her as much as I do."

"I'm sorry."

"Your apologies mean shit," I snarl, lip curling up in disgust. In pure hatred for this piece of shit not worthy of breath. Gino coughs when I remove my foot, but his reprieve is short lived when I lean forward and land the first punch to his face. I don't stop after one and rain down blow after blow to his mouth, nose, and the corner of his left eye.

The skin becomes red, his flesh breaking just above his orb and still, it's not enough.

My fist doesn't pause. My anger won't simmer.

"Por favor. No more."

"I'll only stop when you're dead." The car picks up speed then and I look up, catching Alejandro's eyes in the rear view mirror. He nods and Emiliano turns in his seat, reaching back to open the van's door. "Thank you."

"Enjoy yourself."

"Oh, I will." Then I'm leaning the bitch over and smirk as his screams rend the open road. He's cursing, crying, but nothing fills my heart with peace like the sound of flesh rubbing off on asphalt. His face leaves behind a bloody streak from one end to the other, and back again when we make a circle back. Gino's body convulses in pain, fighting and squirming, and the scent of his piss infiltrates my senses when he soils himself again.

I pull him up, and half his face and scalp is gone. His eyeball is missing.

"..." he slurs, but it's unintelligible and I scrunch up my face in mock concern.

"What was that?" His head lulls back, and spit mixed with blood dribbles down his chin. *So nasty.* "You want more?"

Head shaking, a few tears roll down his good eye. "No."

"Si."

"Please...compassion."

For a second, I nod. Give him false hope before elbowing him in the one eye he has left and lowering him a final time out of the van's door. I'm holding him a little above the moving asphalt. His squinting eye is trying to focus on me, his body no longer fighting.

"Javi, I—"

"Thank me."

It takes him a moment, but he does. It's low and weak and I shoot him twice in the head before dumping his body over.

It bounces off the paved road, lying still and waiting for the birds to arrive. They don't take long; the scavengers wait nearby on trees and watch—wait for opportunities to present themselves.

"Are you heading straight to the airport from here?" Emiliano says as the sight of Gino's corpse becomes distant, and I turn my face to meet his eyes. "Or are you picking anything up? We can handle the cleanup alone."

"I'm taking Chulo. She loves him."

"Then I'll text Lourdes to have him and your bags ready. Let's get you back to Mariah."

Closing my eyes, I nod and sit back. Relax a bit knowing I'm going home.

*I miss you, Muñeca.*

# 25

## Mariah

I T'S ALMOST TWO in the afternoon and I'm restless. Unable to sit still while this invisible pressure weighs on my chest. *What is wrong with me?*

Something inside me is unable to rest, and for a Friday afternoon that makes no sense. Not when I have the weekend off and Malcolm demands I disconnect from work.

No phone calls. No helping with last-minute demands from clients.

My eyes flick to my cell phone, and I glare at the screen. Javier hasn't called in days, and I'm fearing the worst while hoping for the best. This uncertainty is gnawing at my gut, and I'm going to punch him in the mouth before kissing him stupid the next time I see him.

No contact in days is unacceptable. *You go silent when hunting.* One of the few lessons my father imparted that I understand. Distractions can get you killed, and while I hate it—loathe the silence—I understand the why.

Touching someone's mother is forbidden, and when that line is crossed you act swiftly and without humanity. No conscious thought.

*I'm still going to give him hell for making me—*

"You look like you need a coffee break," my cousin asks, standing in front of my desk with a cup of coffee from my favorite shop, but all it does is make me miss Javier more. Wish that he were here bugging me instead; pushing me and taking my body as he did the night before I flew back.

I'll never forget that cabin deep in the jungle. The way he fucked me, then loved me and fed me a delicious dinner in bed afterward.

I want that man again. The side of him that only I'll see when the day is over and we no longer have to respond to titles and expectations.

*I miss him. I love him.*

"Thanks." Grabbing the cup, I bring it to my lips and take a sip. My brows furrow and head tilts to the side; the brew is too perfect. Just the right temp and sugar versus caffeine ratio. It also reminds me of every cup Javier has brought me thus far.

Of his smiles when I'd grumble.

Of his knowing eyes when I'd bite back a caffeinated moan.

"Nice to see you smile."

"Unless you have some kind of cake behind your back, shut it." And the gloating jerk only nods toward my desk and the open light pink box that sits there. They're from the same bakery as my drink, and containing the baked goods I've been craving for the past seven days of this week. "How?"

"Just thought you'd need a pick-me-up. You've been off for days." He's staring at me pointedly, and I feel a twinge of shame. This isn't a life I don't understand, I know to expect the unpredictability, but it doesn't negate that when someone you love is involved, things change.

"That bad?" I ask sheepishly, giving him innocent eyes that he sees through.

"Do you want the truth or a bullshit-praising deviation of reality?"

"Touché." Taking another sip, I breathe in deep and let it out slowly. "Has he contacted you?"

"Not in days, but we both know he's fine." The concern in his tone catches me off guard, and I raise a brow. "Just because I don't cry into my cereal doesn't mean I don't like the guy, Mariah. He's good to and for you. That's enough for me."

"So, you approve?"

"Do you need my approval?"

"No." He laughs at my response while bringing his wrist up, checking the time on his watch. "Shut everything off; we have somewhere to be."

On instinct, I check the notepad to my right and don't see anything scheduled for this afternoon. "We don't have—"

"Shut it down and gather your things. We're cutting out early."

"Sure thing, boss. Let me jump into action," I say with false elation laced with sarcasm.

"Good. And hurry." And to be a jerk, he takes my box of goodies because he knows I'll follow.

I'm half tempted to flip him off but choose instead to roll my eyes and do as he says. There's not much to do and I log off, tear the page off my notepad, and store the items no longer needed. *Clear space, clear head.*

"Where are we going?" I ask a few minutes later as we head down to the main floor and then exit through the back. The employees we pass smile at us—some have a knowing look, but no one stops or asks questions. "Did something happen? Is everyone okay?"

"Keep walking, Mariah. No more questions."

"Malcolm—"

"Trust me." And he hits right where I'll never argue. He's like my brother and has never lied to or hurt me.

"Okay." We walk down a private stretch of sidewalk that leads to the company garage in silence. It's quiet out, the sole noise coming from the distant horn or a street vendor calling out to sell his hot food items.

He doesn't pause at the door on this side of the building, just turns the handle without inputting the code. I'm surprised but don't voice it, choosing instead to bide my time.

"Keys?"

"Sure." Digging them out from my purse, I hand them over and hear the click of my alarm a few seconds later. I don't park far from the entrance and we make it to the vehicle within a minute or two. "Can I have them back now or are you driving?"

He doesn't answer and once again checks his watch. "Give me a sec."

"Malcolm, this is getting weird. Even for you."

"Hush, nerd."

"Suck it, donkey face." I'm smiling at the end of our exchange, more so because we haven't used these nicknames since high school. He was as much a jerk then as he is now. "But seriously, cousin. What's going on?"

"Always so many questions, Muñeca." My entire being freezes, eyes closing as his voice wraps around me and the drink in my hand crashes to the ground. I don't turn to look around for him, I don't so much as breathe, but then he's there. Right behind me. His warmth seeping into my pores. "Aren't you going to welcome me home?"

"You've rendered her speechless, Lucas."

"I should do it more often. Look at that—no arguing."

"I'm going to kick both your...oh shit!" I'm whirled around before I can finish my threat and his lips meet mine, breathing life back into my body. At once I'm hot and needy and I whimper into his mouth, gripping his dress shirt to keep him where he is.

Where he should always be. With me. Touching me.

A sense of relief so profound fills my lungs, and I breathe right for the first time since leaving Colombia. Javier is home and I'm drawing in his taste, clinging to him like the needy woman he's made me.

Our tongues twine, a loving caress and I moan. "When."

"A few hours ago," he growls into my mouth, his kisses desperate. Hungry. "Had to pick up Chulo first, but I'm here. I came back for you."

"I love you."

"I love you too, beautiful."

"And I'm taking the dog home. I don't want to see either of you until next Tuesday." Turning my head, I meet my cousin's stare and there's a warmth there that surprises me. "Go be happy."

Stepping out of Javier's arms, ignoring his protest, I walk over to Malcolm and hug him tight. He wraps his arms around me and squeezes just as hard, and then steps back, grabbing the leash my man's holding.

*Oh shit! Chulo is here!*

"He's already in Malcolm's car with Carmelo. We'll see him in a few days."

"Really?" I'm smiling so big and I know we have so much to discuss, but just having him here, makes my life brighter. Everything can wait. Right now, I just need him. To be us for a few hours, and then I'll talk him into picking up my dog.

Because I'm claiming him. Chulo is mine.

"Yes, linda. He's comfy and warm and getting ready to be spoiled by you."

"That dog is brilliant." Turning my head back in the direction of Malcolm, I find the area empty. "Where did he—"

"He's gone, babe. Now kiss me." Javier doesn't wait for me. His mouth slants over mine and I give in to his taste. The softness of his lips is a contrast to his aggressiveness—as if he can't help himself—and Javier devours me. And I lose myself to him, to the feel of his cock hard and thick against my abdomen. Of the coolness of my car as the metal meets my back, his body covering my front while hands wander.

He's gripping my right thigh with one hand and palming the back of my neck with the other. Dominating my senses. Controlling and pulling moans from deep within my chest.

I don't know how long we stand there kissing and don't care. Either way, this is what I've been missing. That is until we hear the click of a gun and freeze.

"Isn't this sweet," a voice says from behind him, and a quick flash of fear runs through me. Mildred tsks when we don't disengage and turn to face her, but I feel the gun in Javi's jacket and finger the cold metal, gripping it tight right before he turns.

His back is against my front, his muscles coiled tight. "Leave, Ms. Frederick. Killing so soon after being gone so long isn't on my agenda for the day."

"Step aside."

"Last warning."

"Why do you defend the whore?" she spits out, and I take in her appearance. *The hell happened to her?* Mildred is dressed all in black and her lip is busted, a large bruise forming at her jaw. "It's because of her that I've lost it all."

"I thought you were pulling my strings. That I'd be the one to lose it all?"

"You took him from me." Tears fall and leave mascaraed tracks down her cheeks while her hand shakes. She looks unstable. "Had you kept out of my business—had you left Lane alone—I'd be a happy bride right now with a kid on the way. Instead, I'm alone on our anniversary and you'll end up dead by my hands."

"You mean, with you going to jail?"

"With your father burying his child." Something about the way she says *father* catches my attention. It's full of hurt and bitterness.

"Did he leave you? Is that why you're pulling the dramatic act?" Antagonizing her isn't ideal, but right now I'm seeing red. Seething at this bitch for interrupting our sweet reunion and I step from behind my love, standing shoulder to shoulder while keeping his Glock out of sight. "Or is he sleeping with someone else?"

Fury flashes in her eyes, but she tamps it down with a fake smile. "I'm going to enjoy killing you, and then I'll end your mother."

"Mildred, this is your final chance. Walk." Javi reaches for my hand, trying to grip the gun. She's too busy glaring to see the exchange, but he doesn't miss the way I hold on tighter. This kill is mine; I'm not backing down.

"I want her dead," Mildred sneers and lifts her shaking hand with the barrel pointing at my head.

"The feeling is mutual." Still, I hold my ground without showing my weapon. Showing your hand before it's time can be a costly mistake. "But I'm going to give you the opportunity I never offered Lane. Walk, run...leave Chicago and never come back."

The mention of his name cuts her deep; I've come to understand within the last few weeks that she did love him, just had a shitty way of showing it.

"Fuck you," she screeches and the gun in her hand goes off, the bullet aimed at me while I return fire with a quick flick of my wrist. It all happens so fast. One second she's standing, while the next, her vacant eyes watch us with three bullet holes decorating her head.

"I keep warning people that my shot is better than most." Her discharge never touched me and I smile, until I look over and catch the sight of red on Javier's shirt and the sudden buckling of his knees. "Baby?"

"I love you," he whispers, and my world stops. This can't be fucking happening.

"Look at me," I yell out as footsteps approach and then surround us. They're barking out orders and closing the garage down, and while I'm somewhat aware of Malcolm's voice through a phone's speaker, I don't react. My sole focus is on the man gritting his teeth as the stain grows. "Javier, baby...focus on me."

"I love you." He slumps back and I help him against my car, cradling his head as paramedics arrive with the police close behind. They load him on a stretcher and I try to follow, but with me being the shooter, one of the officers arrested me without questioning or watching the video recording.

Javier is taken to the closest hospital.

I'm being taken to the nearest precinct.

*God, please let him be okay. Please don't take him from me.*

# 26

## Mariah

I HAVEN'T FULLY stepped inside the precinct when I catch sight of a man I know and well. His eyes meet mine and they widen, then narrow on the man beside me walking as if he's made the bust of the century.

"What's the meaning of this!" Captain Hall bellows and all movement inside ceases; the man he's talking to also turns to look and grimaces at the image of my tears and the handcuffs on my wrists. "What the hell are you doing?"

"Captain, we answered a call for help at the garage for Asher Holdings," Officer Millstone answers, his chest puffing out with pride. He's young. Too eager. *Moron.* I'm seething in these cuffs, but I keep my composure. The faster we get things cleared up, the faster I can get to Javi. "Shots were fired as reported, and we discovered a deceased female upon arrival. There was also a wounded man nearby who's been taken to Northwestern Medical. She—"

"Is the fucking victim."

"What?" The hand on the small of my back shakes. "She's our suspect."

"No, she isn't." Hall flicks his eyes to me, and the look in them is apologetic. Embarrassed. Scared. "Had you done your job properly, you would've asked for video footage and known that the deceased shot first and accosted the couple. Ms. Asher acted in self-defense and if you don't get those handcuffs off within the next fifteen seconds, the only job you'll have in my department is in clerical."

Millstone jumps into action and the restraints come off; his face is ashen when I turn to raise a brow. "Ms. Asher, I apologize. This was a huge mistake and I—"

"Drive me to the hospital and we'll be even. No stopping for shit."

"Captain, can I—"

"Go." Hall is exasperated, embarrassed, and I'll talk Malcolm into not retaliating. But later. Much later. "Get her there and back quickly. Head straight to my office. I'll be waiting."

"Yes, sir."

"You'll be arresting me again if we don't get to that damn hospital, Officer. And that is not an empty threat." He gulps, then nods. Hall turns, and I catch a hint of a blush on his cheeks and it takes everything in me not to snap.

*Lord, now is not the time to test my patience. Please get me to Javi.*

I breathe a little calmer once we are on our way.

---

"WHAT THE HELL HAPPENED?" Malcolm hisses beside me the second I walk through the emergency rooms doors. He's been waiting outside, knowing I was close after Officer Millstone was kind enough to return my belongings that he confiscated from the ground near my car. "Who the fuck arrested you?"

"Not now."

"Mariah, I need—"

"To give me a moment to see if the man I love is okay." The tears come then, and I'm pulled into his chest, his lips at the crown of my head, but I don't understand what he's mumbling. "What?"

"I said, he's—"

"Malcolm, I swear to God if you tell me he's anything but fine, I'll shoot *you*."

The man chuckles and gives me another quick squeeze before stepping back. He looks amused, mostly angry, but there's a hint of mirth there too. "So this is why he finds your threats so amusing. I get it."

"You are skating on very thin ice."

"*You* have anger issues, dear cousin."

"It's hereditary." I close my eyes and breathe in and out. And in and out. *Until you know everything is okay, you keep your composure. Rip him a new one later.* "Now... Where. Is. He?"

"Getting the wound cleaned and stitched up."

"So, he's okay?"

"Yes." Malcolm entwines our fingers and pulls me along behind him. I'm not paying attention to the where or if we turn right or left and how many doorways we cross; I feel lost until his eyes meet mine and his lips stretch into a soft grin. "Go on. I'll be in the waiting room while you two talk. And don't worry, Carmelo has Chulo."

My feet are rooted to the ground, though, and Javi gives me a concerned look. "Come here, Muñeca. I'm okay." A sob catches in my throat, and the nurse tending to what I now see is a large shoulder wound gives me a sympathetic look. It's just all too much. So much could've gone wrong. "Stop for a second."

"Sir, I just need to close the last two stitches. It'll be...never mind."

With his warm brown eyes on my seafoam ones, Javier rips off the medical tape and the dirty gauze used to clean up the wound. There's a green nylon string with a small pair of scissors clamped in place for her to administer the next suture, but he lets it dangle while walking closer.

Another step, and tears drip down my eyes in relief.

His scent infiltrates my senses, and I shake with this profound need to grab him and never let go.

And then he's the one touching me.

Javi's hands cup my face while ignoring what I'm sure is searing pain. He doesn't care. He only rubs his thumbs across my cheeks and collects my tears with soft brushes before his lips meet mine and soothe the ache that's making it hard to breathe.

"I can't live without you, Javier. I'm sorry I didn't see—"

"Shut up and kiss me." And just like a few hours ago, I give in to my need and kiss him with everything I am and what I'll be by his side. Each swipe of my tongue is an apology for not being careful. Each nip of his bottom lip is a promise to never leave his side. "Fuck, I love you."

Pulling back, I rest my forehead against his chin. "More than my own life."

We stay that way for a few minutes, his presence helping me calm down, and then I take his hand and walk him back toward the bed. I peck his lips and instruct him to lie down. I lay my head beside his ear while the woman works, and it's while his hand plays with my fingers that I get the courage to ask the one question that's been plaguing me since coming back from Colombia.

It's what I need. How I want to spend the rest of my life.

"Javier Lucas," I breathe out slowly against his cheek, and his head tilts in my direction. "Will you marry me?"

"Yes." No hesitation. No doubts.

"Today?"

"This very minute if we can find someone to officiate."

"Thank you."

Plump lips curl up into the happiest little grin. "Shouldn't it be me who thanks you?"

"No." The shake of my head is minute, and I use the movement to nip his jaw. "Because I feel like the luckiest woman in the world right now. You've given me you, and that's all I'll ever need to be happy. To feel complete."

"I'll never stop loving you, Muñeca."

"And I'll be more than thankful to have a good shot." His boisterous laughter fills the room and I smirk. No more of the heavy for today. Not when I'll move heaven and earth to marry him today. "Scare me like this again, and I'll shoot you. That's a promise."

"Wouldn't dream of it, dear." Javier rolls his eyes but in them, I see nothing but love and devotion. The same emotions I'm drowning in. "I'll just have to find other ways to annoy you."

"Good boy."

# Javier

*A sinful sixteen months later...*

"W HERE DID YOU go?" Mariah asks, her voice thick with sleep as I kick off my boxer briefs. She's naked and warm, much like I'll be in a minute, and cuddled up on my side of the bed. I find the action amusing—sexy. "What could he have possibly needed at this time of night?"

"I visited the Foster residence to extend a formal invitation to his house tomorrow."

Mariah lifts her head and arches a brow. "At this time of night?" Why would he—"

"Because he's interested in one London Foster."

"Say what, now? He's interested in the sister?" My wife turns in my arms, her lips spread into this megawatt smile that means nothing but trouble. "When did they meet? Is she as pretty as the picture in her file?"

"What file?"

Her grin is sheepish and her eyes wide with mock innocence. "I might've made one after they moved to town cataloging the terms of their agreement. The men in that family are shady, low-end criminals, but the girl is not involved. If anything, she's too sweet and afraid of them."

"Does Malcolm know this?"

She scoffs, squirming a little closer, and my dick perks up at her nearness. At the way her ass jiggles while she plays the *I'm only trying to get comfortable* card. Brat. "Of course not. That man is too stubborn for his own good."

"What's that supposed to mean?" My hand falls to her hip and then lower to her thigh; I lift it, and she moans when my cock slips between her bare lips. When the head kisses the wetness that is only for me and settles at her entrance. The tiny hole clenches in anticipation, but I don't enter. Just touch it. Savor the feel of her sweet juices coating my tip. "What are you planning, Muñeca?"

"Nothing."

Lying is a mortal sin for me, and yet she pushes. *So bad. So mine.* "Liar."

"It was just in case they meet, or something goes wrong."

"Like what?" I slam in to the hilt and she clenches, her breath caught in her throat from the force of the punishing stroke. "Tell me." No response. Not so much as a breath escapes her, and I take that as a challenge. "This one is on you."

Pulling out, I push Mariah's hip forward and pin her there. Her back arches while she tries to fight my hold, wanting to be fucked for being bad, but unwilling to give in.

Good thing for her she has a husband who doesn't mind dominating, bringing her to tears with his cock.

"Javi, I—"

"*I* what?" Short little jabs slip the engorged head just past her opening a few times, but I don't penetrate. I want to hear this explanation. *Why is she keeping tabs on that family when I'm doing the same for our family's sake?* "Tell me."

"Please fuck me."

"Answer the question, Mariah." Fuck, she looks so good like this. Needy and hungry and her entrance clenching in search of me. "Tell me why you've been—"

"Because Earl asked me to make sure she doesn't get mixed up in their drama. He's a family friend on her mother's side and is worried. *Christ...*" She's struggling against me. Her eyes over her shoulder meet mine and they're angry and desperate "...keep denying me, and I'll take care of this myself."

"Is that a threat?"

"Yes." My smirk is dark and my intentions dirty; she knows this. Lives for it. "You can't stop...oh *fuck!*"

"Louder, baby. Scream for me." My thrusts don't allow her time to adjust or take a breath; I'm fucking her fast and hard and holding her down with my weight after spreading that thigh higher. I hold it to the bed, fingers digging in, and yet, my precious doll only whimpers out a *"More."*

Always more.

"Javi, I'm..." she trails off, lips going slack when I slip a hand between us and touch her throbbing clit in time with my thrust. No lead in or gentle circles. I press two fingers down and use every punch of my hips to massage—bring her closer to the orgasm I denied her earlier in the night.

She's hiding something from me, and I don't like it.

"You close, Mamita?" Her response is a whiny, keening sound. She loves it when I speak Spanish and I'm not above using it when necessary. "Tan bonita mi muneca. Tan rica."

"Oh God..." another delicious clench and I feel her clit swell the second goose bumps erupt all over her heated flesh "...just need—"

"What?"

"Tell me."

I smile against her sweaty neck, closing my eyes as the power I hold over her slams into me and rocks me to the core. I'll never deny how heady it is to own her love. To experience her greed for me every single moment of the day.

"I love you more than my own life." No sooner has the last word slipped past my lips than Mariah comes and hard—her pussy tightens around my cock like a vice and I find myself holding still—letting her fuck herself back on me with short strokes.

She's massaging me. Her heat enveloping me.

And when her small hand slips beneath her hips and holds me to her, I come.

Spurt after spurt rushes out and deep into her core. I fill her and still, it's not enough.

I want her round with my child. I want to have everything she's not ready for...*yet.*

"Javi, I'm dead," my girl whimpers a while later and I laugh, pulling out and falling beside her on the bed. She's insane and a little mental at times, but I wouldn't change a single hair on her head. "I needed that."

"You ready to tell me what you're hiding now?" Secrets and lies are the one thing I'll never allow between us. Not with how far we've come. "Are you still—"

"I found my mom."

That's the last thing I expected and I sit up, pulling her into my lap in the middle of the bed with the sheets strewn around us. Her mother's disappearance has been bugging her since the last time she spoke with her father.

A man whose body, sans head, was found in a lake by the police a week after we said *I do.* No motive or suspects have been found, but that's because Malcolm is nothing but an irate perfectionist. Especially, after finding out the black roses were coming from him and his whore as a scare tactic.

The flower shop owner was a friend of her father.

Moreover, I took pleasure in hanging the widowed-shop owner and watering the sunflowers with his blood.

"Where is she?"

"In Indiana." She buries her face in my neck; I feel the few tears fall and begin to think the worst. "She's living under an alias and working as a caretaker in a women's shelter. The kids love her, and she seems happy. Happier than I've ever seen her."

"I can have the car ready in ten minutes, linda."

"That won't be necessary, Papi. I'm not going to see her."

"Why?" I'm surprised by this. I'd give anything to see my mother again.

"Because she's at peace, and I never want to take that away from her. I'm okay as long as she's safe."

We've had people look into her whereabouts over the last few years. We've dug and dug and searched high and low, but the truth is she's hiding and doesn't want to be found after Mariah's father forced her into a mental institution in London. For seven months under the guise of her being schizophrenic, her Mom was forced medications and endured treatments not meant for someone with a clean bill of health.

A lie he told after slipping those in charge a few bills, and it wasn't until the owner went to trial for a wrongful death case that my mother-in-law escaped. Vanished without much of a trace.

Tipping her face up to mine, I kiss her nose and then peck her lips. "Are you sure?"

"I am."

"You're amazing, sweetheart. She's lucky to have you as a daughter."

"And I am blessed to have you as my husband. So lucky that I want to start trying for that baby?"

"Yeah?" My grin matches her. It's dopey and happy and I'm fucking hard again. "Right now?"

"Why not?" Mariah laughs, turning her in my lap to straddle my legs. "I want a little mini Javi throwing tantrums and harassing kids on the playground."

"What about a mini Mariah threatening to shoot everyone she meets?"

"The possibilities are endless." It leaves her on a moan, her hips gyrating against the bulbous, angry tip. "But as long as I have you—"

"I want them all," I finish for her and then take those soft lips with my own, sending a silent vow to God above to never let me lose her. Our connection. She's my life, and I plan to spend my life showing her each day that I live and breathe for her love.

# Mariah

*Two years later…*

"**R**EADY TO COME CLEAN, little cousin?"

My head whirls back, a gasp slipping from my lips at the sight of Malcolm. He's the one I've been worried about the most, disappointing him by not confiding a secret we've kept long enough.

That I've made Javi keep.

*You hurt him, too.*

Christ, my eyes well with tears and my lips open to speak, but no words come out. How do I explain my selfishness? How do I explain that I kept them away from the happiest day in my life?

"Malcolm."

"Stop," we say in unison, but the annoying jerk just wipes off my eyes with a soft expression. "I'm not mad."

"You're not? And what exactly are you *not* mad about?"

"I was there the night you said your *I do's* in the hospital room."

*What the?* "But we never saw you." It's the only thing my brain can muster. That, and a contrite expression.

He's always been there for me.

More like a brother than a cousin.

"It's a lucky coincidence that I was." He's smiling and relaxed. No anger or reproach in his tone. "After dealing with a phone call from the DA's office over the incident with Mildred, I stopped to check in on Javier. To thank him for saving someone I love."

"London's made you a softie with emotions," I tease, not used to seeing this side of him often. Malcolm shows his affection with actions and not words, unless you're his wife. The way he fawns over her is quite adorable to watch.

"I'd shoot you, but your husband might quit."

"That's my line, jerk!" I yell in mock-indignation. "Besides, Javi always double-crosses me."

"Do I?" The man in question wraps an arm around my waist then, pulling me against a hard chest. One I love. One I can't sleep without cuddling on. When I don't answer, he chuckles against the crown of my head. "What's freaking her out? Coming out, or the pregnancy?"

I've never turned around so fast in my life. My eyes meet his: my wide ones on his soft, molten chocolate ones. "You know?"

"I do." Javi brings both hands up to my face, cupping my cheeks. His lips are spread into a wide smile, the softest expression over his chiseled features. "At first, it was just a suspicion, but after the week of nothing but Buffalo wings for dinner with a coconut cake for dessert, I knew. You love coconut, but not in a cake."

"I'm sorry. I—"

He shuts me up with a kiss. It's soft and sweet and warm; our lips connect, and all my worries disappear. I'm tethered to him. My world begins and ends with him.

Softly, Javier nibbles on my bottom lip before pulling back when a throat clears, a sheepish grin on his face. "My apologies for forgetting you exist."

"I'll remember that the next time London comes to have lunch at the office." He's trying to sound annoyed, but I hear the happiness in his tone. Real happiness, and after nipping Javi's jaw and removing his hands from my face, I turn to face him. "Take a moment and come inside when you're ready. We'll keep them inside."

"We?" I squeak, worried someone else knows.

"London knows, Mari. And don't worry, no one is upset, nor will we let them give you shit."

"I'm sorry I hid this from you."

"Shut up." Pulling me in for a quick hug, he kisses my forehead before gently pushing me back. Right back where I belong. With Javier. Always my Javier. "Congratulations, Lucas family. I'm looking forward to meeting my godchild."

"I didn't ask you?" I laugh, feeling so happy to finally share this.

"Not asking. I'm claiming my rightful spot." With that, Malcolm turns and heads back inside, slipping into the kitchen through our sliding glass doors.

"How far along are you?" Javi asks. His hands grip my hips, fingers expanding to caress my small bump.

"A little over a month."

He hums in the back of his throat. "And everything is okay? You've seen the OBGYN?"

No anger. Never reproach.

"We're healthy and right where we should be." Closing my eyes, I inhale deeply and let it out slowly, savoring his manly scent. Javi is my home, and being close to him gives me the peace and stability I need at the moment. He centers me. Assuages and fortifies my soul. "I'm sorry for not telling you sooner, but so much—"

"I'm not upset, Muñeca. You've been nervous and taking on so much." His words soothe me. Calm me of the fear I've been trying to fight against. "But I need you to understand that no matter what, you're not alone. We handle this together. Everything together."

"In sickness and health, we are one."

"We are one."

We've been here before, eight months ago when we lost our first little one. It was an accident. One of those things you can never prepare for—it's out of your hands—and no matter how much you think *what if the drunk asshole who slammed into my car didn't drink that night,* it's useless.

Nothing changes the outcome after the fact.

He decided to drive drunk after a coke bender.

He decided to hit his wife and then leave her locked in their basement.

He made a decision that changed our lives.

But more than that, we faced the heartache on our own, while Javier made an example of the unscathed driver. He made sure the man never made it to court, killing him outside his home with an old rusty ax his wife provided.

"I love you, Javier. So much." My voice breaks a bit, and he turns me, wrapping me in an embrace. His forehead on mine. "Please know that I never meant to hide you or our babies. Both of them," I whisper, tasting his every exhale. Letting the tears fall, because I know no matter what, he's my rock. My haven. "All I ever wanted was a bit of normalcy. To keep this perfect little bubble we've created where I'm me and you take me with every quirk."

"I do that with pride, Mariah. You're mine."

"Always yours."

Warm fingers sweep across my cheeks, clearing the traces of my emotions and then healing every fear with a kiss on my lips. Just one pec settles me. Just a simple touch to let me know he's here.

I'm not alone. I'm loved. I'm protected.

"Are you ready to let them know?

"I'm ready to marry you again." He tilts his head, brows furrowed, but before he can ask, I'm slipping to one knee. Our new rings are in my pocket; a special set I had made with our wedding date inscribed along with our babies' due dates. "So will you make an honest woman of me again and renew our vows?"

"You had this planned." Not a question. I see the small shiver that rushes through him.

"Yes."

"Yes."

"Yes, you will, or yes, I'm crazy."

Javi doesn't respond. Instead, I'm lifted off the ground and swept off my feet. He's a determined man with a smile on his face that sends my heart into a frenzy as he rushes inside and comes to a stop in front of our family.

Everyone watches us with a smile, not understanding his erratic breathing and my goofy grin.

"We've been married for over three years now and I'm sorry we've kept it hidden. I don't apologize for loving her, for living for her, and anyone who gives her shit will deal with me." My face heats up while silence surrounds us. I peek up and catch a few people with surprised expressions and others that look smug. My aunt and uncle look smug. *Do they know?* "Now, I'm going to take my *wife* upstairs, thank her for giving me this beautiful life—the baby growing within —and then renew our vows. Do not interrupt, or I will shoot you."

"Oh my God!"

"My baby!"

"Jesus, Javi," I giggle, smacking his shoulders while those in the room begin to protest. However, one look from the man I love, and they file out and into the backyard with London leading the pack. She's smiling, winking at me, and gives us a thumbs up before closing the door.

The music begins a second later.

Laughter seeps through the glass.

And it's exactly how our first wedding should've been, surrounded by those we love. Full of happiness and... *oh fuck!*

"But first, you'll choke on my cock..." Javi's lips are at my ear, nipping and teasing with the tip of his tongue "...while I eat your pretty little pink pussy. I want your juices on my face, your release on my tongue before I impale you and watch you shatter all over again. I want your sobs of pleasure and sweaty skin. I want to worship, then fuck you until you break, and then, *I do* is the only thing that will slip past those lips."

"Yes, please." It leaves me on a moan. A breathless plea, and Javier nods against my neck.

"Your wish will always be my command, Muñeca."

# MALCOLM

I'M STANDING JUST outside of Javier's hospital room with a man I'm all too familiar with.

I caught him here, wandering down the halls and stopping just outside this room where I have just enough space between the door's opening to witness what's happening inside.

My little cousin is incredible, and I smile.

"She's always done things her way," I say, and the man tries to answer but I push the barrel of the gun deeper against his neck. "You should be proud of the woman she is, Uncle."

"Let me go."

"To your death, sure." The wedding officiant begins to speak, and I listen, taking in the goofy smiles on their faces and the way her eyes light up with laughter when he pokes her side. And while I'll never admit this to her, hiring—arranging that first meeting with Javier has been my wisest decision to date.

He's good to her. Has taken away the sadness that lingered in her eyes for so long after Lane and her parents betrayal.

"You need to stop this. That man—"

"Is your future son-in-law, although you'll never meet him."

The man dressed as a priest begins to read from his bible about love. He explains that the emotion is given freely and is honest—it's not jealous and does not boast nor does it strike down or hurt the other person. He talks about kindness and hope. Of unity and family.

A tear falls from Mariah's eye and she catches it before Javier notices. His eyes are on the officiant while my cousin shows a moment of weakness, of missing her family, but when he looks over and sees her frown, his concern erases all traces of hurt.

He mouths, *are you okay?*

And she replies, *always with you.*

"The rings?" the man asks, and both have sheepish grins. "You don't have any?"

"This was a last-minute thing, and she proposed." Javi shrugs, his grin cocky. "Ms. Mariah here stole my thunder, once again."

"I did not. You're just slow."

"You two will be just fine." He produces something from his pocket that looks like small rubber bands and places one in each hand. "Now, repeat after me and use these as place-holders. I'm sure you'll have your real sets before the week is over."

"Guilty." Javier looks at Mariah with a soft expression. One you don't see in men who hold no qualms in ending a life. Who's itching for revenge. "I brought my parents set home with me. I'd like to use those for now."

"I'd be honored, babe."

"You see that, asshole?" I hiss into my uncle's ear, my finger pulling the trigger but no bullet dislodges. The clip inside has three at the most, and he got lucky this time. "That's love. That's the look she'll wear on her face for the rest of her life."

"He's not worthy."

"And these are your last few minutes on this earth," I remind him. "I'm considering this a wedding gift to the happy couple after all the trouble you've caused with your deceased whore."

"What?" The gun is pressed so tight to his jugular that it comes out a low garble. "What did you do to Mildred? Where is she?"

"Dead." Javi looks over and I catch his minute nod of approval. The evil in his eyes, a quick flash that's gone before Mariah notices the exchange. "The same your friend—the supplier of the black roses —will encounter. Mariah killed Mildred. Javier will end Grant."

"No. No, she can't be—"

"By the power vested in me by the state of Illinois, I now pronounce you husband and wife. You may kiss the bride." Their lips meet, and I hit my uncle across the forehead with the butt of my Desert Eagle, creating a nasty gash right across the bridge of his nose. And as they kiss, I drag him back toward the stairwell where Carmelo stands guard. He sees the unconscious man and jumps into action, carrying his weight like a sack of potatoes over his shoulder.

"Where to?"

"My home. I'm in the mood to play."

# Javier

"**T**HIS IS UNNECESSARY, Javier." It's the eighth time she's said this since I placed her inside my SUV, adding kidnapping charges to my already long rap sheet. *Fuck it.* I don't care and my cock enjoyed the way she pouted at the end of her ridiculous statement.

Now, what's unnecessary is her notion to fight my every gesture. She's stubborn. Always on the defense.

*You like it, though.* And fuck me, I do.

Besides, this complaint falls on the nicer side of her conversational skills at the moment; a monologue I hum to here and there, so she knows I'm listening. And I am...

Each objection.

Each annoyed sigh.

Each curse.

Each motherfucking time she bites her bottom lip in exasperation, I'm left fighting the demonic urge to pull over and take her over the center console. Or part those glossed lips and let her feel the weight of my cock on her tongue.

She has no idea how each provocation heightens my need for her.

How hard I am behind my zipper.

"Time to get this over with," she whispers under her breath, but I hear it loud and clear and there's a lilt of anxiety that doesn't sit right with me. Mariah fidgets a bit in her seat, the just above-the-knee skirt she's wearing in a soft pink shimmying up her thighs, exposing more flesh. I swallow hard and she sighs. "No time like the present since I wasn't given a choice."

Pulling into the parking space closest to the E.R. entrance, I shut off the ignition and turn to look at her. Fully appreciate the vibrancy of her eyes, the high rosy cheeks, and then the curve of her pouty, sensuous lips. "I am your choice."

"Says who?"

"Me." I'm attuned to her moods, react to her emotions and right now, the little coquette is fighting back a smile. And yet, there's a hint of unease there I don't like. "Are you—"

"Have I ever told you that I despise hospitals and needles?"

"No." That's not something I'd forget about. Ever.

"Well, it's true." My eyes narrow and hers widen, giving me that phony innocent look all women use to their advantage at some point in their life. "Can I come back another time? I'm not ready."

Oh, she's good.

"Whatever you want," I croon, reaching over to tuck a stray piece of hair that's fallen from her high ponytail. Then, I begin to play. Tit for tat. Tilting my head to the side, I furrow my brows and frown. "You do look pale. Are you okay, Muñeca?"

I don't miss the small shiver at the nickname or the way she bites the inside of her cheek. "If I am, it's because needles squig me out. Just not a fan of being poked and prodded."

Her lips turn into a small frown and it hits me: she's serious. Mariah's uncomfortable and that creates a pang—tightness in my chest—and I rub the spot. "Why didn't you tell me, sweetheart? I'll never make you do something you don't want to do."

Her shrug is sheepish. "Couldn't give you more ammo to use against me."

No sooner has the last word passed through her lips that Mariah jumps down from the SUV, and rushes inside. For a second, I'm lost to her words and the way her answer makes me feel, but I'm hot on her heels the moment that car door slams closed.

A nurse inside the lobby looks up the second we almost run into her desk. I'm breathing hard and Mariah is slightly glaring—we don't look like the most trustworthy individuals—and the woman merely raises a brow in question.

"I'm here to get my stitches removed."

"They can wait a day or two," we speak in unison and the lady continues to just watch us. The expression on the poor nurse's face would be comical any other day, but the tremble of my muñeca's hand evaporates any amusement.

*She really does hate this.* Moreover, I'm the asshole forcing her.

"Babe, we really don't—"

"Is Samuel available?"

"Who the fuck is—"

"He's on shift tonight. Let me page him." The nurse is quick to press a few buttons on her phone, cradling the receiver when the link clicks. "Dr. Pains, are you available for a suture removal? Umm, I don't…let me ask her." She makes eye contact with my girl. "Name, ma'am?"

"Mariah Asher."

"He'll be right up." The young woman looks like she ate a lemon, her lips pursing a bit. "Must've heard you because he didn't give me the chance to finish."

"Thank you. I'll wait over—"

"What in God's name are you doing in my E.R., squeaks?" *Who the fuck is he calling squeaks and why is Mariah smiling at this clown?*

"Need these out." My muneca holds her palm out, showing the small line of stitches from her accident at the restaurant. The day I came into her life like a frustrating hurricane and she broke a glass, according to Malcolm. He snitched the next day with another threat to treat her right. "Can you help?"

She bats her lashes and my eyes narrow. She leans over a bit and

I nearly pick her up, throw her over my shoulder, and march the fuck out.

"Mariah, I think it's best if we leave," I grit out and all three heads turn my way. Two wary, while she's all innocence. *And wasn't she afraid a minute ago?* "Trust me on this."

"No."

"Yes."

"Mariah..."

"Javier..."

"Do you two need a minute?" Dr. Pains asks, his lip twitching. "Or can I take care of *my* patient?"

The way he says *my* almost costs him his life, and were it not for Mariah, I would've shot the prick. Her hand grabs mine, entwining our fingers, and the harsh squeeze she gives them settles me—calms me down enough to not open fire inside the public building.

"Come on," she sighs, rolling her eyes and I'm tempted to bite the brat. "Let's get this over with."

"Fine."

"Good." Pains walks toward the two doors with the keycard access needed and waves the plastic square in front of the reader. They open and we walk through, following the prick to an empty room near the back of a long hall where he points to the bed. "Sit and breathe. You know the drill."

I cut my eyes to him; eyes narrowed. "Say it politely or I'll—"

"Ms. Asher, can you please sit down and extend your palm facing up over the tabletop?"

"Thank you, Sam." *Now she calls him Sam, too.* This woman is pushing my buttons. All of them. "Anything else you need me to do?"

"Muñeca," I warn, this is past the realm of what I can take. "Quit it."

"Quit what?" She bats her lashes and looks at me with that wide and innocent look that stirs something within. The kind that makes me want to drop to my knees and worship at her altar. "You brought me here. Isn't this what you wanted?"

"I'm—"

"Close your eyes and breathe," the doctor interrupts and Mariah's bottom lip trembles. She does as he asks, but the sudden jitters make me feel like shit all over again.

I'm going from jealousy to anger to guilt all within the span of a few minutes; she's going to drive me insane. Certifiable.

A lone tear falls and that's it. That's my limit.

"Touch her and I shoot." Fuck it, I use her line. "We're out, babe. Grab your things."

"But, Javi—"

"No but, Mariah. I will not sit here and let you be miserable." Cupping her face with one hand, I wipe her tear with my thumb. "This is unacceptable."

"It is." Another tear falls from her eye and my chest constricts. *God, what is she doing to me?* "But you know what's even more messed up?"

"No," I whisper, afraid to further upset her.

"It's messing with my desk, you jerk. Don't. Touch. My. Stuff."

"What did you just say?" The doctor is laughing beside us while her eyes are alight with mischievous amusement. "Muñeca, I'm—"

"What my cousin is trying to say," Samuel interrupts me once again and I'm close to snapping his neck. I'm trying to compute, but coming up short past the tears and threat over her desk and—"

"Your desk."

"Si."

"This is over your desk?"

"Once again...*si*."

"And he's your cousin?"

Mariah tries to smirk, but it comes out as a squishy grin when I squeeze her jaw. Not hard, but enough to create a kind-of-cute ducky face. "He is."

"Are you fucking kidding me?"

"No." Turning her face with my hand still holding her jaw, she waves at Samuel. "Meet Dr. Samuel Pains. He's my mother's late sister's son."

"I'm going to kill you."

"Not really."

I turn her attention back to me and laugh. The chuckle is a bit dark. A little sinister, and when she raises a brow in challenge, I let go and step back. "Run."

"What?" A shiver rushes through her. My threat excites her.

"Run, Muñeca. Because I plan to do more than bite."


The End.


*Turn the page for Beautiful Sinner + BOOK News…*

# MY SINFUL VALENTINE

The only thing that can crumble a KING is disappointing his
QUEEN. So what do my Beautiful Sinners do on Valentine's Day for
their women? They spoil and lick and eat...

Worship: Malcolm and London
Say My Name: Casper and Aurora
One More: Thiago and Luna
You've Been Bad: Javier and Mariah
Pretty Doll: Alejandro and Solimar

*Available Now*
https://books2read.com/u/bprv29

# BEAUTIFUL SINNER SERIES

EACH BOOK IS A STANDALONE.

NOW LIVE!
SIN (#1)
COVET (#2):
MINE (#3):
YOURS (#4):
RISQUE #5
MY SINFUL VALENTINE

BEAUTIFUL SINNER SPIN-OFF:
CORRUPT

# NEW DARK ROMANCE

LITTLE LIES
BUY HERE: https://books2read.com/little-lies

I AM DARKNESS.
I AM SIN.
I AM YOURS.

A truth imprinted onto my skin—its sharp vines digging into my flesh as our bond strengthens with each shallow intake of breath my love takes. Her life is intertwined with the devil, a man who hungers for depravity and death, and yet, I bend my knee for her.

Only her. Always her.

She is mine and I will kill to protect. Kill to own her.

Gabriella Moore will never leave me. Not by choice or circumstance.

Elena M. Reyes is the epitome of a Floridian and if she could live in her beloved flip-flops, she would.

As a small child, she was always intrigued by all forms of art: whether it was dancing to island rhythms, or painting with any medium she could get her hands on. Her passion for reading over the years has amassed her with hours of pleasure, but it wasn't until she stumbled upon fanfiction that her thirst to write overtook her world.

She's a short and sassy Latina with an adorable pup, a kiddo that keeps her on her toes, and a husband who claims she'll cause him to go bald prematurely. Lol

**Email: Reyes139ff@gmail.com**

**Elena's Marked Girls.**
**Come join the naughty fun.**
**Link: https://www.facebook.com/groups/1710869452526025/**

**NEWSLETTER SIGNUP:**
**http://bit.ly/2nHJxTI**

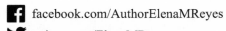

facebook.com/AuthorElenaMReyes
twitter.com/ElenaMReyes
instagram.com/elenar139
bookbub.com/authors/elena-m-reyes

ALSO, BY ELENA M. REYES

FATE'S BITE SERIES
LITTLE LIES
LITTLE MATE
HALF TRUTHS {COMING 2022)
OMISSION {TBD}

SERIES:
BEAUTIFUL SINNER SERIES
Each book is a standalone.
Now Live!
SIN (#1)
COVET (#2)
MINE (#3)
YOURS (#4)
RISQUE #5
Beautiful Sinner Spin-Off
CORRUPT

(Marked Series)
Marking Her #1
Marking Him #2
Scars #2.5
Marked #3

(I Saw You)
I Saw You
I Love You #1.5

(Teasing Hands) Re-Released
FREE Teasing Hands #1
Teasing Hands #2

*ALSO, BY ELENA M. REYES*

Teasing Hands #3

SAFE ROMANCE:
Taste Of You
Doctor's Orders
Back To You

STANDALONES:
Craving Sugar
Stolen Kisses